THE QUILT GARDEN

THE BRIARWOOD SERIES ~ BOOK TWO

GINI ATHEY

Cover design by My Author Concierge.

ABOUT THE BOOK

Change is her only option...

After decades in an emotionally abusive marriage, Tina Montgomery has finally found the courage to break free. For solace and security, she returns home to the small town of Briarwood, Wisconsin, but struggles to redefine herself, her career, and her place in the world. Within weeks, Tina faces a second loss.

After the death of their father, Tina and her older sister, Helen, are forced to take over management of their legacy, the business their father built from the ground up. If they fail, they'll lose everything their father worked for.

Tina's passion has always been quilting—teaching, creating, and designing—but her brand and skills have become sadly outdated and now she's lost the respect of her peers in the quilting world. When an opportunity opens up at the quilt shop in town, Tina is at a crossroads, torn between working with Helen in the family business or following her true calling as a quilter and teacher.

Then there's John Delaney, her childhood friend and secret crush. He's back in Briarwood after years on the road as an internationally renowned photographer. Whether John's home to stay or on the road again tomorrow, Tina has an opening to learn the truth about his feelings—and if the door is open for a second chance at love.

Tina finally has an opportunity to decide what kind of life she wants, but it will only happen if she has the courage and resilience to change.

Congratulations to newlyweds, Chad and Nicole L.
Best wishes for a lifetime of happiness and joy.

ACKNOWLEDGMENTS

First, and always, to my husband, Gary. He listens to my joys and fears and encourages me to follow my dreams.

Thank you to the many readers who have purchased my books and written reviews. As I write, I always think of entertaining you.

It is very difficult to remember all of the people that have contributed to this book, from the librarian who searched for a special book to the conversation I overheard in the grocery checkout line that I used to make a character in the book more interesting.

A special shout-out to Virginia McCullough, my first content reader. Her "yes" here and "no" there encourage me to strive deeper into my characters' backgrounds and desires. Every writer needs a person like you, friend.

There is one person, Maria Connor, virtual assistant and production manager, that I send loads of joy to every month with our conference calls. She keeps me on track and solves numerous problems with her positive attitude and energy. This book is because of you. Thank you.

Gini Athey
2021

NOTE TO READERS

Dear Readers:

Welcome back to Briarwood, Wisconsin, a small fictional community near Green Bay.

After many years away, Tina Montgomery has finally returned to her family home in Briarwood. She barely has a chance to experience the relief of her hasty divorce from an emotionally abusive man before she's coping with the death of her father. Tina and her older sister, Helen, soon find themselves at a make-or-break crossroads. They'll either learn to manage Montgomery Enterprises, a business their father started and the sisters' legacy, or they'll lose it—and with it, the source of their income. Sadly, their dad has never shared the inner workings of the company, a reality with enormous practical—and emotional—fallout.

Tina has taught quilting for decades, but she's allowed her lectures and samples—and even her signature vests—to become seriously outdated. But she feels a special joy when she is working with fabric and teaching quilting and must decide if her desire is strong enough to do whatever it takes to claim a new place in the quilting community.

John Delaney, an internationally renowned photographer, has spent much of his life traveling the world on assignment, but he's ready to come home to Briarwood and forge a new direction. Now that Tina is divorced, John's ready to find out if Tina will ever return the love he's secretly carried in his heart for over thirty years. Tina has loved John for as long as she can remember, but after he broke her heart, she's all but given up hope that he'll ever fall in love with her.

But now, will events of the past continue to keep them apart?

I hope you enjoy your visit to Briarwood. Please stay in touch —you can find me online at https://giniathey.com/, Facebook, BookBub, and Goodreads.

Gini Athey

2021

You build on failure. You use it as a stepping stone. Close the door on the past. You don't try to forget the mistakes, but you don't dwell on it. You don't let it have any of your energy, or any of your time, or any of your space.

~Johnny Cash

1

I SLIPPED ON ONE OF MY HANDMADE QUILTED VESTS, INSTANTLY adding color to my solid white capris and short-sleeved shirt. I had a special fondness for this vest with its scrappy style of squares of different fabrics sewn together in a random design. It had become a signature item that'd helped build my reputation as a quilter, but now, I worried it was outdated—and dated me. I was staring at myself thinking about all this when I heard my older sister, Helen, frantically calling, "Tina? Tina?"

I turned around, and she was in the doorway of the room on the lower level of our family home. Three months ago, I'd taken over this space, originally our childhood playroom, for my quilting studio when I'd returned to Briarwood after my hasty divorce. I might have stayed decades too long in a bad marriage, but I'd put my divorce in motion and had it finalized in record time. Thankfully, I was already in town—barely—before Dad died unexpectedly just shy of three months ago.

"What's up, Helen? Is something wrong?"

"Did you forget our virtual meeting with Doug?" She had an uncertain edge to her voice, not typical for Helen, who was normally cheerful. "I've been reminding you for the last two days, but you don't seem to understand how important this is."

What? The meeting with Doug Baker, our friend and attorney, would help us fill in some details about our immediate future—specifically, our financial future. That was about as important as it got. If I were like Helen, and prone to be on the dramatic side, I might have said it was life or death. "I most certainly have not forgotten it. Don't you think I know what this means? We're lucky this meeting is with Doug and not a stranger."

When our pillar-of-the-community dad, Maxwell Montgomery, died, he left his business affairs for Helen and me to figure out. That alone mystified us, although it shouldn't have. At various times over the years, both Helen and I had tried to talk to Dad about his business, Montgomery Enterprises—ME, as we called it—but he'd always told us not to worry. He'd assured us that Doug knew the state of the business and was a hundred percent trustworthy. After all, he and Doug had been friends and confidants since they were both young, ambitious, and each set out to make his mark in the world.

Apparently, Helen was taking my reassurance to heart because the tension had drained from her face. But now she was staring at me. Feeling self-conscious, I glanced down at myself. "I need your opinion. Truthfully, do you think my clothes look old?" I was nervous getting the words out, but my fears eased when I touched the diamond earrings Dad had given me last spring on my fiftieth birthday. I really did want an honest answer, and Helen wasn't one to mince words.

Helen gave me a disbelieving look as she twirled her hand as a signal for me to turn a full circle. She crossed her arms over her chest. "Well, since you ask, the clothes don't look *old*, exactly. Only outdated." She narrowed her eyes and stared, making me feel the weight of her scrutiny. "You have good legs, Tina, so show them off in skinny jeans or ankle pants, or if you like capris, make them the skinny kind. And you could vary the shape of the vests, right? Longer in the back, shorter in the front—that's the trend now. Maybe less voluminous—you don't need to hide your body. Experiment with the cut and see what happens." Helen lifted her hands in a helpless gesture. "But then, what do I know about wearable art?"

Helen's emerald tunic and slim pants accented her summer tan. Green earrings sparkled between strands of shoulder-length auburn hair. "I guess it depends on who you're dressing for. Maybe people who attend quilt shows dress the way you do. I can't say, but you can." Suddenly, she planted her hands on her hips. "Why are we talking about your fashion sense when we should be talking about how we're going to survive?"

She didn't hang around for an answer because the front doorbell rang and after a hard pivot, she scurried up the stairs. I turned to my suitcase filled with vests that I had worn over the weekend at the quilt show. I'd chosen vests to match my branding – Vested in Happiness and Joy – with each one showcasing a different quilt design as its focal point. No one who saw my vests or remarked on my upbeat branding knew that I'd come up with the theme during one of the low points of my life. A time when all I had was hope.

But now, Helen was right. Maybe the vests had once been fit for a quilt show, but each one I removed from the suitcase was hopelessly out of style. True, vests were classic, but some of the fabrics I'd used weren't even available anymore. Fabric in quilt shops tended to change with the pace of women's fashions. Bright colors and geometric patterns trendy one year gave way to florals and neutral tones the next. The cycle never ended. I grudgingly admired Helen. She adored clothes and always showed up in the latest colors and styles—at least the styles that showcased her great figure, pretty hair, and creamy skin.

"Tina? Doug's here," Helen yelled from the top of the stairs, a note of surprise in her voice.

I took one last look in the mirror and lifted the legs of my capris. Hmm...Helen was right. I did have good legs. Smiling to myself, I turned off the banks of bright lights as I left the room and headed upstairs to the kitchen where I heard Helen and Doug talking. Helen held out a cup of coffee for me while I greeted Doug with as much positive energy as I could muster. As usual, he dressed for comfort and was successful enough not to worry about creating a stuffy corporate lawyer image, which explained the khakis and sky-blue, short-sleeve shirt. If I hadn't known better, I'd have guessed he was heading out for an early morning round of golf. Standing opposite us on the other side of the center island, he looked entirely comfortable leaning against the counter with his legs crossed at the ankles. The sun coming through the windows behind him highlighted streaks of gray at his temples.

"This is a surprise. I thought today's meeting was going to be virtual." I eyed Helen over the rim of my cup to let her know I'd been paying attention to her reminders.

"Well, we planned it that way, but I was in the area and hoped you'd have a pot of my favorite coffee brewing," Doug said with a laugh. "Even if it is July, and it's going to be hot today."

"We don't care about Wisconsin weather," Helen said. "Tina and I both like a cup of roasted almond to start the day. Let's head to the office." She didn't wait for agreement. Adopting a take-charge attitude, she picked up her cup and led the way down the short hallway toward what had been Dad's home office. His only office. He'd started working from home decades before it was a trend.

In the room, Helen swept her arm over the two client chairs across the desk before settling herself behind it. "Have a seat."

Wow. It took me back to see Helen so easily claim Dad's chair, although who else? Doug wouldn't have done that, and as much as I loved this office, the idea never occurred to me. My grief over losing Dad so suddenly was still raw, and, at times, it surfaced before I could control my emotions. That day, with Doug in the room, I put my loss aside to focus on this meeting.

Dad added the office years after the house was built, and it had always reminded me of the old English libraries I'd seen in movies or on TV. Dark wood and built-in shelves covered three of the walls. Dad had received all sorts of awards for his business and service to the community, and now they sat on the shelves and marked the spaces between his books—an eclectic collection. The office might have been dark but for windows on the front wall and the French doors leading to the gardens in the back. That day the sun poured in and brightened the room. The space where he had worked felt warm and inviting, much like Dad himself, at least on the surface most of the time.

Outside the French doors, a small patio also offered an invitation to sit and gaze at the large yard beyond. Numerous beds of flowers in full bloom added a riot of color to the lush green grass. Pergolas and a gazebo provided resting spots with benches and rocking chairs. Thinking came easy in the gardens, and I had spent many hours there since my return.

Helen pushed coasters across the desk for our cups as she asked, "Is this a social visit instead of our scheduled meeting, Doug? I don't see your briefcase."

"We might as well start as if this was being done over the computer." He smiled at Helen and then to his left, where I sat. "So tell me, how are you two adjusting to being business owners?"

Not exactly the smoothest dodge of a reasonable question. Doug dropped in on us instead of showing up on our screens. Why, I wondered?

Helen ignored the evasion and raised her hands in the air and shrugged. "We're doing okay." She picked up a pencil and nervously fidgeted with it.

Why was she nervous? I'd never seen her uncomfortable around Doug before. Maybe something had changed, and she knew more about the state of things than I did.

"Before he died, I promised your father I'd help guide you —if needed—through the estate issues, but especially with Montgomery Enterprises."

"Sure, Doug, we know that," I said. It wasn't the first time we'd heard his I'm-here-to-help speech. Doug had always played the role of an uncle who wasn't really an uncle. At least when I was a little girl, the uncle designation fit, and then he was a friend when I was grown and making decisions, some of which were not particularly productive or wise. Then, he was my steady presence when I needed him most, as a lawyer I could trust to quickly untangle me from a marriage that never should have been and that had lasted way too long. Thankfully, he accomplished that feat in record time, and just before Dad died.

"We're doing okay," Helen repeated. I saw her hands tremble.

"Maybe so, but that's not good enough, Helen." Doug moved forward in his seat. He grasped the edge of the desk. "I've *seen* the bank statements." His words carried a tremor of frustration.

The jolt in my gut came on like an SOS. "What about the

bank statements? What are you talking about?" I looked at Helen, then Doug.

Doug turned in his seat to face me. "Look, when it comes to ME, I've tried to stay hands-off. I thought the two of you would open the books and figure out what to do to keep the business going." Doug lifted his hands in frustration and focused on Helen. "To be blunt, you two will be broke within a year if you don't start to actively manage Montgomery Enterprises—and *soon*."

Doug's words hit hard and threw me off center. Broke? How was that possible? And why had Doug waited so long to deliver this news? Dad had told us the story of how the business started. It was a treasured family tale of preparation and opportunity colliding. Our neighbor had been denied a $5,000 loan from the bank to buy his wife a car. She needed the car so she wouldn't have to take public transportation home after her evening shift at the local paper mill. Our dad overheard the man talking about it with another neighbor and quickly stepped in and offered a loan—he thought it was a good will gesture, nothing more significant than that. He enlisted Doug to draw up a simple contract with terms the man could handle.

Dad didn't know it at the time, but he'd unwittingly launched his new business, which had helped numerous small businesses and families in Briarwood. Sometimes, he heard about a need and offered to help, but most often the person with the need came to him. Within a few years, what started out as a small-loan-hobby had grown into a full-scale business, and one day he realized he could leave his job as an assistant manager of Briarwood's only grocery store. After our mother's death, he'd invested the life insurance money into the business so he could make more loans, help more people, and expand the business.

Early on, I referred to the company as ME, because Montgomery Enterprises had been too much of a mouthful for a little girl. ME stuck, and in our world of acronyms it wasn't long before everyone referred to the business as ME.

"Broke?" I squinted at Helen across the desk. "What is he talking about? Do you know something I don't?"

"No, no...I...I didn't...You and Alex divorced. Dad died." Tears filled her eyes. "I don't understand the business, at least not the way Dad organized his books." She looked at me with pleading eyes. "He had his own set of terms. It's like a code. Just because I lived here with Dad doesn't mean I worked with him." She shifted her gaze from me to Doug. "Dad never told me how all this worked—I was the *public* face of the company. Dad's representative with the charities and on boards."

What? How did I not know that was the extent of her involvement? "You mean Dad didn't tell you what the recordkeeping required or how he made decisions about when to okay a loan and when not to?" Why had I assumed Helen held the key to my understanding what was ahead for us? I had many questions flying around in my head, one being why Helen and I had waited so long to ask for help. Of course, that led to a sense of failure on my part. I hadn't probed into the workings of ME, either.

"Dad put money in my account because I put my energy into the volunteer work in town." A sad smile crossed Helen's face before it disappeared. "He used to tease me about being the PR director for ME. But, teasing or not, I was good at that role, and he knew it."

"You might have been good at the business end, too," I said, still confused. "Did you ever ask?"

Helen jerked her head back in surprise. "Of course, I asked. But he spouted the same answers he gave the two of us years ago. He told me not to worry about it. He wanted me to keep on doing that public work. So, that's why I don't know anything about the way he organized the business." Helen's mouth tightened into a grimace. "Dad never changed, you know. When we were kids, he was never interested in hearing about our career dreams. It's like we were smart, but not worldly or capable of being street smart like him."

Oh, boy. Helen hit a nerve. All my muscles slumped. "I understand the feeling...believe me, Sis." If I hadn't held myself back, I'd have pounded my fist on the desk in frustration that was about so much more than this meeting. "When was someone going to tell me we're broke?"

"When were you going to ask?" Helen shot back.

I had no comeback for that. Since Dad died, I'd gone passive. I figured someone else would explain all this. Did I assume these loans were on autopilot? Apparently.

"Look, you two, I never understood why your father didn't make his intentions for ME clear, not even to me." Doug shook his head and huffed air out of his lungs in a heavy sigh. "I encouraged him to talk with you about what he envisioned. Did he think the two of you would jump in and run the business together, or just Helen, or what?"

"That's what we thought you'd tell us," I said, glancing at Helen, who nodded.

Doug simply shrugged.

"That's the past," I said, glum and defeated. "But logically, once all the current loans are paid off, what did he think we'd do? I mean, what would the source of our income be? Dad's income came from the steady stream of loans he made."

"Exactly," Helen said, folding her arms and leaning back in the chair. "Dad always acted like the money would always flow. But, Doug, you're saying we have a year or less and then the flow stops, the loans run their course and logically, the business shuts down?"

Doug flopped back in the chair. "More or less, although some loans won't come due for a number of years. Just not enough of them to provide the kind of income Max produced year after year." He held up his hands defensively. "I shouldn't have waited all these weeks to talk with you about taking over the business. I thought you'd both see the situation immediately."

Talk about feeling small. I stole a glance at Helen. She lowered her head and was studying her hands as she rubbed her thumb across her perfect salon-polished nails. My hunch was she felt like a chastised kid, like me. The fact is, we should have known better.

"But since Max worked with our firm, the financial statements come to us," Doug said. "Max knew that, and we have a CPA and other people who manage business and personal accounts." Doug frowned. "Didn't you wonder how Ivy was paid after your dad died? Or how you kept the lights on in the house—literally?"

Helen and I glanced at each other. I assumed she knew how the household money worked. She'd lived in our childhood home, but for the years I was married to Alex, I was on the other side of the state. I hadn't asked because it had been easier not to. Besides, I didn't think much about the business. Since I'd been home and Dad died, I'd spent too much time fretting about what I was going to do next. Sometimes, to give myself a break from endless looping thoughts, I pulled a few weeds in the vast gardens we had. That wasn't a particularly valuable use of my time, and I lost interest once the landscaping crew came in and spruced everything up.

"I asked Ivy if her checks were being deposited as usual," Helen said to Doug. "She said everything had continued as before. The household account she uses to buy groceries and other supplies was operating as well."

Helen was wringing her hands by this time, showing on the outside what I'd been feeling on the inside. Shallow and complacent pretty much summed up the two of us, at least when it came to money. In my marriage, I'd never been "allowed" to be in the know about finances. Helen, who'd never married, was in the same situation, more or less, with our dad. What had he been thinking?

"That's what gave me the idea that you were left in charge of the business decisions, Doug. I see now how wrong I was." Helen cupped her cheeks in her palms and lowered her head.

"Me, too," I admitted.

"I suspected as much," Doug said. "That's why I thought we should have this pre-meeting, more or less. I was talking to Steve, our CPA, and we thought the two of you would need a true organizing meeting before you even decide how to go forward. Whatever you decide, it's time to bring in the experts."

"When you say go forward, do you mean you'll show us how to run the business?" Helen asked. "In the short term—I mean now—we even need to get a handle on the household accounts. For all these years, I've known that Ivy does the cooking, shopping, and light cleaning." Helen waved toward the French doors. "She straightens up the gardens and patio. But landscapers do most of the work. Every month for all my life, I've watched the cleaning service arrive to do the heavy cleaning."

"Didn't Dad ever explain *anything*?" I asked. I assumed he had filled Helen in on these details, and eventually, she'd feel up to talking about it. As for me, I needed time to get over not only Dad's death, but also to recover from the demise of my awful marriage. I needed to examine everything in my life and try not to sink even deeper into the muck of regret.

Helen gave the desk a whack. "No, he didn't. But I tried. I

asked the right questions, but he always teased about there being plenty of time ahead for us to talk. He implied that my questions meant I was afraid he was about to die. So, it was better not to make him think I was waiting for him to pass away." She slapped the desk again. "And that's why I stopped asking."

"What you two are describing is exactly what I was afraid of," Doug said sadly. "Fortunately, he had a will—you two own everything, as you know. That's not the same as understanding how to keep it. A possession isn't worth much if it erodes away over time."

I let out a long, heavy sigh. Much as I wanted to, I had no business blaming Helen for this mess. Whenever I came back for visits, I saw the household run smoothly and neither Helen nor I lifted a finger. I never asked how it was managed. For me, being home was like being on vacation.

"So, once I know what *you* want, I can set up a meeting. You don't have to make up your mind to keep the business. It's possible it could be sold as a small loan company, most likely, swallowed into a bigger firm." Doug frowned when he said that. "Or you could keep it as ME, a local loan company you operate out of the house here, just like your dad."

"You're implying we have choices, Doug," Helen said, quicker to piece all the implications together than I was. "Am I right? Are you sure our ignorance hasn't let this operation wither on the vine?"

Doug waved away Helen's words. "No, no, it's not too late to turn the ship around. That's why I'm here, Helen. Our firm would never have let it get to the point of no return. But we were waiting for you to come to us. I'm here because we *don't* want to let it get to be too late." Reeling in his impatience, Doug lowered his voice a notch and again said, "So, let's be clear about this, Helen, it's *not* too late."

Helen and I exchanged another look, and I suspected we both had the same hunch. Doug was upset with our dad. He was probably not happy with himself and probably regretted that he didn't push Max into leaving behind instructions for Helen. She was the one still at home, the logical heir to the business itself. For years, I was married, and Dad acted as if I was set for life. He didn't much care for my husband but commented little about him. He wasn't thrown by my divorce but didn't ask me about it. When Dad talked about Helen and me as being free, what had he meant? At the moment, this freedom felt a lot like we had been left in ignorance and not encouraged to become educated.

Doug shifted in the chair and finally stood. "I want you to call the firm and ask for Steve Anderson. I'm on my way over there now, and I'll tell him to expect your call before the end of business today."

Helen jumped to her feet. "I'll do that. Will he know what we need?"

"I'll fill him in, but he's someone who can help you figure out the business and get on a path *you* choose," Doug said. "You can't make decisions with your eyes closed. Steve can help you open them."

Suddenly, I was confused. Or maybe overwhelmed. But alarm bells were going off. "What exactly can he do for us?" I'd finally found the nerve to speak up after my initial panic quieted. When I was alone and calmer, I'd have to examine what this alarm was all about. For right now, I needed to keep my head in the game.

"Excellent question," Doug said. "Like I said, we have a couple of CPAs on staff, and Steve is one of them. He's been with us for over twenty years. He helps clients correct business problems, as opposed to legal issues. He's upbeat and easy to work with. Let's give him a chance to evaluate the financials."

"I trust your judgment, Doug." I looked across the desk at Helen, who had her hands braced on the desk. Her downcast expression aside, she nodded in agreement.

Doug pulled out his phone and sent a quick text, effectively drawing the meeting to a close. "Good. He'll expect your call today."

Doug went back to his role as Dad's friend and more or less a member of the family when he gave both of us a goodbye hug before hurrying to the door. "This is good. I'm glad you've made the choice to go forward. I'd rather see ME continue than be forced to advise you about shutting it down. With the right help, I'm sure the two of you can give ME the shot of energy to make it chug along again."

One of the most frequent guests in our house for many years, Doug didn't linger. He knew his way out.

After he left, Helen flopped down on one end of the couch in Dad's office. I settled in at the other end and curled my legs up under me. We sat in silence as the shock wore off. That was much easier to cope with than the deep embarrassment bordering on shame that set in. At least that was how I experienced this wake-up call. Waking up on many levels. More than anything, though, I was struck by Helen's sad expression, as if she had more regrets than I did.

A few minutes passed. Clouds covered the sun and the gardens darkened, but it brightened again when they passed. The breeze rose and fell, making the flowers sway one minute and stand still the next. As beautiful as the gardens were, it didn't matter. I tugged at the front edges of the vest I'd settled on. Its outdated look didn't matter. My out of style capris were of no consequence. Skinny jeans weren't going to solve my problems. Neither would Helen's fashion magazine style.

For the first time in our lives—and not young ones, either —we had to rely on ourselves to make a living. What counted now were the actions we took that would support us indefinitely or until we made a decision to go in a different direction. I'd long dreamed of turning my passion for quilting into a business. I didn't know about Helen, but she was a crack fundraiser and PR person. We might not know much about applying them to our current situation, but we had skills.

Right now, our dad's life work, his legacy, was at risk. I knew two things for sure. It wasn't entirely Helen's fault, or mine, that we were ignorant about the business and the systems that kept it moving. That was on Dad. But the second thing I knew for sure was that whatever our dad had done, or failed to do, was irrelevant.

What happened next was on us, Helen and me.

2

"I SUPPOSE I SHOULD APOLOGIZE FOR BEING SO UNAWARE OF THE business and how it functions." Helen's voice was low and halting, barely above a whisper. She stared off into space. "I've always had a *vague* notion that ME was our future, but I was under the illusion it was a reliable source of income, like it ran itself."

"I assumed it was like a trust fund that had regular payouts," I said, "although now I see what a silly assumption that was. Where did I think the loans came from?" The truth was not pretty. I'd counted on Helen to be more in the know. Proximity, I suppose. But that was putting a burden on her.

Helen's deep frown reflected her refocused energy. No longer focused on being helpless and sad, she'd morphed into deep-in-thought Helen.

"Do you remember when we briefly talked with Doug after the funeral?" Helen asked, still frowning.

"I do." Memories flooded in about the days that followed burying our dad. He might have been a man up in his seventies, but he wasn't ready to die. Maybe that's why he'd been so careless in preparing us for the business. He might have had his affairs in order, as the saying goes, but he'd been secretive about them. I couldn't help but imagine Dad wondering how death could have happened, even during those final seconds when the life drained from his body. Or maybe that was my projection, my way of explaining Dad's lapse in judgment, or more accurately, his years of avoiding the way he'd either dissolve or pass on the business.

"I obviously misunderstood and chose not to press the issue," Helen said. "During our conversation with Doug right after the funeral, I got the impression Dad's estate had loads of money in it. I didn't question the arrangement Dad and I had because it hadn't changed in years. All our lives, Dad had household accounts that operate on autopilot. We've seen that for ourselves."

"True, enough. The cleaners show up, Ivy gets paid, the lights stay on." I laughed from embarrassment. "Meanwhile, I've had the luxury of hanging out in what I'm calling my studio. You know, thinking about what to do with my life now that I'm free."

Helen leaned back. "Do you remember when I started doing the volunteer work, sort of as an offshoot of the business?"

"Of course, I remember," I said. "It seemed like such a good idea, and you were like me. We didn't really prepare for careers."

"Well, Dad assumed my volunteer work was just a temporary stop in my life."

First I heard of that notion. "Why? What did he think was going to happen?"

Helen held up her left hand and wiggled her fingers at me. "He assumed I'd be married. He had a few blind spots, our dad, and preparing his two daughters to be independent and on their own was certainly one of them." Helen shrugged. "I suppose I thought I'd get married, too, and that would be all I'd need. I can't believe I bought into Dad's assumption that being married would mean being taken care of. So stupid."

"I can see why he didn't include me in the business," I said. "I did get married and was off his hands—at least that's how he saw it. I didn't realize until years later, that women could stand alone and on their own."

"And single or married, women our age have their own careers," Helen said. "That's how I looked at the volunteer work."

"My quilting turned into my work eventually, after many years of living with a man who had no regard for me," I admitted. "But making it into a career to fully support myself will be tricky, especially with doing my part of the work for ME."

"I got so complacent," Helen said. "Since I'm the oldest, Dad probably expected me to get married before you did." She gave me a pointed look. "I fooled him, huh? I never met anyone who I really fell in love with—not enough to give up my life in this house." She gestured around the room and out to the gardens. "I love this house."

I got it. I loved the place, too. It was more than the place we grew up. It provided a sense of security, the place where Dad worked and Ivy made sure Helen and I had everything we needed. The house was also a gem, especially because of the gardens that set it apart from other houses nearby. "I've missed it all these years." I flashed a cynical smile. "Lucky for me, Dad didn't care about having a bunch of grandchildren, so even after I married—the wrong man, as we know—I never felt pressured about producing grandkids. But now, looking back, did Dad think this was the extent of the lives we'd have?"

"He never said one way or the other, did he? And I never asked." Helen banged her fist on the cushion. "I loved Dad, but he wasn't exactly a man you could describe as approachable. He was so completely wrapped up in the business."

I sat quietly and let Helen vent or reflect on or examine, whatever word she wanted to use, our dad's actions—or lack of them. All the while, I questioned my own lack of curiosity about Helen's life—or how she felt about it. She always seemed cheerful and happy. Maybe that was because she knew so many people in town through her work. Regardless of anything else, she had an identity based on service work for ME.

"Seriously, Tina, I've never had to manage finances. I've lived here all my life with the expenses covered. Dad put money in my account every month for personal needs. I used to think it was compensation for running the household—ha! I never had to direct Ivy, except to get a tray of coffee ready if Dad had a meeting in his office. I never dusted a vase or mopped a floor. I washed my own clothes, well, at least some of the time. That's all Max's daughter, Briarwood's Volunteer Queen, was expected to do."

"We don't have time for guilt or blame, Sis." I pulled my vest tighter across my chest as if hiding behind it. "Or shame. And I have a ton of that. Since I've been back, I've been preoccupied with my divorce and then Dad's death. I haven't done any real planning either. I've been locked in my own world, not even asking if you needed help with ME. I figured you had worked closely with Dad at some point."

I suppose my brain wasn't completely idle. I'd been spending a lot of time downstairs in my quilting studio, initially a place I stored my supplies and those vests I was beginning to question. I had new ideas in mind, and I missed teaching, although it didn't seem to have the same impact now as it once had. If women were talking behind my back about my outdated fabrics and designs, I wouldn't last long in Briarwood, with its growing reputation as an arts and crafts community. A well-known designer and pattern publisher lived here, and the town had a quilt shop large enough to attract out of town visitors, and it did a good online business as well. I wasn't sure how I would fit into this community, but it felt like the right place to be at the moment. Besides, I had no real expenses. The savings I had from my quilt business could sit for the time being. Eventually, I'd have to throw myself into ME—at least I'd see if I had any talent for it.

Helen laced her fingers around the back of her neck and blew out air. "Go ahead, you can say it. I was never the independent daughter I pretended to be. What a fiction...oh, sure, I came and went as I pleased, but that's hardly the same as being independent." She picked at the hem of the gorgeous silky emerald-green tunic. "Do you like this? I never thought twice about buying it and all the other things stuffed in my closet and dresser drawers. I had all that money magically appear in my account every month."

I shrugged. "I'll bet everyone in town thought you were paid staff of ME—the PR arm of the business. I think everyone knew I was more or less trapped with Alex, although I could have sprung that trap many times, but didn't. Fear, I guess. But I didn't want for anything material, not really. It just wasn't my money. Only the quilting gave me a taste of that kind of independence."

I paused to consider the odd situation we found ourselves in. Odd for twenty-first century women our age—fifty and fifty-two years old, respectively. But watching Helen, I knew my sister was being harder on herself than was justified. But the only thing different between Helen and me was my ill-conceived and ill-fated marriage. Big mistake. It took me away from Briarwood, but the silver lining was the chance to rediscover quilting, my passion. That alone helped me escape and at least start to find my own way.

"Look, we can go back and forth about what we should have done. We could go all the way back to graduating from high school without true goals to see our mistakes," I said. "But let's get real about this. Dad hired Maggie to oversee the business. She was both his administrator and sounding board. He didn't need us. When Maggie died, he didn't replace her. I suspect he never thought he could find anyone else like her."

Maggie Delaney and her children, John and Susan, came into our lives when our father hired her to be his assistant. When she first arrived, I had no idea about the important role she'd play in our lives. She was just a part of Dad's business. Even so, I knew in an instant I liked her. And I fell in love with John when he held out his hand like a grown-up man. We shook hands like we were making a pact. And maybe we were. He was ten, his sister was seven. I was eight and when I met John, I believed the world had finally righted itself.

"I've struggled with why questions all my life," I said. "The answers aren't easy and if you let them, they'll pull you down a rabbit hole."

Helen let a burst of cynical laughter escape. "Is there a pot of gold at the bottom of that rabbit hole?"

I grinned. "We can only hope the pot at the bottom includes instructions for running ME. Whether Dad brought us into it or not, he'd created ME and made it a big hit in town. And it supported the two of us growing up, and gave us Ivy, who raised us. That's not to mention this big house and its gardens, and Maggie, of course. He paid a full-time assistant as salary that allowed her to support her kids." John, like Maggie, practical, with a restless and artistic side, had never wanted for anything. "Dad made this life possible for all of us by lending money to businesses and families right here in town. We're sitting in this house and enjoying everything in it, including the most beautiful gardens in town, because of Dad."

As for the real rabbit-hole, I summed it up as: How did I get to be fifty years old and was still hiding under a shell after spending more than half my life in a bad marriage? How was it possible I was afraid of a spreadsheet? I'd avoided those questions far too long.

Helen's voice turned serious again. "Do you want to call Steve Anderson?"

I nodded once and then shook my head. "Yes, I want to have a meeting or a series of meetings or whatever it will take to gain an understanding of this business. But I'll leave it to you to take care of setting up the appointment, Sis. I don't have a schedule, but you come and go, so I know you do." At some point, I'd need to ask Helen about her boards and committees and afternoons spent volunteering here and there. "You can trust me to do half the work of whatever comes of the meeting."

"You got it," Helen said, allowing her shoulders to droop as if she would finally allow herself to relax.

I rubbed my temples. "I'm going downstairs to evaluate my outdated vests."

"Tina?" Helen drummed her fingers on a nearby pillow. "Why now? What happened to make you question your clothes?"

I let my head fall back and stared at the ceiling. "Lots of reasons, but I don't want to talk about them now. Let's just say, I need an update in more ways than one." I shook my head. "I think it means I have to head down the rabbit-hole, but this time I'll be prepared for the answers."

Helen smiled the same sad smile I'd noted earlier. Then

she nodded. "Go do what you have to do. I'll call Mr. Anderson."

AROUND NOON HELEN CAME DOWN THE STEPS TO MY QUILT studio. "What in the world have you done?"

I straightened up and planted my hands on my hips and surveyed the piles I created when I emptied my suitcase full of vests. I used a rolling suitcase to transport my vests from the car to the hotel and down the halls to the meeting rooms where I set up my classroom or to the expo where I had my own booth.

"It seems I've gone down one of those rabbit holes I mentioned." I pointed to the largest pile of vests. "I'm donating those." I moved my hand to the second stack on the floor. "I want to keep those for teaching. At least until I can make new samples." Finally, I nodded toward the smallest group. "And... well, those I want to keep because I like them so much. But at least I'll have lightened my load of vests by about half."

Helen leaned against the doorjamb. "Whatever. But to use Doug's words, 'That won't make Montgomery Enterprises chug along.' Steve's coming on Thursday. He'll be sending us an email outlining our first steps. He sounds nice on the phone, but you know how wrong first impressions can be." She sighed.

Right. And Helen should know. Sadly, Helen and I are a lot alike that way. A couple of years back, she'd been engaged to a man who seemed like quite a catch. Even Dad agreed he'd be a good partner for her. At one time, we thought that when it came to his daughters, Dad's trust level was on the low side. Or, put another way, we believed he had high standards for us. It turned out he wasn't paying much attention. Whenever I thought of that, it wasn't so much a criticism of Dad as an observation.

One day Helen was at the beauty salon and overheard the woman in the next chair chatting excitedly about her move to Briarwood. She rattled on about finally being closer to her fiancé. A little detail here and a familiar fact there caught Helen's attention. Putting it all together, it soon became painfully clear that Helen and this woman were engaged to the same guy.

Needless to say, that was the end of Helen's wedding plans. My dramatic sister hadn't waited for weak explanations and more lies. She'd thrown the diamond ring back in his face.

"Apparently, we'll have homework," Helen said, bringing me back to the present.

"How so?"

"He's sending us lists of what he wants us to do to prepare for the meeting." Helen stared off into my studio, looking around, but not taking much in.

"We'll do whatever is required," I said with a shrug.

Preoccupied with my quilting, I filed the meeting prep work, whatever it was, in my mental to-do file, tucked back behind some more pressing matters. As I stood surrounded by vests, I asked myself if my sister likely considered my quilting too frivolous. I mean, could I make a living through quilting?

Well, yes and no. Obviously, people did—the quilting world was filled with career quilters, legendary designers and teachers. But at the moment, I couldn't elevate my reputation into that top group, especially after hearing some women bluntly critique my outdated samples. Even worse, I couldn't disagree.

At least for the time being, I couldn't concern myself with my quilting passion. Besides, what did she mean when she quoted Doug's words about ME chugging along? I had to rethink her words. Did she mean the CPA we had yet to meet thought Helen would have to give up her volunteer work and I'd have to give up quilting in order to run ME? Was that the bottom line?

"What's this all about, Tina?" Helen asked flapping her hand at the piles. "I don't understand why you're preoccupied with the vests when you know what Doug said. We have a business to salvage. Doug was pretty frank when he gave us the ugly truth. If we can't keep the business going, we'll have no income. True, we don't have a mortgage to worry about, but given property taxes and upkeep we'll still need to sell the house. Maybe our priority ought to be not going broke. I'd just as soon not lose our home."

I started to answer, but I couldn't put my thoughts together fast enough, and Helen wasn't done.

"Why now, Tina?" She raised her hands in the air and let them flop to her sides in frustration. "With all that's going on, why are you questioning what you wear and what has essentially been a hobby?"

I couldn't answer her question about timing. I'd always assumed I'd keep quilting and teaching, no matter what. Like I'd keep breathing. But I was confused, too, and it was useless to think I could hide the truth.

"Coming back to Briarwood from the quilt show last weekend, I overheard two women on the charter bus whispering about my classes and sniping about my clothes." I shook my head. "They weren't shy with their comments, either."

I repeated every word: *Tina's given that same class so often even I could teach it. And what has her so sour lately? She never smiled at us or cracked a joke.*

Her companion delivered another blow: *Her vests are so outdated. She hasn't mentioned any new gadgets or notions either. She... She...blah, blah, blah.*

Standing with Helen, I crossed my arms tightly across my chest and hunched my shoulders as if trying to shrink and disappear. My eyes filled with tears. Since coming back to Briarwood, and getting that fast divorce, I'd managed to scrape together a few dollars teaching at quilt shows or at guild meetings. That didn't count the money Dad had started giving me every month, like he'd done for Helen. Obviously, he died so quickly, that wasn't relevant, but I now realized that had he not died, he'd have likely kept that up forever. But oh, it hurt to be confronted with all the questions that came up around the fact that two middle-aged, capable women relied on dear ol' Dad to support them, one long-term, and me very short-term. And I hadn't been surprised by Dad giving me that money.

Wow. I had to push all that away. I just couldn't sink deep into the place within me where I'd have to figure out how that happened. That was a major rabbit hole.

My marriage to Alex, an obvious and prolonged mistake, taught me all I needed to know about enormously selfish, petty people. Among other things, he had been threatened by my early successes as a quilt teacher. He liked a woman—that would be me—to be at his beck and call, so when I left for quilt shows he'd pout like a child until that turned into ugly temper tantrums. Not physical abuse, his controlling behavior certainly fit the definition of emotional abuse. In some ways, that tricked me into thinking he could and would change. Not so. Ultimately, he tricked some other woman into catering to him.

Alex kept a tight rein on our finances, primarily by keeping me in the dark. Of course, I later learned he was a major league liar. Little white lies were only a warm-up act. As the divorce went forward, Doug was able to get a court order to review all our financial documents, going back years. Naturally, Doug asked me if I'd known we went through long periods when Alex relied on plastic to pay for our most mundane expenses—even the utility bills. His latest credit card spree spanned the last year of our marriage. Alex had sold only enough insurance policies to keep his job, but not enough to support his lifestyle. He took cash advances on the cards, so he could keep up the fiction of handing me cash to pay for groceries and miscellaneous household items.

When I knew for sure I couldn't stay married to a man who, among other things, had left me demoralized and dependent for years, I packed the only things that mattered to me, primarily related to my quilting life, and came home to Briarwood.

Moving back into my family's house and living with Helen and Dad again wouldn't have been my first choice, but at the time it seemed like my only option. It was the choice that kept a roof over my head while I took a deep breath and began to piece back together the life I unraveled. When in doubt, I hung on to hope that I could reinvent myself.

Apparently, seeing me standing in the middle of my studio in defeat was too much for Helen because she crossed the room and grabbed my shoulders. "Hey, Tina, stop this nonsense. You're smart and talented and could teach anyone to sew...quilt. Even me." She gave me a sly smile.

I tilted my head and in a dry tone asked, "Want to try?"

She raised her eyebrows and looked as if she might burst out laughing any second. "One day. *Maybe*. But that wasn't my point. You identified your own problem. You need an update. What business doesn't need updates now and again?" She pursed her lips. "Even ME, or so it seems."

"True enough," I said.

"Not important now, though," Helen said. "We need to get our finances in order first before we make other plans."

"Right." I took a step back. "Knowing how to quilt isn't a

critical skill if you're broke." I swung my arm wide over the mess I'd made on the carpeted floor. "Doug was very clear that the only way we can come to terms with the business, and what Dad did or didn't do to help us, is to take this one step at a time."

Helen nodded and then turned toward the door. "Ivy has lunch ready. You coming?" She was humming something. I couldn't identify the song, but typical of Helen, it had an upbeat, happy melody.

I wouldn't keep Tilly Iverson waiting. She'd asked that we call her Ivy when she first came to our house after our mom and baby brother died in childbirth. Dad quickly realized he needed help to manage two young daughters, Helen, nearly five, and me, three. At the time, he was building a fledgling business and working a full-time job as an assistant manager of Briarwood's grocery store. Operating on a shoestring, he'd also bought and sold a couple of pieces of property, which was how we happened to have such large home. It had plenty of room for Ivy to have her own private space. I hadn't known life without her.

Ivy was a young widow when Dad hired her. She'd lost her husband in a military exercise overseas and becoming a nanny was ideal for her, at least until she figured out her next step. The job description included being a housekeeper and nanny, and she'd been twenty-four years old when she became more or less our mom. Dad hoped he'd found someone who would want a permanent position and paid Ivy well. As it turned out, she didn't need to figure out her next steps and settled into her job with us and made herself indispensable. Meanwhile, Dad's business had thrived, so he could keep her on. Now, she was a youngish seventy-one. She'd never stopped taking care of us, and that made her more like family than an employee.

Embarrassing as it was, it didn't occur to me to ask how Ivy was being paid after Dad died. Like everything else, I assumed it was all part of some internal organizational system. Pay the property tax, sign the annual contract with the landscapers, direct deposit Ivy's salary...all of a piece. As it turned out, my assumption had been on target.

As usual, Ivy made our chef salad lunch into an occasion when she added her hot rolls to the menu. She made the platter of fresh fruit the centerpiece on the table, which sat near the window. The tall glasses of iced tea were so chilled they were beginning to weep.

Ivy was the chattiest at the table, telling us all she'd accomplished that morning. She'd fixed our supper, but we'd have to heat it ourselves. "I'm joining friends for a boat trip and dinner on the river tonight."

I'd noticed during visits and when I moved back in that Ivy was open about her plans with her own friends. When we were still kids, Ivy was more private about her plans outside our house. We never imagined Ivy would have plans...really? To us, Ivy was like our teachers. She had no life except the one that revolved around us! When she'd stayed on to tend to the house, Dad, and Helen, she relaxed that policy and Helen knew about her life apart from us. Ivy had an enormous number of friends and took vacations with them—she'd met some on winter tropical cruises and hiking trips in Europe.

On the issue of men, however, Ivy maintained her privacy. If she had a man in her life, or wanted one, we never knew it. Helen might have gleaned more information, but neither of us would invade Ivy's privacy by delving deeply into her personal life.

"That means you'll need to fend for yourself, Tina," Helen said. "I have a dinner meeting with the committee to organize the annual benefit for The Briarwood Youth Club. Hopefully, the country club will host again this year."

"Oh, okay," I said, pretending to be put upon. "I guess I'll have to eat alone, again. That makes three evenings this week you've both been gone." I stabbed a cut of tomato and held my fork over my plate. "Someday I'll surprise you both and announce I'll be gone for the evening." I, too, benefited from Ivy's well-run household. Buttering the hot roll, I realized how fortunate I was.

Helen reaped the rewards of staying in her homeplace of Briarwood, one of which was cultivating tons of acquaintances and several close friends. Some went back to her high school days, but most were accumulated over the course of what amounted to a full-time job as a volunteer. Dad had also kept up our family membership at the country club, not because he cared about golf, but that's how he stayed in touch with clients and referrals.

ME had a connection to the charitable work and other issues in town that kept Helen in the loop. These contacts and friendships made up a large network that were her lifeline to what looked like a full life. My sister had inherited our mother's legendary talent for bringing together committees and sponsors to make any benefit a success. For sure, I'd always envied Helen's people skills, which were what had enabled her to remain the public face of ME for so long.

When I was living across the state in a terrible marriage, Helen's life looked so good to me. At first, I resolved to try to create a wonderful life of my own away from the shadow cast by Dad and Helen. As that became more difficult to pull off, I tried to hide what was happening. Somehow, though, I'd long known that Helen's life wouldn't have suited me. Eventually, quilting saved me from sinking deeper into unhappiness. In the end, on some level, that bit of independence gave me the push I needed to leave Alex.

LATER THAT NIGHT, I READ THE LAST PAGE OF A ROMANCE NOVEL by one of my favorite authors and just as I reached to turn off my bedside light, I heard the front door close. A few seconds later, a light tap sounded on my bedroom door.

"Tina? It's Helen. Can I come in?" She had an upbeat lilt in her voice.

I hadn't heard that for a long time, certainly not since Dad's funeral.

"Sure. What's up? You sound excited."

She opened the door with a burst of energy, her words tumbling one over the next. "You'll never guess who's on the benefit committee." She perched on the edge of the bed. "Drum roll, please." She slapped her thighs. "The one and only, Steve Anderson. Turns out he volunteers at the youth club two evenings a week. He sings its praises. He said he's met the nicest people there."

Even in the dim light, I saw a light blush cross her face. "You said he sounded friendly this morning on the phone."

"Friendly, polite, creative, considerate. What's not to like? We all stopped for dessert and coffee after the meeting with a couple of parents and the kids who hang out at the center."

"Good. You always enjoy doing the events connected to the youth center," I said, recalling that this annual event was one of Helen's favorites. Dad benefited through his association with country club and was well known by many families around town, even if they'd never been ME clients. From what I knew of my mother, this is exactly what she would have wanted. "You've seen the kids of our old high school friends have some benefit from it, and now their kids," I said. "You have such deep roots here."

"True," Helen said, but she didn't stop to consider the

import of what I said. She jumped immediately into Steve's apparently great sense of humor. "He's hilarious when he talks about the kids." She grinned. "He's one of those rare people who can tell amusing tales about things kids say and do without sounding condescending."

"He must be a really valuable volunteer then," I said.

"That's a given. But I can't stop thinking about how he had us all laughing 'til our faces hurt." She stopped and frowned. "I guess you had to have been there, because I can't tell you exactly what was so funny. But you'll see what I mean on Thursday."

"Now you've whetted my appetite for more," I said.

Helen fluttered her fingers in a quick wave. "'Night." She almost closed the door behind her but opened it again. "Oh, by the way, I saw lights on in John's house when I drove past coming home."

3

If I thought I'd get a good night's sleep after hearing that John Delaney had come home to Briarwood, I was mistaken. Memories whirled through my mind like the fast turning of a Ferris wheel. I couldn't remember a time when John hadn't been the best part of my life. I could almost reconstruct in my memory whole days spent with him, entire conversations. We laughed, we argued, and we were so in sync with each other, I assumed we'd share a life together. Well, at least those were my dreams.

Following his sister's death from leukemia, John had become a quiet, too serious kid who found an outlet in photography. Maggie, their mom and Dad's assistant, had brought him a camera as a gift the previous Christmas and he carried it with him wherever he went. I knew that because I'd loved nothing more than following him around. I don't think anyone imagined that camera, meant as a distraction from grief, would end up a passion that dominated his life. John spent his last three years of high school behind the lens of his camera documenting everyday life in Briarwood, as well as the town's special events for the *Briarwood Gazette*.

Two years ahead of me in school, I was devastated when John announced at his graduation party that he was leaving Briarwood. At sixteen, all my assumptions about first love had been false, or at least that's how I saw his announcement. We were so close. I assumed there was more to it, but it seemed, to John, we were only friends. In my dreamy teenage world, John and I would be married one day and have a family together in Briarwood. I saw him making a career as the newspaper reporter in town—or maybe at one of the bigger cities nearby. I hadn't even thought of equivalent dreams for myself. I'd entwined my life with John's.

I cried for a week after he left. Now, thirty-four years later, the hollowness left in the aftermath of his leaving remained in my heart. How crazy that was, especially since other than his mother, Maggie, I was the one person John had stayed in touch with over the years. We started as friends, and friends we remained.

I couldn't wait to see him.

After tossing and turning the rest of the night, I was still in bed when my phone chimed with Helen's ring tone. "Hey, sleepy head. You going to stay in bed all day?"

"Be right there." I grabbed my sweat suit and headed to the bathroom. No more than ten minutes later I walked into the kitchen.

John Delaney leaned against the counter, all lean and tan, smiling that crooked smile that had always made my knees buckle. I'd learned to hide it, or at least thought I had. He held his coffee cup backwards, handle pointing out, a habit he'd started years ago. Faded jeans and a gray T-shirt fit his body like they had been made for him.

"Hey, Tina." His smooth, deep voice filled the room. "I figured I'd see you here."

My sister held out a cup of coffee. "Drink this," she ordered.

I might have fooled others, but never Helen. She had a talent for reading people, including me. She failed to hide the Cheshire cat grin crossing her face. She knew I still held feelings for John. He was the first person I'd texted when I moved back into the house and again when Dad died. Knowing he was gone most of the time, I had no expectation about when I'd finally see him.

I grabbed the cup and brought it to my lips. The almond flavor was a favorite of mine, and I closed my eyes with the first swallow. "Okay, tell me everything I've missed." I perched on one of the counter stools. I couldn't take my eyes off him, nor could I stop the joy that traveled through me.

John dipped his head. "Nothing much. Got in too late last night to stop for groceries. Couldn't sleep much either. I'm still on Jakarta time, so my body thinks I should be wrapping up a night out with friends and heading to bed."

"But here you are," Helen said, giving him a knowing look.

"I knew there'd be coffee in this kitchen. Besides, I'm going to do my best to stay awake and get back to good ol' Central Standard Time. I figured someone in this house would be awake by now." He held his cup out when Helen offered more from the carafe.

"How long are you staying this time?" I covered my mouth. Why would that be the first thing I asked him? "Sorry. I'm not fully awake yet. It was a long night."

"Don't know for sure, but it was a long, complicated assignment in Indonesia. I've been doing a lot of environmental shoots, and that has its ups and downs. I haven't committed to a next step yet. I turned down a quick trip to the Canadian Arctic. Those come along fairly regularly." He set his cup down and pushed away from the counter. "That should keep me awake for a few hours. I'd better do some shopping. Need anything from the store?"

I wanted to ask a million questions, and talk to him about Dad's death, and the predicament Helen and I were in, but I held my tongue. He needed time to get his body caught up to the time zone before we caught up on the real stuff. He knew the basic facts of all that had happened, but I'd not had a chance to talk with him about what it all meant. That was what I missed the most when he was working in remote places, and I couldn't count on a phone call long enough to really connect.

"Thanks for the offer," Helen said, "but Ivy still has that covered. She had a grocery delivery yesterday."

"Ivy...of course. Every time I come home, I expect to hear that Ivy's retired, but I never do." He sounded genuine when he said, "You are two very lucky women."

"She's still spoiling us." Helen gave John a hug. "I'm glad you stopped over. Don't be a stranger." She topped off the coffee in her cup and left the room.

John turned toward me and held out his arms. I didn't hesitate to step into them. "I'm sorry about Max, Tina. I would have been here, but I was deep in the jungle and didn't get your message until after the funeral. But because of your texts, I you'd moved back to Briarwood before you lost Max." John pulled back long enough to say, "Do you want to talk about Max?" He paused. "Or Alex?"

I shook my head. "Not now. We can talk about Dad and ME and what's going to happen another time." I shrugged. "And as for Alex, I'm trying to put him behind me." I stepped away from him and jabbed my thumb in the air over my shoulder. "Way behind me."

Ignoring my gesture, John looked at me through curious

eyes. "Decisions? Do you mean about the business? How did Max leave things?"

"Not nearly as clear as we imagined he would. In fact, we're having a meeting with a CPA at Doug's firm to get a clearer picture. It's about time Helen and I learned how this machine stays oiled." I cocked my head. "It's embarrassing how little we know about ME and how it works."

"We'll have plenty of time in the days ahead to catch up." He couldn't hide the yawn that escaped.

I nodded and gave him a big smile. "Go. Go, before you drop."

I watched through the kitchen window as he walked on the stone path Dad had built to connect the Delaneys' house with ours. Their house sat on a smaller lot than ours, which looked like an estate, but was really just one of Briarwood's larger than average houses. I recalled Maggie walking to work every day on that path.

I took a settling breath, topped off my coffee cup, and went to find Helen. She was in the home office, with a frown so deep it made me laugh. "What could possibly be so frustrating, Sis?"

"John's gone? Already? He looks great, huh?" she said, glancing up. "Oh, did you read the email from Steve? It came in late last night."

The casual way she referred to our new CPA, anyone would have thought he was an old friend and not someone assigned to become a business advisor. "I scanned it, but I planned to take a closer look. Now is as good a time as any." I went to retrieve my computer.

A few minutes later, I was back in the office sitting opposite Helen with my laptop, taking in Steve's list of instructions —or what Helen called our homework. He provided passwords and links to accounts we'd had no access to before.

"We'll get into the business," Helen said, "but let's take a look at the household accounts first."

I let out a hoot. "Great minds...I need the warmup. I mean, how complex could the household accounts be?"

"Famous last words," Helen said dryly.

Using the links and passwords Steve provided, we soon found ourselves looking at a spreadsheet and list of automatic withdrawals and transfers. Like clockwork, money was transferred from Dad's account to the one he used for the household expenses.

"Here it is," I said. "Month after month, Ivy's salary is withdrawn and deposited to her bank."

"Right after Dad died, I asked Ivy if I needed to talk with Doug about the household accounts, including her salary," Helen explained. "Ivy assured me all those expenditures had been on autopilot, as she put it, for years. Dad had it set up for Doug to keep all the transactions activated for continuity. Ivy's been using a debit card for groceries and other household items."

"Good. One less thing for us to concern ourselves with," I said. The minute the words came out of my mouth, I heard them on playback in my head. "I can't believe I said something that ridiculous."

Helen rolled her hand at me as if encouraging me to explain.

"We don't know how this amount of money is put into the household account, Helen," I said. "It's one thing to note the regularly scheduled payouts, but it's another to know how Dad determined the lump sum he deposited into his personal account, his business salary."

Helen looked back at the screen and then scrolled. "Well, here's a last-day-of-the-month transfer from one of the business accounts into his personal one. Then he had the household funds transferred from there."

I laughed again. "Good. One more step, Sis. Gosh what geniuses we are, huh? We found the household spreadsheet and the account transfer notation. Whoopee." I was half laughing, but it was as much from embarrassment as anything else.

"Make fun if you like, Tina, but I'm marking off one item from the list." Good as her word, Helen dramatically picked up a pen and slashed through a line on the to-do list she'd printed out for each of us. "We may not understand how the set amount of money gets into the account from the business and then to Dad's personal account, but at least we know that the cleaning crew and Ivy are paid."

"Odd to think that hasn't kept me up at night," I said, puzzled at myself.

Helen thought I was joking, because her guffaw told me she'd gotten a big kick out me.

"No, I'm serious, Sis. Really. I'm surprised that I never gave it a thought or asked the question." It was my turn to stare into space. "It's not that different from Alex handing me cash for the groceries. He handled the bills from a household account I never saw. It was years before I questioned that."

Not waiting for Helen to feel obligated to comment, I clicked on another link, and sure enough, the household bank statement reflected recent payments to the three different markets in Briarwood, plus some online sources for paper products, specialty foods, and spices.

"We didn't want for a single thing," I said flatly. "Still don't. At least for the moment."

"Why do you sound sad?" Helen asked. "That's a good thing, isn't it?"

"I suppose. But it feels strange not to know how the food I

happily consume at every meal is paid for. I only know who makes the meals. And even that I take for granted."

Helen glanced at the time on the computer. "Ivy will be knocking on the door to tell us lunch is ready at the stroke of noon." She grinned. "You know Ivy. Nothing's changed. We still have to show up with clean hands and on time."

I suggested we go through the household accounts and take a look at the expenses over the previous year to get some idea of what it really cost to keep this large house going.

"Okay but prepare to be surprised by the numbers. I've been living here all these years and I can't believe what I'm seeing." Helen pushed her chair back from the desk as if not wanting to take in more information.

My gut churned as we looked at the totals. We hadn't even looked at Dad's accounts to get a true picture of the business income, but we already knew it took a lot of money to run a house the size of ours.

A couple of minutes before noon, we both put our computers in sleep mode and stood and simultaneously stretched our arms over our head. I hadn't noticed before how cool and comfortable Helen looked in her halter-topped sundress. The floral pattern suited her. Her look was casual, not a hint of fussy, but it was obviously chosen rather than grabbed. I looked down at my khaki shorts and T-shirt. Definitely pulled on without much thought.

We left the office and ran into Ivy halfway to the kitchen. "I was just coming to get you for lunch," she said.

"We thought we'd save you the trouble," Helen said.

"We need this break," I said. "We're halfway through the work, but this afternoon's project is the hardest."

Helen shrugged. "It would be much more fun to swim at the country club, but duty calls."

I wasn't big on the club, but it sounded more interesting to me, too. I couldn't fault Helen.

Ivy had made BLTs piled high with tomatoes and crispy bacon. She'd also put out dishes of yogurt, peach for me and strawberry for Helen.

"Some things don't change," she said. "These were your favorite flavors when you were kids, and I know they still are."

We agreed. Helen was used to Ivy's thoughtful ways. The woman who raised us had a knack for adding special touches to make everything fun or even elegant, including the paper-thin orange slices she'd added to our ice water. Ivy led off our lunchtime conversation by speculating when John would leave for his next assignment and where he might go this time.

"I'm sorry I missed him this time, but I suppose I'll have a chance to see him before he takes off again," Ivy said. "Always liked him, even as a boy. He found his passion early and went after it."

Ivy was right, but that didn't stop the little arrows of sadness from piercing my heart. Again. Always. He wanted a more exciting life than Briarwood could offer. He was like the person in the song who was off to see the world and had managed to cover much of the world there was to see. I had enormous regrets about marrying Alex and staying almost to three decades, but one of the biggest was that I never had the chance to travel other than to some quilt shows. As Helen and Ivy chatted, I stayed silent, making my vow that I wouldn't let the rest of my life pass me by without seeing more of the world.

Helen didn't waste a minute lingering over lunch. She was the one who put her napkin next to her plate and pushed her chair back. "Come on, Tina, let's get to it. We have a lot to do this afternoon."

She poured herself a mug of the fresh coffee Ivy had made

and headed down the hallway to the office. I don't know why, but I expected to be the one to drive this train, mistakenly assuming Helen would lose interest by the afternoon. Instead, I was the one who sighed as I grabbed my mug and followed. I would have liked to do and be anywhere else but staring at a screen in Dad's office.

Helen decided to print copies of the first of the spreadsheets that summarized income and output. As we waited for the copies, I couldn't keep a lid on my curiosity about Helen's sudden interest in working so hard on ME. "I need to ask a question. I hope you won't be offended. But I heard you go on about Steve. You obviously like him. Are you doing this work for us or to impress him?"

She flashed an annoyed look. "What difference does it make, and why do you care? This has to be done in any case."

"Oops, like I said, I didn't want to rile you up." I raised my hands defensively. "And you're right. We have to do this for our own survival. That's a fact."

"That's the point. Frankly, Tina, I don't know what I'd do if we ran out of money. Honestly, I saw the books this morning, same as you. I *live* here." She flicked her hand in the air. "Think of what this looks like to the outside world. For years, I've seen the cleaning crew come and go. The guys come to mow and weed. Everything runs on schedule—and it's Ivy's clock. The carpets are cleaned in the spring and fall, the gutters are maintained, and the furnace is checked." She flopped back in the chair. "I don't think you had a good sense of this household, either."

"How can I argue? I obviously lived in my own little externally comfy world without being allowed to know any of the details." I still wanted the answer to my question. "And Steve?" I prompted.

A smile crossed her face before she twisted in Dad's chair

and looked out the French door windows. "He sure is easy to look at."

I didn't have a chance to agree or probe further because my phone buzzed, and I decided not to let the call go to voice mail. "Hi, Heather," I said, surprised to see her name pop up. "What's up?"

Heather Grant had been a lifelong Briarwood friend. We'd both learned quilting from Maggie Delaney, John's mother. During my visits, we'd get together, and our conversations inevitably got around to quilting. Even at Dad's funeral we'd found a quiet corner to talk about shop in town, Janet's Quilt Shop, the go-to place for quilting supplies. Heather was teaching classes there.

"I *desperately* need your help, my friend." Heather's voice had a raspy edge that told me she was really stressed.

"If I can, sure. You know that." I walked over to the bookcase that had a picture of our mother on the shelf next to the old-style leather and cloth-covered ledgers Dad had used when he started Montgomery Enterprises. I put my hand out to touch the glass over her face. I had only a few wispy memories of her, only a couple of images that had real memories attached to them. Some of the fleeting memories were likely of Dad showing me pictures and telling me about her.

"Valerie broke her arm and wrist this morning and is having surgery to put it back together later this afternoon. She'll be in the hospital for a couple of days." Heather paused to take a breath as she explained her youngest daughter's emergency. "I'm scheduled to teach a beginners' class on Saturday at Janet's. Someone has to stay with Valerie, and Dewayne has to leave town on business."

"You need me to cover for you?" I asked, wanting to get to the point. "If that's what you need, sure."

"That's fantastic," Heather said with a heavy sigh of relief.

"Janet doesn't want to cancel or reschedule the class unless she absolutely has to." Her words were still rushed, probably like her day had been.

Helen was looking on, curious about what I was agreeing to. "Look, Janet, I can't talk now. I'm in a meeting. I'll call you back this evening to get the details. I hope the surgery goes well." We said quick goodbyes, and I tagged off the call.

Helen laughed. "A meeting? So that's what this is?"

I mulled that over for a couple of seconds. "Well, yes, what would you call it? It's literally a business meeting. Why else would we sit at our computers on a gorgeous day like this?"

"Ah, yes, that pesky little detail about supporting ourselves and this household," Helen said, smiling.

"Seriously, Helen, we have to be ready – or as best as we can be – when Steve comes. We need his help to keep ME running, so we need to understand the business enough to ask the right questions." There, that was about as succinct as it got.

It's no exaggeration that the morning's work was child's play compared to what we faced in the afternoon. Together, we tried to follow Steve's logical instructions, written to help us sort all this out. But his use of certain terms relating to the types of loans and interest rates stumped us. We followed along his detailed explanation of a couple of sample loans, one long-term, and one short-term, both of which fit typical models of ME lending. But we were in over our heads.

We knew there were loans, lots of them, and they all fell under the ME umbrella, but Dad had used different models with varying terms based on other factors.

"From what I can guess, this short-term loan was to meet payroll," I said, "but I believe Dad did business with this plumbing company for years. Don't you remember hearing the owner's name? We might find a long-term loan in the files, too."

Helen shook her head. "Nothing sounds familiar except the company name. They've been around for a long time."

"Thanks to Dad," I said. "When we dive into the piles of loans, we're going to recognize more names, but not because Dad ever said anything. He was good about privacy."

"Maggie, too," Helen said. "She was privy to all this information."

Suddenly, the fog began to lift on the magnitude, not only of the job ahead of us, but on the impact ME had on our little hometown. Wow. "This is a huge responsibility, isn't it? Dad ran this business from right here in this office, with Maggie's help. Imagine a small loan company never having an outside office. Amazing."

Seeing the household accounts that morning was shocking, especially my own ignorance about the simplest financial decisions. When I married Alex he set the rules, and his rule number one was "I manage the money." I never argued, assuming that he had a clue about what that meant. A terrible mistake. I thought I needed to be more aware of our basic financial picture, but Alex didn't like questions. I was as much at a loss as Helen when it came to accounting and investments.

"So, at least we know what Steve wanted us to see." Helen's tone was somber. "I wonder if he realized just how little we understand about ME."

I reached over and lightly slapped the table. "Past tense, Helen. Even after glancing through this long list of loans, we aren't sure how Dad made lending decisions, but at least we have some idea of the scope. We understand a lot more than we did when we started." We even saw that Dad had widened his territory, so to speak, into nearby towns smaller than Briarwood, but that did business here.

Helen closed the document on her screen and rested her elbows on the desk. She held her head in her hands. "You're right, but I'm still frustrated, embarrassed, flummoxed. You pick the words. After putting in around six hours today, I'm done." Helen straightened up. "My head is swimming." She let out a cynical laugh. "That's why I'm going for a swim at the club. Do you want to come along?"

"No, I'm not much for lounging around the pool. I don't even have a decent bathing suit." I paused before I said that Steve would likely understand our lack of business and accounting knowledge. "My quilting money and expenses were like a mini-mini-version of the expense side of ME's ledgers," I said, "but Steve's examples and explanations are a start. Imagine having someone to walk us through this minefield. Talk about luck."

Helen pointed to her head. "Somewhere inside my brain I know you're right. But I feel deflated. I can't help it. I need to go swim off this sense of total inadequacy." Helen put aside Steve's list and the printed spreadsheets from this morning. "Oh, by the way, I won't be here for supper. I'll tell Ivy on my way out."

She dashed away before I could ask where she was going, leaving me alone to wonder how we were going to become competent business owners almost overnight.

The room felt empty and extra-silent without Helen's energy, even the concern in the air about our ability—or lack of it—to manage what Dad created. The sun had shifted in the late afternoon and the office was darker than before. All day, the flower gardens had been tempting me from the windows of the office, and I needed the solitude and quiet they offered. I wandered to the kitchen to pour a glass of chilled white wine and wind down from the day. Ivy's note caught my eye. Like Helen, she'd be gone for the rest of the day, but as always, a meal was ready for me when I was ready for it.

Outside, the intense humidity that had hovered over Briarwood the past week had subsided, replaced by a cool breeze. I slowly walked to an area of the gardens Maggie had dubbed the resting area, probably because it had two rocking chairs shaded by a tall oak tree that had once held a swing for Helen and me—and John and Susan. One of the gardens had blossoms struggling to survive in the overgrowth of weeds. I had to smile to myself. I knew from the household books the landscape crew was due in a week, but I bent over to pull a large weed near the edge of the bed. When I pulled, a slosh of wine dribbled over my hand.

"That's a waste of wine."

I recognized the rich voice without turning to see who was standing next to me. I looked up and found John partially silhouetted by the late afternoon sun. Drops of water in his hair sparkled. He looked rested and refreshed from a shower.

I laughed. "That silly weed was more stubborn than I gave it credit for."

"Mom always said that after a rain was the best time to weed." John leaned down to pull more weeds, but they held tight to the ground. "Maybe watering the gardens would work." He flashed a sly grin. "Or maybe we should let the professionals handle it."

"Sounds like a plan," I said. "I was just thinking that Maggie had started the first flower garden the second summer after coming to Briarwood to be Max's assistant. Helen and I hinted that we wanted a swimming pool where the boring old lawn was, so when the grass was removed and the undersoil dug out, we thought we'd won. We jumped up and down and pranced around."

"I have a vague memory of two very disappointed girls," John said. "Really crabby when the load of black planting soil was delivered."

Maggie didn't get far with Helen, a true water-lover and swimmer, but she coaxed me into kneeling next to her in the evenings planting seeds and putting starter plants into the soil. Every day I checked to see if the seeds had sprouted. After weeks of waiting, the garden became filled with colorful flowers. By then I had forgotten about the pool and picked bouquets for Dad and Ivy.

Maggie planted more gardens every summer and the showpiece gardens soon became more than she could handle, especially when she planted flowers alongside the stone pathway through the backyards that connected the Delaney house to the Montgomery house. That marked a shift for me. A sign that the Delaneys were here to stay and almost like family. Maggie turned over much of the work of the gardens to the company doing the yard work, but they were schooled in exactly what she wanted—and how she wanted it done.

John stretched out his leg and sent one of the rocking chairs nearby in motion. "Were you planning to sit for a while?"

"You bet. I've been working my brain so hard I need to give it a rest." I moved to the rocker and settled in. After taking a sip of wine, I said, "Helen and I are getting ready for our meeting with the accountant, and we're trying to get a handle on Dad's loans. We're starting from scratch, so it's been a trying day."

"I get it," John said. "Mom used to say ME was a complex business and much of it based on hunches. Objectively, Max should have said no to certain loans, but if he knew and trusted the person he said yes."

Bingo! That explained, at least in part, why we had trouble

making sense of the way each loan was individualized. "I had a feeling Dad bended the conventional rules pretty much all the time. But not being financial wizards—a serious understatement—ME is a challenge for us." I put the edge of my hand to my forehead to block the sun from my eyes. "I wish your mom was here to teach us about ledgers and loans."

John nodded. "I realized later she talked very little about her work."

"Probably because of the privacy factor. Helen and I noticed that," I mused.

"Mom never mentioned a name, not once in all the years she worked for Max," John added.

"I rarely associate Maggie with the business, even though I know Dad trusted her completely. But when I think of her, I see her in the gardens after work. In my mind's eye, she's either planting new beds or tending to some corner she thought needed extra attention." I rocked as I spoke, thoughts of Maggie swirling through my head.

"Hold that thought. I'll be right back." John turned and jogged toward his house and returned with a glass and an opened bottle of wine. He tipped the bottle to refill my now empty glass. "Don't know if it's to your liking, but I'm sure the weeds would appreciate it if you don't."

I took a sip and let the smooth wine roll over my taste buds. "The weeds aren't getting any of my share."

John sat in the other chair and began rocking in rhythm with me. We sat in comfortable silence. I wasn't sure where to begin after such a long time apart. That was always hard for me because I had to remind myself that as close as we were, John and I were friends, just friends. It had been over a year since I'd seen him, so occasional phone calls had been our way to connect.

After my marriage finally came to an end and I'd returned

to Briarwood, John had been in some remote areas and we hadn't talked in a while.

"Tina?" John started.

"John?" I asked at the same time.

We laughed. It reminded me of our years growing up and palling around together when we'd be thinking the same thought and finished each other's sentences. Maybe that's why I'd been crushed by his announcement that he was leaving Briarwood with no plans to return. It had felt like a betrayal, and that hadn't healed so much as faded as life took us in different directions.

"Ladies first." His foot nudged the rocker into motion again.

"So, tell me where you've been. You mentioned Jakarta, but what were you doing this time? What brought you home?"

It wasn't what I really wanted to ask, the question that still haunted me. *Why don't you love me the way I love you?* How many times had I asked that question?

"*Home*. I like the sound of that word." He waved his hand across the distance to his house and then gestured across the yard to take in the gardens. But he didn't elaborate.

"The last assignment was for a travel publication called *Street Life*. We were doing a follow-up on a story about Indonesian markets—apparently surviving and doing well, even though a couple of fast-food joints opened up down the street," John said. "They'd done a piece on the tension between traditional diets and the Westernized diets that support tourism—and the demands of young people. So, this publication promotes regular life outside of hotel rooms and expensive restaurants."

"Hence, *Street Life*," I said. "Great title for a global travel magazine."

John's face lit up. "And believe me, there's nothing more

colorful than street markets—I must have taken tens of thousands of photos of them all over the world, from Helsinki to Johannesburg."

"You look happy just talking about it," I said. His clear gray-blue eyes brightened when he talked about his work.

"Well, not always," John said, frowning. "I've documented the shrinking of big open markets in many corners of the world. Imported food and fast food change the health of locals, and not in a good way."

"Progress isn't always progress, is it?" I had a feel for what he meant, even if I hadn't seen it for myself. I'd read a lot about the places John visited, partly out of my own interest, but also because I wanted to vicariously experience what John had. It was a way I could fuse our decidedly unfused lives.

"The fact is, old cultures can teach us a lot," he said, "but they have to fight to stay relevant when young people everywhere live on their phones."

"Like here."

"Exactly, and like our kids, they can't prosper and be part of their country's economy if they're stuck with yesterday's tech." John shrugged. "I've been at this long enough that I can see the differences, good and not so good, from decade to decade. I'm not sure it's wise to have one country or culture exerting that kind of influence over other countries, but no one asked me."

"That's not true, John. You're hired to tell stories with your photos. You are being asked to comment with images if not words." The wine had mellowed me, and for once I didn't have ME or my dreary divorce or my outdated vests dominating my thoughts.

The sun was setting behind the trees. It was time to warm up whatever dinner Ivy had left for me. A yawn escaped, but I quickly put my hand over my mouth in hopes John wouldn't see me. No such luck. He nearly laughed out loud.

"So much for philosophical musings," he said.

"Oops, sorry. It's been such a long day and tomorrow will be... well, I don't know what it will include, and I need to call my quilting friend back." I got to my feet. "But I love our musings, philosophical or otherwise."

"I like sharing my work with you." John looked away. "Over the years, I've seen so many things I thought would fascinate you. I'd wish you were there to see what I was capturing on film. Our phone conversations weren't enough to really give you a feel for what it was like to hunt for the perfect shot."

I swayed forward and pulled myself back to regain my balance. *He wished I was there...with him?* What did that mean? He'd never said that before. I was tongue tied and couldn't respond to his actual words, so I babbled something about Heather Tucker. "Your mom taught Heather to quilt at the same time she taught me. You might remember her husband, Stuart Grant."

John tried to look interested, but he still had the faraway look in his eyes that came with talking about his work.

I hurried through the reason I had to call her, from the surgery to needing a substitute for her class at the quilt shop. "I have to be ready to teach a class for beginners on Saturday, but it should be fine."

"I bet you do a great job," John said, rising to give me a quick hug. "Mind if I sit here for a while?"

"No, not at all." *Of course, I mind. How can I mull over what you said if you're still here?* "You can always make yourself at home in the gardens. We only have them because of Maggie." I stopped or I'd have rambled on again.

I headed into the house but saw him sit back down and resume his rocking. I sat at the kitchen table and called

Heather, who sounded weary but said it was as good a time as any to talk. She spoke in quilters' shorthand about the class and said she'd send me a handout.

"Naturally, Janet is trying to attract more customers, and once quilters visit her shop, she wants them coming back. She hopes the beginning students will want more classes, which means they'll consider her shop central to their lives as quilters." Heather chuckled. "Translated, that means she wanted me to make it fun. You know what that means."

I laughed lightly. "Sure. I can do that." Thoughts of my classes at the quilt show and the women on the charter bus mocking me and a couple of them willing to say out loud they regretted spending the money raced through my mind. I had to up my game. And fast. I hope I sounded confident when I wrapped up our conversation with, "Fun it is, then. If I have questions I'll call."

"Best to text or email. The surgery has been bumped to the first thing tomorrow morning, so I'm not sure where I'll be the next couple of days," Heather said. "It's hard to know how long they'll keep her."

"Don't worry about a thing." I spoke with more confidence in my voice than I felt inside. "You take care of yourself, my friend."

Heather hadn't been her typical chatty self during the call. Maybe she was stressed about her daughter's accident. Maybe her husband was impatient that she had her quilting business to consider in the midst of the emergency with their daughter. Like Alex and a lot of other quilters' husbands, Stuart had never shown much interest in her work. She'd mentioned that some time back, but I'd dismissed it, as had Heather herself. Sadly, some men had little use for what they deemed as women's arts and crafts and, therefore, not of any particular importance.

After Heather and I ended the call, memories of Alex's anger over my quilting surfaced and stubbornly took up way too much space in my mind. He'd never encouraged me or supported my success as a teacher or a presence at weekend quilt shows. After years of struggling to live under distressing conditions and unable to have a job because he objected, he complained that what he called my little hobby took my attention off of him.

I caught myself going down that particular train of thought and shook my head in a weak attempt to derail those memories of Alex for good. Unfortunately, I'd never be rid of the anger at him, but mostly at myself, for wasting decades trying to appease a man who was selfish and mean and had no true regard for me anyway.

When I'd packed up and moved out—finally—I'd vowed to make the most of the next decades and stop regretting my mistakes. Easier said than done. John's presence, as much as I craved our conversations, not only brought up the past, but triggered thoughts of a future with him. Even after John left, I'd spent my teenager years with those fantasies, and I couldn't afford to lose myself in them again.

The real issues in my life were right in front of me. First on the list was the meeting with Steve and facing the truth about my capacity to do my part to maintain ME. Maybe I'd be good enough to take on the job, or maybe I wouldn't. Steve was due to arrive at nine a.m., and, like I told John, I wanted to be focused and clearheaded. I rinsed my wine glass and put it in the dishwasher.

I glanced through the open doors to the patio and gardens and saw that both rocking chairs sat empty. At some point during my phone conversation John had left. The gardens looked empty without him.

4

THE NEXT MORNING, I COULDN'T HELP BUT LAUGH. THERE SHE was, my confident older sister, changing her clothes for the third time. Finally, she settled on a multi-colored T-shirt with a gauzy over-blouse. Her flowing teal skirt hit mid-calf. I didn't need to be a mind-reader to recognize her preoccupation with a man. She only tossed clothes around her bedroom when she was anxious, and I'd only seen her anxious a few times in my life. All were related to feelings for a man. Steve had thrown her like no other guy had in years.

I sat at the breakfast counter and enjoyed my whole-grain toast and yogurt. Ivy filled my coffee cup and tried to suppress a smile, but she saw what was going on. Helen wasn't good at hiding her feelings.

Steve arrived dressed for a casual day, gray jeans and a short-sleeved summer shirt. He carried a large briefcase with him, though, which gave him the look of an up-to-date professional.

"Coffee, Steve?" Ivy asked, after Helen introduced them.

He waved her off. "I downed two mugs of my favorite roast

and that's enough caffeine to keep me going all day but thank you."

Helen introduced me to Steve, and we exchanged a quick handshake. He was all smiles, especially for Helen. Hmm... this could get interesting. I hoped his upbeat manner would continue once he realized how little we knew about ME.

We moved to Dad's conference table, which was big enough for our three laptops. Helen and I were silent, and when we exchanged a glance, I saw the fear in her eyes. That fear had nothing to do with Steve as a man but was all about Steve-the-accountant. I had the feeling our fate was in his hands, primarily because my sister and I didn't know enough to take care of ME on our own. Somehow, like Helen, I'd given him power he hadn't asked for.

I started by telling him what we'd done the day before. "We started with the household accounts so we could get a handle on how the bills are paid." I hesitated, but kept on going, explaining what we saw from the examples Steve had pulled from the loans. I fed back to him the answers to the questions he'd asked us in his list. "Overall, though, we assumed Dad had a system that applied across the board to loans, including standard interest rates and duration of the loans."

Steve frowned and glanced at his screen.

"In other words, we thought we were learning Dad's guidelines," Helen said. "It didn't take long to realize that Dad didn't have obvious guidelines."

"And that was news to you?" Steve sat back in the chair and shook his head.

"Yes, it was." Talk about annoying. "How would we have heard that so-called news?" I asked, not hiding my own sarcasm. "Didn't Doug fill you in? Dad never told either one of us anything about the business." Maybe Helen was enamored with the guy, but that didn't mean I had to be.

"Of course, Doug filled me in about Max's stubborn ways," Steve fired back. "Look, I don't pretend to understand why Max would have been so silent. But the lack of standardized policies that applied to all his loans was the *point* of ME. That's why he was able to loan very small amounts of money to some and large start-up and expansion loans to others."

Steve glanced at me and back to Helen. "I'm the messenger here, remember. I didn't set up Max's books or his company policies."

This meeting hadn't started well, and it was my fault. I cleared my throat. "My apologies. I didn't mean to imply that any of this mess is your fault. You can't know what was in Max's mind."

I glanced at Helen, whose face had visibly relaxed.

"I understand this is stressful for the two of you." He gestured to Helen. "I knew Helen by reputation because of her volunteer work and the way she represents the company. But I didn't know anything else about the family, Tina, so I'm coming into this blind."

"I think Steve assumed that because I've been the face of ME's charity work, I would naturally have been part of the business." Helen offered a weak smile. "But Steve, we need you to start from scratch. The reasons Dad did or didn't train us—or me—in his business can wait for a later time."

"Right," Steve said. "We need to make sure you two don't have to sell the house just to get enough cash to start new lives."

That hit hard. So hard, that the color drained from Helen's face. The idea of selling the paid-for house had occurred to me, but I'd pushed the thought away. Because of the gardens, it was more like an estate than a house. Even if we wanted to sell, that process could take some time.

Having achieved a baseline, mainly zero, Steve fired questions at us to make sure we understood the essence of the business. When we broke down the two loans we'd studied the day before, Steve looked pleased and said we'd made a good start.

"Being relatively new to Briarwood, Doug gave me an overview of the company and I've gone over ME's bank statements, the same ones I sent to you." Steve smiled broadly. "Your dad had a *unique* idea for a business—very creative. And he was always fair. You'll notice, he wasn't like a high-interest finance company or a payday loan operation."

Helen almost shrieked at that notion. "Wow, I'm glad you recognized that. Dad might not have told us how the business worked, but I can tell you I run into people all the time who tell me their bakery or cleaning service or even their law firm would have gone under without Dad's loan."

"That's precisely why I thought you knew how it worked," Steve said dryly. "I have a feeling once we get you trained, you'll be able to keep this business humming along."

"Really? Humming along? Do you honestly think we can pick up where our dad left off?" Even after my apology I was still uneasy with the way the meeting was proceeding. On the other hand, I had to give Steve credit for recognizing ME for the unique business our dad had created.

"Dad liked helping local people," Helen offered, "and I'd like to keep that going." She raised her chin a little defiantly, but I still saw fear in her eyes. I understood.

"According to the estate papers at the time of his death he was helping thirty-one businesses or individuals," Steve said, looking at us for verification. "The number matched what I saw in the files. Did you see that in the totals?"

"That's the number Doug said, but we didn't go through each one," I said. "We stuck with the one small short-term loan and the larger long-term loan you gave us as samples."

"But we didn't...don't...understand why Dad okayed those loans," Helen said, "and we saw that in years past, he'd managed many more loans."

"Good that you walked your way through the two samples." Steve reached into his briefcase and pulled out two files. "Here are hard copies of some other loans I'll walk you through." Steve handed us each a file and kept talking. "You'll see the direct income from the loan payments. The payments are all sent electronically in most cases to your father's bank. A few are still mailed in, but that's coming down to close to zero now. We'll quickly go through each one today, but over the next couple of days you should take a much closer look."

As soon as I started perusing the hard copies, I had an unfamiliar sense that we held our future in our hands—these printed sheets seemed to hold the key to everything. I glanced at Helen intently studying the pages. Curiosity had replaced the fear. I willed myself to mirror my sister. If we failed, though, I'd still put the blame on Dad for keeping the workings of ME to himself. I was filled with anger, but at the same time, now was not the time to be consumed with fear and regret, let alone resentment.

Steve explained the way he'd organized the files and then he started in. Within minutes, Helen exclaimed, "This is astounding!" She patted the center of the table. "I knew that Dad worked with local people—we saw two of the deals yesterday. But holding a sheaf of papers with the names of so many businesses and individuals we've known all our lives makes what Dad did come alive."

It was true. "It also sheds light on why Dad was almost secretive with us growing up."

As I spoke, Ivy came into the office with a tray of glasses and a pitcher of ice water. She put them on the end of the desk since we'd spread out and used up all the space at the table. No one spoke until after she left.

"Dad used to visit people at their places of business, at least until he slowed down some," Helen said. "He kept ledgers in locked drawers." She pointed to a glass cabinet. It had always been locked when we were young. "Growing up, he made sure we didn't know he'd issued a loan to the principal of the school or to the family that owned the diner, or the insurance broker."

"I'll give you that," Steve said. "Max had these clients because he was discreet and maintained confidentiality. It was good business practice to keep his girls and the nanny in the dark." He pursed his lips and shook his head. "But you grew up, he didn't change, and here you are."

Steve didn't give us time to respond but moved quickly to pick up the conversation by explaining the way the deposits worked and how ME figured its profit each month. Interest rates were negotiable, at least in part based on the prime rate. He had built in late fees and a loan could roll over if necessary. He painstakingly pointed out what part of each payment was interest and what was applied to the principle. Taxes were another issue.

Steve had been holding a pencil and suddenly he tossed it on the table and his shoulders tensed. "You're both smart women," he said. "Nothing I explain here is meant to make you feel inadequate or plant any kind of seed that you're not up to running ME."

"Then why do we feel that way?" Helen's voice quivered.

Steve shrugged. "Easy question. You're scared because everything is riding on this. It's your livelihood. Your future. So, no matter what mistakes Max made or the folly of leaving you in the dark, that's the past. ME isn't something you can brush aside." His tone became gentler as he finished his thoughts and relaxed back into his chair.

The earlier tension fully eased; I could smile without the sense I was pasting it on my face. "Okay. What's next?" I realigned the papers in front of me. If this was going to be our income for years to come, Helen and I would figure out how to join forces and learn how to make ME provide for us the same way it had for Dad. "At some point, we need to issue new loans." I picked up a printout of current clients. "It's time we inform all these current clients that ME hasn't missed a beat and will keep on serving Briarwood."

"I've been confirming that for years at some of the business owners' meetings in town," Helen said. "When I started going in Dad's place years ago, a few people were blunt enough to ask if he intended to shut down ME. I always responded the way Dad asked me to, but now we have to decide what to say."

Steve tapped his pencil on the first entries on the page and noted the dates. "These will be paid up before the end of the year. No payments, no interest, no income." Steve nodded at Helen and then at me. "You're right. You'll need to send out a mailing as soon as possible to make sure everyone is aware the business is continuing."

"But is it?" No matter how charming Helen was, she didn't know the day-to-day operations any better than I did. "It's one thing to say we're in business," I pointed out, "but it's another to make that so."

Selfishly, I thought of my quilting supplies and bins of fabric—outdated or not—in my studio below. I had a class to teach on Saturday and updates to do. I had decisions to make about my brand. Did I still want to be known for my vests? I knew the older versions were yesterday's news.

With a heavy sigh, I turned to Helen. “Are you up for this? Steve is convinced we can learn, but do you want to?”

That question got Helen’s attention. And Steve’s.

Two hours later after going through the details of a list of loans, we took a break. Fortunately, the interest on three large, long duration loans would keep the household going for now. As for personal expenses, Helen and I agreed to drastically cut the amount Dad had direct deposited to our accounts.

Everything looked rosy in one way, in that the business of processing the loans was on autopilot, more or less. Our job was to find clients and negotiate terms that gave them what they needed while we received income. A few loans were behind, but fortunately, not too many.

“You two will need to contact the individuals and make sure they get current,” Steve said. “A few might have thought their obligation changed when your dad died, but that’s not so. Those loans are mostly the personal type and will need to be fulfilled.”

Steve had double-checked with the bank to make sure the few remaining checks for ME’s mail-in accounts had been updated. “Doug and I checked all the paperwork. You’ll need to go to the bank and have your names put on the account. Doug’s name was the default in case of Max’s inability to handle his affairs, and had legal power of attorney, which is why Ivy and the household services were paid.”

It was obvious something was bothering Steve when he shifted in his chair and avoided looking directly at me. He pulled another file from his briefcase and held it up. “Before I leave, I need to ask you about this one expense, which was filed with the loans, but was a personal matter and never processed like ME’s other loans. Doug said to ask you about it, Tina.”

Steven handed me a printout titled: *Alex: son-in-law*. Rows of figures showed money paid out, but no amounts coming back in.

I clapped my hand over my mouth to keep a sound from escaping—a scream, a cry, or something in between. "No!" I shouted as I waved my hand in the air as if I could bat away the truth. My face burned. "Dad gave Alex money? He's my ex-husband. Doug just handled my divorce. He hadn't uncovered this, or he surely would have said something."

I covered my face with my hands. The room was so still I could hear Helen and Steve inhaling and exhaling. Finally, I straightened up. "Why?" For some reason I looked to Helen for an answer.

She raised her hands defensively. "Whoa, don't look at me. Dad never said a word about Alex, at least not to me."

I put my hands to my temples to quiet my pounding pulse, and then swiped beads of sweat forming on my forehead. Steve busied his hands as he waited for me to get over my shock of learning Dad had sent money to Alex. Neither Alex nor Dad had ever told me. They were direct deposits into Alex's account. "All this money went to Alex, but it wasn't for loans. No payments are listed here."

"I couldn't find a business contract to go with this account," Steve said, "so I'm guessing your father classified the money as a gift. Doug helped him with all the business and the household accounts, but Max had personal accounts, too. Steve looked at me, waiting for a response. "I'm not sure if you need to do anything about it. I noticed the money stopped the same month you arrived home and started your divorce."

I slapped the table. "Half of that money is mine. Well, ours now, Helen, if it was part of ME."

"Technically, maybe, but not on a practical basis," Steve said. "This money was withdrawn from Max's personal account, like the household expenses. We never would have discovered it in the business documents used for tax purposes. Max probably called it a personal gift."

I couldn't stop shaking, just like I couldn't make the facts go away. More than anything I wanted to pick up my phone and shout at Alex and rundown every injustice, every mean remark he'd sent my way, every slammed door, and denied pleasure. I managed to hold back. I couldn't very well rush off and accuse Alex of taking money from Dad, not if Dad thought he was helping me by helping Alex. Dad never asked about the marriage, and I never supplied information. I knew Dad didn't like him, but since we seldom visited together it didn't matter.

"Maybe in Dad's distorted thinking, he considered it a way of being fair. Money to Helen, money for Tina. Dad must have assumed I knew about it." I lowered my voice as I spoke, as if all my energy was circling the drain. "But why would he give money to me through Alex, a guy he never liked in the first place?"

Steve sighed. "All I can say is that Doug didn't have any explanation for this. Your divorce was straightforward, and you basically had no assets. He took his car, you took yours. You left the furniture and the apartment. The money Max gave to Alex was small amounts so no one would notice it in an ordinary account."

I let my head drop back and looked to the whirring ceiling fan for answers. "What this comes down to is the sad truth that Dad thought of me as a child who couldn't manage money. He saw me as dependent on Alex, and that was that."

"So many things raise questions about Dad," Helen said, glancing at Steve. "Don't worry we won't drag you into this, but I realize now Dad didn't think we were capable of handling a business, or even independent careers." Helen closed her eyes and in a shaky voice added, "He was content to let me think I was doing my part by representing the company, but I was window-dressing."

"Helen, no, no, that's not true." I was insistent in my tone, but unfortunately, I was hard pressed to defend my position. It was difficult thinking about any of this. I had to face that my own father gave money to my emotionally abusive, controlling husband. Behind my back. Didn't Dad ever wonder why I never thanked him? Did he truly mean this money to be a gift to me or was there some other reason?

I needed to give my next step some thought and then confirm the basic facts with Doug. He'd seen Dad's business taxes and advised him about any decision that would have legal implications. I folded my arms over my chest and lowered my head.

"We've done all we can today," Steve said, his voice low and kind. "I'll leave you to it. For now, nothing changes, except for your banking. I'll go with you to change the accounts if you'd like. That way, I'll have a working relationship with your business banker. No matter what you decide to do in the long run, you need this update now."

Helen and I had to make calls to a couple of accounts that had fallen behind, but our main job was to study the loans and draft a letter to current and past clients. We agreed to meet again in a week or two.

Helen walked Steve out, but she was back in a matter of minutes and took her place at the table. She rubbed her cheeks and her eyes and held her head.

"You look the way I feel," I said with a scoff. "Lucky you."

She lifted her head to look at me. "Big shocker about Alex, huh?"

"*No*...I wouldn't put anything past Alex. He's a terrible person, a liar and probably fits the clinical definition of a narcissist." I choked getting my words out and put my hands over my eyes, as if I could keep myself from seeing the truth. "It's Dad who shocked me."

"Maybe so, and believe me, I'm seething at Dad right now." Helen grimaced and narrowed her eyes. "And I'm kicking myself. But, Tina, *Alex* spent the money and kept the secret."

"I want to make my miserable ex pay my share back, but I know in my gut he never will. No matter what, it will always appear that whatever he earned or whatever money Dad gave him was used to support me." I loathed the idea he could claim that he'd provided a good home for me.

Helen reached across and gave my shoulder a squeeze. "At least you're free of that loser." Her tone was unmistakably filled with total disgust.

"I wish I'd faced that earlier in our marriage. I would have bailed out years ago. All that time lost." I felt old burdens weighing me down and I didn't like it. "Instead, I held on to the hope he'd change. That if he felt successful in his job, he'd be nicer at home." I shrugged. "And then there was a matter of commitment—I said the vows all those years ago, after all." Surprised that my emotions were so close to the surface, I reached across the table for a nearby tissue to catch the tears.

"Hey, that wasn't completely lost time," Helen said, covering my hand with hers. "Eventually you found your strength and turned your quilting hobby into a small business. Not everyone can do that and become as successful as you have." Helen's voice grew louder with every encouraging word.

"But I wasn't enough to keep a man from..." I stood up. "I need some space. I'll see you later."

Helen gave me a hug. "We can pick up our work on this tomorrow. I understand Steve's urgency about us not getting further behind on ME business."

I nodded. "Alex doesn't matter now, anyway. When it comes to ME, we're in charge." I heard the despair in my voice.

"You're right. It's you and me, kid," Helen said, giving me a mock salute. "It's up to us to decide if we even want to keep ME alive and well enough to provide us with an income-producing business. *We* have to support ourselves and pay Ivy. We need to either keep up the house or go ahead and sell it now. That's even before we can consider Dad's motivation for starting ME, which was to help a few people close to home in Briarwood."

Helen's words were true enough. It's as if she faced reality and, on some level, trusted us to succeed despite Dad's failure to prepare us before his death. But her encouragement fell short, at least after such a long dreary day. And Dad's betrayal hung over my head. "Dad's mission, so to speak, to provide a useful service to Briarwood, is what makes any of this seem worthwhile." I opened the French door and went to rock in the gardens.

5

FRIDAY DIDN'T START WELL. I ASSUMED I'D HAVE RECOVERED from our days of "home-school," alone and with Steve. Not so. I had a night of fitful sleep. I went over and over the realities of my dismal marriage to Alex. The torch I still foolishly carried for John intensified knowing he was only next door, but likely planning his next escape. He could have been on the phone that very morning accepting another assignment that would lead to packing up and taking off. Sure, it was his work. I got that. John had the ability to wander and create. At times over the past years, I envied that freedom and fantasized about my quilting skills allowing me to travel to the far corners of the world. At the same time, in my real life I struggled to create a relationship with Alex that would give both of us what we wanted and needed to be happy together and as individuals.

As I dragged myself out of bed and slipped my phone into the pocket of my robe, I faced—again—that my marriage was over and done. That was the good side of my current state. I never had to deal with my lying, controlling, and deceptive ex-husband ever again. I might not be free to wander the world, but my passion for quilting, triggered in me as a child by none other than John's mom, gave me the chance to create beautiful things.

Underneath the conglomeration of thoughts flitting around in my head, I was anxious about agreeing to fill in for Heather. I couldn't shake the comments from the ladies on the bus, either, which had led to my crisis of confidence in the first place. As if all that weren't enough, I both missed Dad, the only parent I ever knew, but I was also teeming mad, furious with him. I didn't know where my anger at him ended and my fury with myself started. Why had he left ME a more or less rudderless ship? Great, Ivy and gardening crew and the utility companies were paid like clockwork. A relief, yes, but not good enough. Still, with Steve's help, Helen and I were unraveling the threads that formed ME.

In my sleepless state, I got no answers to my questions about the money Dad sent to Alex from his personal account and, therefore, unbeknownst to Doug. No matter how many times I demanded answers, of course none came. But that didn't keep me from asking the question again. By the time I got to the kitchen to pour some coffee, I'd already created more stress than I thought I could handle.

I took my coffee downstairs to my studio and took Heather's call where I knew I wouldn't disturb anyone, including Ivy, who liked to linger over a cup of coffee in the kitchen before jumping into the day's work.

It didn't help that when Heather called, she also sounded frantic on the phone, and way too stressed from working out the logistics of her life. Heather promised to drop off copies of the handout for the class at Janet's Quilt Shop later that afternoon, along with samples and supplies. She'd send me a copy of the handout by email attachment earlier in the day, giving me a chance to look it over. "I don't know why I'm worrying so much," she said with a quick laugh. "You could walk in the door and give this class off the top of your head. I know you're that good. Anyway, have fun."

I had a hard time thinking of the class as a chance to have fun, although I always got a rush from teaching. But Heather's request came at a bad time. Emotionally, that is. The week showed me that I still needed time to recover from what I realized were years of frustration and feeling low.

Later, after I worked up my nerve, I called Doug's office, only to learn he was gone for the weekend. I put on hold my hope to probe into Doug's knowledge of Alex and the money. I started to dial Alex's number a couple of times, but put that off, too. Helen had meetings with other volunteers from two non-profits, so I put off more work with ME. If I felt up to it, I'd make a stab at drafting our letter to assure clients we were open for business.

That left me with my quilting studio mess, but before I could clean it up, I had decisions to make about the new direction I would take my work. I couldn't shake off the past or slam the brakes on my worries about the future, but I could choose to turn to what had become for years my only source of immense joy.

Since I'd be teaching at Janet's the next day, I treated myself to a trip to a couple of quilt shops in Green Bay. I hadn't visited either in years. The great escape. That's what I called the days spent immersed in quilting. With any luck I'd come away with ideas for new samples along with the fabric to bring the ideas to fruition.

When I pulled onto the street from our circular drive, my heart was lighter than it had been in months. I couldn't control much else in my life, but what I did with my quilting was all up to me.

On Saturday morning, three other cars were already in the lot when I arrived at Janet's Quilt Shop just before opening time. I hoped they were students, and their early arrival foretold their excitement to soak up what I could teach them. I remembered my first class. It had been after Alex and I had been married a few years and had moved away from Briarwood. I'd been nervous and anxious but didn't know why. Perhaps it was because I hadn't quilted for so long, not since sessions with Maggie when I still lived with Dad and Helen. I'd bought a couple of quilting magazines and scoured the library for up-to-date how-to quilting books, so I'd reignite my earlier passion for it.

Now, all these years later, Janet handed me Heather's tote bag overflowing with samples and supplies. When I followed Janet into the classroom, the size of the room came as a shock. It was much smaller than I remembered. As if reading my mind, Janet spoke up. "We needed more floor space, so we halved the size of the room last year."

What could I say? The four tables with two chairs each were evenly spaced in the room with a longer table crosswise at the front. The room began to fill with students, some of whom looked around with intimidated expressions. Beginner's anxiety. I knew it well.

Janet handed me the list of registered students. "There should be eight women this morning." Janet had one arm wrapped around her middle, the way pregnant women often do. Her baby bump was covered—sort of—with a sunflower patterned apron.

"Eight students? For a beginners' class?" No wonder Heather was stressed out. I wanted to tell Janet that four students were the maximum that any teacher could handle for a room filled with beginners, but she'd already left the room. Students starting out also needed extra time with the teacher in order to become comfortable using the equipment and learning the techniques. Not to mention the lingo. Quilting had a language of its own, complete with shortcut phrases and quips.

Soon, the rest of the class filled the vacant chairs, and Janet came back to introduce me and give a welcome speech. She also explained why I was teaching instead of Heather. Fortunately, she added, "Tina has been teaching for years, so she has lots of experience."

Good...emphasis on lots.

"Enjoy the morning. I hope you'll be inspired to take more classes in the future." With that, she left, and I had the floor.

I'd already unpacked Heather's tote, and Janet had left the handouts in a stack. I launched the session the way I always did and asked each woman why she'd signed up for the class. About the time I gave a quick summary of my experience, I started to relax, and a sense of pride filled my body head to toe.

Students had a variety of reasons for not only wanting to learn to quilt but to take action to make it happen. Or, in the case of a woman named Clarice, she signed up because her friend Donna didn't want to come alone.

"That's me," Donna said. "I really want to make a quilt, but I've never done any sewing before."

Others like Nancy were looking for a new hobby. She wasn't an experienced sewer, but at least when I asked, she could laughingly say, "I can hem a skirt and sew on a button. It's a start."

Indeed, it was. As the others introduced themselves, the knot in my stomach tightened and my pride drained away, and a real crisis of confidence replaced it. Had I come down with a bad case "impostor syndrome?" Was I good enough to engage eight beginners to learn the fundamentals of quilting? Luckily,

I fingered the earrings Dad had given me. For some reason, they were my touchstones for strength, reminders of who I really was without this overlay of challenges—and grief. My anxiety eased and the strength I'd felt as a quilter and teacher seeped back into place.

When the last student had made her introduction, I reached for the stack of handouts and distributed them. "We'll take a few minutes to go through the steps of cutting fabric then you can practice."

It wasn't that simple—the pages of the handouts were mixed up and it took a few minutes to make sure everyone had a complete set. I thought of Heather hastily putting the handout together as she waited for word about her daughter. If mixed up pages were the only problem I encountered, I'd consider myself lucky.

I hand-pressed a piece of fabric on the cutting board and gestured for the women in the back to come closer to get a clear look at what I was doing. "Your handout has more detail, but I'm sure you want to do some actual cutting, so I'll take you through the steps." I grabbed the quilting ruler and the rotary cutter. "Using the rotary cutter..."

"What's a rotary cutter?" one woman asked.

I took a breath and started over to explain some of the tools, starting with the cutter. "Your scissor isn't as accurate as this round blade that travels alongside the ruler's edge and cuts the fabric. The blade is very sharp so be careful."

"My grandmother used scissors and she made beautiful quilts." The woman, Amy, spoke in a challenging tone.

I smiled and gave her my stock answer. "True enough. Before this cutter came along everyone used scissors. But this newer tool allows us to get more cutting done is less time, often with more accuracy." I held the ruler down and made a cut and then pointed out the evened the edge of the fabric.

Next, I measured the length of fabric needed and made a second cut.

I had looked up for only a second in order to see if everyone was following along with me. As expected, the ruler shifted at the end of the cut. That was perfect for the moment because I held up the cut fabric and pointed out the narrower end. "This is what happens when you aren't paying attention."

That won me a few chuckles.

The practice came next, with the group taking turns with the rulers and cutters Janet provided. That was another reason beginners' classes were small. Participants were rarely fully equipped with all the right tools and Janet didn't have enough to go around. But she had provided practice fabric. The women were more good-natured about sharing the tools than I'd have been. I didn't care for classes where I had to sit and wait for my turn to use the supplies. Because of that, I'd always been a stickler for maintaining my supplies. I scoffed to myself. Let those women on the bus criticize me all they wanted, but they could never claim they had to share equipment.

I walked past each table, offered hints that would make the cutting easier. One of the women was left-handed, but she'd reversed my process and was cutting accurate strips. "Good job with that," I told her.

By late morning the students – well, most of them – were ready to cut squares from their own fabrics.

"Ouch!" The exclamation came from one of the back tables.

I went to see the cut—they seemed to be inevitable—and pulled a Band-Aid from my apron pocket and put it over her small cut. "Bet you never make that mistake again." I waved a second Band-Aid in the air. "See? I never teach a class without a supply. I've put a few on myself over the years."

"I started talking to my friend next to me and looked away for half a second," Joan said. "Hurts like the dickens, but I'll survive."

The women continued cutting their fabric into squares, which they'd use for the second session the next weekend. I hoped Heather would be available to teach that class. If all eight students returned, it would take a lot of patience and skill to get them hand sewing their squares together.

Most of the students left shortly after noon, but a couple stayed into the middle of the afternoon to get their squares cut. Although I'd tried to be upbeat and casual, I wasn't happy with the class, too big in the first place. I hung around so I could tell Janet my thoughts before I left. I'd had no control over planning the class, but I was still associated with it.

Unfortunately, Janet had left the shop for the day. I didn't know the woman at the check-out counter, but she whispered, "Pregnancy issues," and nodded her head like that told me all I needed to know.

I was about to leave when I saw the HELP WANTED—PART-TIME sign tucked next to the register. My mind jumped to an image of greeting customers to Tina's Quilt Shop, a long ago dream I had once made the mistake of telling Alex I wanted to pursue.

"You'd go bankrupt the first month," he'd said with a sneer.

I never mentioned the dream again, but that didn't mean I'd let go of it. But could I revive it? I took a deep breath when I saw two cars parked in front of the house when I arrived. I didn't recognize either of them. All I wanted to do was have a long soak in the tub. But when I walked inside, I heard laughter—not a common sound in the house lately. I didn't have to see them to identify the sound as coming from Helen, John, and, I was certain, Steve.

Helen met me at the door. "We thought you'd have been home earlier." Helen grabbed my tote and ushered me into the living room. "I didn't want to interrupt you when you were teaching, but we made a plan and I know you'll go along with it. Steve invited me to dinner and then when John stopped over, we decided to make it a foursome." Helen talked so fast she ran words together and left me no room to argue, not that I would have. "We'll give you a few minutes to freshen up before we leave. But hurry. John is going to talk about some upcoming assignment. I told him you would want to hear all about it."

"John's leaving?" My mind, already cluttered, tripped over that news. "So soon?"

She pushed me toward my bedroom. "Not now. Hurry."

Arguing with Helen that I didn't want to go was fruitless. But that was only my bad mood talking. The less than satisfying teaching day and John's plan to leave didn't make me happy. But neither would my sending the three off to dinner without me. I decided not to change clothes, but I added a gold chain necklace and a multi-colored beaded bracelet John had given me years ago. I wondered if he would remember the gift. I gave my hair a quick brush-through. My customary short hair was longer now. I had yet to take the time to find a hairdresser in Briarwood since my return.

"Tina? We need to leave now. They're holding a table for us at the club."

At the last minute I grabbed a shawl. During the summer the club always kept their air-conditioning on the icy side. I'd decided to enjoy the evening without being on the edge of too cold.

Helen was all for us going in one car so we wouldn't have to repeat our conversations. Feeling contrary, I wanted to ride alone with John and find out why he was leaving so soon. We hadn't connected for a couple of days and my time with him was quickly evaporating.

"Steve offered to drive, so you and John can jump into the back seat," Helen said, ushering us out the door. She was flushed again, the way she'd been the other day around Steve. The man had a major effect on her equilibrium.

"Helen told us you were teaching quilting to some beginner students today. How did it go?" John asked when we'd settled into the back.

All thoughts vanished when I looked into his gray-blue eyes. Eyes that had seen both tragedy and happiness. Eyes that I had fallen in love with when I was eight years old.

"Um. I never should have agreed to substitute for Heather," I said. "Too many students for one teacher in a small space, so no one got the full benefit. I doubt the women learned much. I could spend all evening running down all that went wrong and what I'd do to fix it." I grinned. "Don't worry, I won't bore you to death."

"I can tell you have an edge on you," John said. "But it wasn't your class material, was it?"

"Nope, it was Heather's, but my name is going to be attached to that class."

"So, the fault lies with her, not you. You didn't organize the class." John touched the bracelet on my arm. "I remember this."

Subject changed.

It was a short drive to the country club from the house, and as usual, others greeted Helen like an old friend. Because she stopped to talk to each person our trip to the table was slow. When I recognized one of the women from the morning class I wanted to hide, but I waved instead.

"Great class, Tina," she said loud enough that I heard her over a couple of tables.

I didn't know if she was being truthful or facetious, so I stepped away from our group and navigated around one large table to get to hers. I stood behind and off to the side. "Did you honestly think it was a great class?"

She pursed her lips. "Oh, please. It was a waste of time, mine and yours." The disgust in her voice wasn't subtle.

"Would you be willing to meet with me and talk more about your expectations? Soon?" I glanced across the room to a table where my three companions were laughing—again. I wanted to join them and laugh off this case of the blues.

"Anytime. Really. Give me a call." She turned away when someone grabbed her attention from across the table.

"Thanks," I said, but I doubted she heard me. It was a blow to hear her blunt words. I'd never have described the class that harshly.

There was a glass of wine waiting for me when I joined the table. "Sorry. She was one of the students from this morning."

"Well, don't keep us in suspense," John said. "What did she think?"

"Exact words, 'waste of time'. I was almost afraid to come to that conclusion, but she's not wrong. I'm going to call her and ask her more specific questions." I took a sip from my glass and glanced at John. "So, what's this about you leaving us again?" *Leaving me...no one else cared like I did.*

While he described what he expected to be his next assignment for a travel magazine my attention bounced back and forth between his voice and my feeling like a failure as a teacher that morning. Wow, I was ripping myself to shreds. No one else had to do it for me. But once again, the women's remarks on the charter bus haunted me. And I concluded I wasn't anywhere near ready to own my own shop. Too big a leap, especially since I had no income source other than ME, dwindling at the moment unless Helen and I could turn it around. Besides, if I was having trouble handling a bad class, how would I handle a week of dead sales?

I finally put aside my distractions and focused on the people at my table. John recounted his experience narrowly escaping a deadly street fight in Morocco. He'd wandered off the beaten path, as usual, looking at street life. That night, he'd ended up having to duck down a narrow stone street and dodge scooters and bikes in order to escape a gathering mob of young men facing off against each other for reasons John couldn't surmise.

"Exciting life," Steve said. "Maybe a little too exciting for me."

"But what did you find on the other end of the path," I pressed.

"Kids playing soccer in the street," he said, his face lighting up. "One of the most common sights in the world, even in refugee camps." John sighed. "I've found myself in so many contradictory situations like that. Threats and danger on the one hand, and kids making their own fun in spite of everything."

"I've seen those soccer game images on TV," Helen said, nodding. "It makes my plans for the Youth Club benefit seem pretty tame."

"But the kids at the Youth Club are terrific," Steve said. "Give those kids a basketball and they're off and running for a whole afternoon. They're good at refereeing themselves, too, like the kids you're talking about, John. Good prep for life, I like to say, no matter where they live."

John nodded, a little weakly, I noticed. Maybe the memories of the harshness of some of life he'd seen intruded on his thoughts.

We shared a laugh when the waitress took our order and we all chose the same dish, cold marinated salmon salad with a side dish of fruit. That took John on a side-trip down his own memory lane about the dozens of ways he'd eaten fish during his travels, especially coastal Asian countries and South America. "The various kinds of fishing boats are as interesting as the fish," he said.

"Have you been to all seven continents?" Steve asked. "I have that on my bucket list."

"Six. No excursions to Antarctica yet. The research organizations do their own photography to document their work, and earlier in my career, I didn't make the cut on the projects freelancers were invited to apply for." John gestured across the table at Steve. "If you really want to go, take a cruise. Relax. As for me, I've decided to skip that region. I'm not that fond of cold weather."

"Me, neither." Helen shuddered to emphasis her point and made her dangly earrings swing.

"When I get a chance to travel to different countries, my dream is to bring back lots of fabric," I offered, revealing one of my main motivations to travel.

"I see. You want to see the world just to buy fabric?" John kidded.

"Not only for that," I replied, "but I'll admit I'm pulled in that direction. Of course, I'd want to do some sight-seeing, too. I mean, why go to Paris without going to the Louvre or the Eiffel Tower, but I don't want to miss a stroll along the Rue d'Orsel."

"Uh, translation, please?" Helen said, looking slightly annoyed.

"It's the major street of the fabric district in Paris," I explained. Then I laughed. "I was just showing off the list of places I'd like to hunt for fabric. Seeing bolts of cloth displayed on the street sounds incredibly appealing, just like searching for fabric-making and fiber arts exhibitions."

Helen gave me a curious look. "Odd. I never heard you talk about travel. Fabric and quilting, yes, but never in connection with travel outside the country."

"I've always yearned to travel, Sis. Once I started quilting again those old dreams of mine came alive." Divorcing Alex cleared the way for all kinds of longings, but I wouldn't say that out loud.

"Sounds like you have an amazing list, Tina," John said, smiling. "Once you get Paris scratched off your list, you can head to fabric markets in every corner of India."

"And spend the rest of my life exploring them," I said with a laugh. "I've done the research. I know what you're talking about." No one knew I'd done research online and gathered books from libraries all over the state. I could plan that trip in a day.

"I'll bet you have," John said with an understanding expression on his face.

"Back to the near future," I said, lightly touching my warming cheek. "You haven't told us where you're off to next." I didn't want my dreams scrutinized by anyone, even John, when I knew how flimsy they would seem at a time when Helen and I were trying to keep ME alive.

John shrugged. "A couple of things in the works, but nothing definite yet. I should get more information within the week, unless there is a major event in the world somewhere. In that case, it's not all that unusual to learn my exact destination when the tickets and itinerary arrive. That's how I knew I was heading out to cover one of the earthquakes in Haiti and the tsunami all those years ago."

I shivered thinking about fires raging in so many places, storms always imminent, drought, and on and on.

Steve added his take on the last-minute travel. "Man, it

must be hard to pack. I debate each item I toss in my suitcase." He laughed. "Uh, not that I really toss the clothes in."

Helen and I shared a laugh over the sheepish way Steve shared a slice of his personality. But John took the topic more seriously. "Everything needs to fit into a backpack, so I can leave my hands free for cameras and the computer—tablet and phone, nowadays." John's twinkling eyes challenged me when he cast a sidelong glance. "Of course, now that we know about your travel fantasies, you could come along and help me carry my gear."

That's how my dreams started, you fool. "Sorry friend, I'm in the middle of reviving not one, but two businesses."

Steve frowned and leaned forward and rested his arms on the table. "Two? I know about ME, Tina, but what's your second business?"

"Fiber arts, specifically quilting. I've done custom pieces, but the heart of my business has been giving classes and lectures at quilt shows and guild meetings. My teaching examples served me well, but they're outdated now. So, I'm in the process of overhauling my presentation—a fancy way of saying I'm remaking them using more current fabric."

I caught of glimpse of Helen nodding, her head way up and then way down. She left no doubt about her opinion of what I needed to do.

I scoffed. "As you can see from my sister's enthusiasm, she agrees that I need a change. And I know I must stay up to date on all the latest trends in quilting, the news designs and pattern publishers, plus the latest fabrics, not to mention quilting techniques and gadgets."

Steve nodded. "It's the same in the financial world. There's always a new accounting program to evaluate or the government updates need to be installed in our current program. We have to stay aware of anything new that might affect our clients—in a good way, we hope."

"We need to fill Steve in on a little background info," Helen said, turning to Steve. "Tina learned to quilt from John's mom, Maggie, who was also our dad's assistant. She's the one who started the gardens, which occupied her spare time in the summer. But in the winter, she turned to her quilting. She created many beautiful pieces."

"All her life, Maggie had a love affair with color," I added.

"Where are her quilts now?" Steve asked.

"They're in my house. I'm not there much, but it's still home. It's at the end of the path from the Montgomery house," John explained. "The quilts have been packed away since my mom died."

"We've always referred to it as the Delaney house," I said, "because we associated it with Maggie and John. We'd see Maggie walking back and forth from our house to their place. I went to the Delaney house often when Maggie was teaching me to quilt."

John looked away and seemed to flash back to a previous time.

I touched his arm. "We really should open the totes and unfold the quilts while you're home. It would be wonderful to see them again. Besides, it's not good for the fabrics to be folded for an extended time. It's been years since they were stored away."

Selfishly, I wanted to see Maggie's quilts to get ideas for my new samples, which I'd then reflect in my teaching wardrobe. John had always been protective of them. I doubt he knew until now how deeply I'd absorbed his mother's passion for quilting. I gave it up for a time, but once I went back to it, my life was changed forever.

"Can I tag along if you bring them out?" Steve asked. "I'd like to see them."

"Why?" Helen wasn't shy with her question.

Steve steepled his fingers and tapped his chin. "I haven't had a chance to fill you in on things about my life, Helen. I have a wheelchair bound sister who needs, or I should say wants, a new pastime. A hobby that's meaningful to her." He paused. "I don't want to speak for her, but maybe quilting would be worth a try. She has an eye for beauty and is particular about her surroundings."

"Tina could teach her, couldn't you?"

"I...well..." I frowned thinking of the classroom at Janet's. Such a tight squeeze even for those without a special need. I could teach her one-on-one, but Janet might not go for that, either. So far, my teaching had been for a sponsoring venue, a show, a guild, or a shop. "Let me give it some thought."

We'd almost finished our wine when the waitress came back with our dinners. Digging into our food broke the spell that had started with John's travels and moved into the emotionally tender place that defined Maggie and her quilting. It was hard for John, but it was difficult for me, too. My connection with Maggie hadn't died with her. In the bleakest moments of my marriage, I clung to what I'd learned from her. Finally, Steve and his sister were on my mind, and probably everyone else's.

When we'd eaten the last of the shared desserts, chocolate drenched ice cream and peach cobbler, John suggested we go out again before he left town. I tried to keep my joy bottled inside when he touched my hand to make a point about what a good time he'd had.

We shared hugs at the car before Helen and I went inside. Then Steve drove off and John crossed the lawn to his house.

"What did I tell you? Isn't Steve fun to be with?" Helen asked as she relocked our front door.

Feeling almost lightheaded from the evening, and not only because of the shared bottle of wine, I quickly agreed. "Oh, Helen, I do like him. I see why you've been talking about him. I enjoyed all the different directions of our conversations. And Steve is up on things. He didn't talk about finances and budgets all evening."

"I know. The way he relates to the kids at the youth center touched me from the start." Helen got another faraway look in her eyes as she spoke, as if she were contemplating life's great mysteries.

"Did you know about his sister?" I asked.

"No, he hadn't mentioned her. Maybe his experience with her is behind the reason he volunteers at the youth club. In any case, I hope he'll share more about her," Helen said. "You know, fill in the details. I can think of many reasons she'd be confined to a wheelchair." Helen turned away and headed toward her room.

"Helen, wait a minute. I need to talk about something before we call it a night." I nervously pulled the shawl tighter around my shoulders.

"I'm kind of tried," Helen said. "Can it wait?"

"It could wait, but don't worry, it's not that huge a deal. It's about our income...my income. We need money, right?" I waited, but she didn't seem to want to answer my question. "Right?"

My sister gave me an older sister sigh, as if she'd indulge me even if she'd prefer to walk away. "Well, yeah. Why are you asking this tonight?"

"Simple. Janet has a help wanted sign by the register. It's for a part-time job," I explained. "We cut the amount of ME money going into our accounts, as it should be. But I was thinking that if I worked for Janet, I could use that money to buy the fabric I need for new models. I could still do my part to manage ME. I'd try to work late afternoons and weekends, and keep my mornings open for what we need to do here." To make my argument stronger, I told Helen that Janet was pregnant and would definitely need help when the baby comes.

"Have you talked to her?" Helen asked as she toed off her sandals.

I shook my head. "Not yet. I've been mulling it over. And she had already left by the time I finished up this afternoon."

Helen shrugged. "Right off, I don't see why not. Once we get ME up to date, we shouldn't have to work on it every day." She leaned against the doorjamb. "I don't want to give up volunteer work, so I was thinking maybe we could set aside certain days or parts of days for checking the books and setting up meetings with new clients."

"Are you thinking this could be a part-time business for each of us if we split the work?"

"Something like that. Dad started using Maggie when people were still mailing in checks and they had to make in-person deposits and nothing was on autopilot," Helen said. "But technology changed everything, and now we don't need to allot time for all that extra work."

"But we still have to bring in new business," I said.

"Maybe we could have one quick face-to-face meeting with each client, and then communicate through online chats now and then," Helen said, speaking fast again, the way she did when her enthusiasm was running high. "We could also send a newsletter with tidbits of local news, not about loans, obviously, but the launch of projects and businesses." She tapped her head. "That's a way to never be far from their thoughts."

I could see from Helen's face that she'd already written the first newsletter in her head.

"So, yes, take the job if you want it. Our biggest challenge is going to be attracting new clients and renewing loans," Helen said. "And after listening to you talk about your work tonight, I can see that you need to jumpstart your quilting life."

I swallowed back my urge to describe my vision of 'Tina's Quilt Shop'. It was still a gauzy vision, and maybe it would disappear once I worked in a quilt shop. If the vision actually became stronger, I could ask ME for a starter loan. I laughed at my wild idea.

6

Helen left early Sunday morning. She routinely met a group of friends for brunch first, and then they did various things. One week they might visit a nearby festival, or browse an art show, or take a trip to the botanical gardens in Green Bay. Helen had invited me to go along when I first came back, and I had joined them a few times. But they were Helen's friends, and she had a large circle of them, many new, but some were high school buddies. I couldn't help but envy her for having such a large circle of friends, but then I thought of all the quilters I would meet if I started teaching and traveling again. By itself, a job at Janet's would be an opening to my own new world.

Why was I leaping ahead of myself? I'd call Janet on Monday or stop at the shop to talk in person. I left the kitchen and took the stairs to my quilting studio. I moaned at the mess I'd made when I'd sorted my vests. So, I went right to work. I went through the piles again and moved two vests from the "remake" pile to the "save" pile. I couldn't bear to discard them. I'd worked hard to get the circular design on each of them perfect. Rather than seeing them as outdated, I saw that

I could use them in my teaching. They could be my props in telling the story of my frustration in making them. Or maybe I'd make a video. Other professional quilters did that. Why couldn't I?

I laid out the fabric I'd bought in Green Bay, but with no plan for using it I didn't want to make random cuts. I made a bigger mess when I opened the boxes of fabric I'd brought with me when I left Alex.

For a second or two I reeled, lightheaded, as if I hadn't eaten. But lack of breakfast hadn't caused that sensation. My mind had gone back to Alex's deception. And Dad's. Helen and I had put our dad on some kind of pedestal, like he had with us, which meant he'd raised daughters ill-equipped to handle the nitty-gritty of life.

Did Dad believe my life had been a series of mistakes that needed to be hidden, even from me? Did he think I wasn't capable of handling the truth? I didn't like asking the questions, not only because Dad couldn't provide answers, but because I didn't like any of the responses that came to mind. Helen was probably wondering the same things I was. Why did Dad hold some deep belief that his daughters couldn't understand ME or finances?

I held fabric in my hand but tossed it into the pile yet to be sorted. The feelings within me were so overwhelming I couldn't contain them in the relatively small space of the studio. I needed air and sun. I knew where to find them.

Before I went down a road infested with rabbit holes I rushed upstairs and out to the gardens. Maybe I could work off my frustrations by watering the gardens. Ivy usually set the timer for the automatic sprinklers, but I decided to do it the old-fashioned way. I opened the little-used garden shed. It was filled with tools, but the gardeners used their own. Fortunately, there were also hoses on reels. I remembered where the spigots were and put myself to work.

I ended up laughing at myself when I managed to twist the hose and stop the flow of water. Giving the hose a yank, it immediately freed the twist and drenched me with cold water from the nozzle. That hadn't been part of the plan. Neither was turning the hose on John when he came off the path and into the gardens.

By the time he'd playfully wrestled the hose from me his T-shirt and shorts had molded to his muscled body. I nearly froze in place. When it came to my reaction to John, I might as well have been twenty as fifty. It never changed.

John had his own idea of fun. He held the nozzle skyward, and the water came down like a waterfall. "We did this as kids. Remember?" The water ran down his face and across his chest before dripping to the ground. He gave the nozzle a twist and the water stopped.

"Spoilsport. At least it was refreshing while it lasted." I wiped the rest of the water off my face.

He pulled the hose to the closest flower garden and let the water soak into the dry soil. "It got dry over the last few days."

"We're saving Ivy a job tomorrow if we water today," I said.

Watching the water soak into the soil, it hit me how much I took for granted. John, on the other hand, probably adjusted to every new environment by assessing what resources were scarce. "I bet you've been to places where lack of water is life-threatening."

John expression turned thoughtful as he adjusted the spray and swept it over a new area of the garden. "I've shared my canteen with strangers, for sure, but that was a temporary fix for an immediate problem. But there's nothing quite like drought—and that's affecting an increasing number of people, even fairly close to home. But people in this country who complain about not having much should live where the people struggle to get enough water—and food—every day just to survive."

"You really have seen it all, haven't you?" I asked.

John nodded. "Seen it and chronicled it." He finished watering two gardens while we chatted more about the things he'd witnessed all over the world.

He pulled his wet T-shirt away from his body to encourage air drying. "So, what brought you outside?"

"Oh, this and that. Indecision. Frustration. But also hopes and plans that Helen and I are hashing out." I never had to hide my feelings from John. Well, except the love I carried for him in my heart.

"Sounds like you and Helen are at a crossroads. You have to make decisions, some together, some alone." He planted his free hand on his hip. "We all hit those patches from time to time and we're forced to make a choice."

"Not John Delaney," I said without thinking. "You had your compass set in high school and it seems to have served you well." Did I have to sound so resentful? None of my choices were John's fault.

"That was a long time ago, Tina. Back then all I wanted to do was head out and be anywhere but in Briarwood." He stared at the bed of marigolds and swished the hose like he was angry. "I made the mistake of thinking that I had to leave everything I loved behind and couldn't come back."

My scoff was bitter. I wished I'd hidden it. "I married Alex when I thought..." I twisted away so my back was to him and kicked at the hose, pretending it needed attention. I'd do anything to avoid having to explain that mistake.

"But you're here now. And what about your future plans?"

I gave him a brief rundown on Janet's opening at the quilt shop and the work Helen and I were doing with ME. "Quilting is definitely part of the future. No matter what else I do. Steve and Doug seem to think we can learn to run this business on our own. Even if Dad didn't."

I turned back and caught his slate blue eyes watching me.

"Mom always said a fabric store was her place to escape her troubles."

"Ah, yes, I remember her saying that. It was like Maggie to manage whatever life threw at her. Your mom was so...so together. I guess that describes her best. By the way, I was serious about checking her quilts before you leave us again."

He bent down to pull a weed from the garden. "I'll water again this week and save Ivy the trouble." He waited a couple of seconds before adding, "Do you think Steve was serious about you meeting his sister?"

John's curious expression matched the way I felt. "I don't know him any better than you do," I said. "I'll let Helen probe around a little bit. But I'm happy to meet her, and if she wants a private quilting tutor, I can make time for that. It's possible it's all in Steve's head. Just because she's in a wheelchair doesn't mean she can't act on her own behalf."

"That's what I was thinking," John said. "It wouldn't work if it was really Steve's idea."

By now our clothes had dried in the warm sunshine. Although my outfit was a wrinkled mess, John's clothes didn't even look like they had been wet. "What's with there being no wrinkles in your clothes? Mine look like they just came out of the dryer?"

John waved me off. "Pretty amazing, huh? Almost everything I own is made of fabric that doesn't easily wrinkle. Rain has washed my clothes while I was wearing them more times than I can count. Then the air dried them out."

I laughed. "I'll have to look for clothes like that."

"I've got an idea," John said, "unless you've already made plans for lunch."

"Me? Nope, not a one."

"Let's catch something at The Bistro," John suggested. "Then we can wander around the Richardson Complex. Steve mentioned it at dinner the other night. The guy repurposed the old warehouses into combined living quarters and work studios. Pretty trendy for Briarwood. The complex is near the restaurant."

"Sounds interesting. Do you have thoughts of getting your own studio space?" *And stay here in Briarwood, here with me?* The thought threw me, but I hope my voice didn't show it.

"No, no, nothing like that." John chuckled. "I've had assignments where I went to six countries in six weeks just to photograph new housing concepts. Co-ops and complexes created from repurposed buildings and designed around bikes and scooters and even golf carts." He offered a helpless shrug. "What can I say? I'm curious." He tilted his head. "So, lunch?"

"Give me five minutes."

"I'll get my car. Race ya to see who gets to the driveway first," he yelled as he jogged toward the path.

I rushed inside.

It didn't take long to slip on the best pair of linen slacks I owned. They were fashionably wide-legged and a summery dark tan. I'd bought them after seeing Helen in similar pants. They were perfect with my favorite white lightweight linen shirt. From the back of the closet, I dragged out red espadrilles. At the last minute I'd taken them out of the give-away box and packed them. Nothing was new or even that recent, but I looked in the mirror and felt enough like Helen that I borrowed some of her confidence and stood a little straighter.

I brushed my hair and tucked it behind my ear and let it

fall loose. I smiled at my own reflection and touched my special earrings. Dad might not have known much about the real Tina, but he picked out the perfect earrings.

I opened the front door as John was pulling up. He stopped and reached across the passenger's seat to open the door. "Whew! I call that a tie." I said when I slipped in and buckled the seatbelt.

"And rumor has it women take forever to get ready."

I flashed a long-suffering look.

"Just sayin'."

"You should have seen Helen fuss over her clothes the first time Steve came over to help us with ME," I said, smiling. "She'd already met him and was very impressed. She must have tried on half her closet before settling on a killer outfit."

John turned a corner and drove past Janet's Quilt Shop and slowed down. He wore a secretive grin when he turned to look at me.

"Why'd you go this way? She's not open on Sundays."

"Just taking the scenic route." There was a touch of innocence behind his smile.

He was up to something. "Oh, really? Or did you think that if Janet was there I'd ask you to stop so I could talk to her?"

"Just making the offer. It's early now, but why don't you think about. If you stopped in late, she might stay a few minutes after closing and you wouldn't be interrupted by customers." He drummed his fingers on the steering wheel. "You also had some concerns about the class. Might be easier to tell her what's on your mind when you're alone."

He gave me something to think about and I said so. "But if I recall you invited me to lunch."

"Yes, I did. But if you want to stop back later, all you have to do is ask." Two more right turns and John pulled into the restaurant's parking lot. We'd missed the busiest hours, so we had our choice of tables. John's preference for a table by the window was okay with me.

The waitress brought glasses of water and menus, but John handed the menu back. "Cheeseburger, fries, and an order of onion rings. And whatever dark beer you have on tap." He touched the top edge of my menu. "It's just lunch. Be brave."

I ordered a garden burger and fries but stuck to water. "I'll eat onion rings off his plate," I added. Like old times. Maybe because I was younger, when we were kids, he tolerated my tendency to sample whatever he'd ordered.

"That wasn't very brave," he teased. He played with his napkin folding it into interesting shapes.

I pointed to the napkin. "A little origami?"

"Right. The first time I saw a room full of people producing origami for mass market sale wasn't in Japan, but Las Vegas, of all places." John laughed. "A local cottage industry for custom party favors."

"I never tire of hearing about your exotic life, even origami in Vegas." I leaned back in my chair to give the waitress room to put the platters in front of us. "Smells good. There's nothing quite like the familiar, comforting aroma of burgers and fries."

John grabbed an onion ring and twirled it on his finger.

What was he doing? "Oh, please. How old are you? Six, maybe eight?"

John grinned. "I like it when you smile. It takes away that frown on your forehead. I hope it doesn't become permanent. The frown, that is, not the smile."

"Not much to smile about right now," I blurted. As if his question flipped a switch, I listed all my troubles, from the threat of ME going broke, to my teaching blunder, and I threw in a line about my divorce. "So, I'll either grow or sink into a hole and shrivel up." I took a sip of water. "Not a very pretty picture of a woman's life, is it?"

John dropped an onion ring on his plate "It won't be that long before you're on the upswing again."

I dipped a fry into the ketchup. "I'll let you know." Suddenly, I put my elbow on the table rubbed my forehead. "It sure is fun to take me to lunch, huh? I'm a barrel of laughs."

"Well, I *was* wondering...you know, about your mood." John shrugged.

"Wow. When I play my spiel back, I don't like what I hear either." I shook my head. "I'm sorry.

"No problem...really." He let out a low short laugh. "Lunch isn't over yet. We can turn this ship around." John wiped his hands. He reached into a pocket and slid a business card across the table. "New set of satellite numbers on the back. I upgraded so we can talk more while I'm gone." He took another bite of his burger.

I fingered the card. He was giving me a lifeline whether he knew it or not. "When's the best time to call?" Realizing what I'd asked was nonsensical given the time zones, I finally laughed at myself. "Forget I asked that. You'll tell me where you are, and we'll go from there."

"Let me call first when I get settled." He gave me a reassuring smile. "Well, as settled as I ever get. I don't even know where I'm going yet."

How many times had I heard him say that?

7

THE NEXT WEEK HELEN AND I FOCUSED ON ME, CATCHING UP with Joe Jepson, a client whose loan was sixty days behind. It turned out he'd changed banks, and a glitch in the transfer system had spit back his payments. Joe had heard about Dad's death, as had another client with a similar situation. It still took half the morning to straighten out the problems.

Fortunately, Dad had been lucky to have a great relationship with the personal banker he'd worked with for decades at our local bank. The bank valued continuity, so Helen and I could continue to deal with the same representative. Dad and Doug thought alike in some critical ways, and Helen and I benefitted from their choices. For one thing, why court local business but then take your own money and plunk it in a less personal national institution? Joe rightly assumed we'd contact him and help straighten it out.

We had other jobs to handle on our new path. Helen used her skills to write a letter to send to existing clients to assure them nothing had changed. We could see in a few cases that ME was a source of a few large loans that had helped carry a couple of small restaurants in town through some big crises.

Other businesses needed loans to expand inventory in order to stay competitive in changing markets.

Helen remarked that in all the years of working around Dad, she'd never imagined him being the only source of fast cash in town during a sudden catastrophe. Dad funded the diner for the couple of months it took the state's small business office to process a more substantial loan. "So, this is why we have a thirty-year-old diner in town," she said. "Dad helped it through more than one recession and other threats. It has two payments to go."

Helen's letter also stated that we'd be in touch in the next thirty days to discuss future needs. Somehow, even though it took half a morning to draft the letter, we were able to strike a balance between too formal and too buddy-buddy.

We personalized the letter with a handwritten note to add our greeting and thanks. Somehow, Dad had managed to keep ME going without a master mailing list of clients or software that allowed personal information inserted. "We'll have to update these things as we go along," I said, when Helen had printed the copies on ME letterhead—outdated letterhead that we needed to redesign. Because of my superior handwriting, I addressed the envelopes and Helen sealed and stamped them.

We sat with the pile of more than thirty letters ready to go when Helen asked, "Do you think we should have sent Doug or Steve a copy of the text to review?"

I laughed and pointed to the finished stack. "Now you ask?" Since this was our first contact with the business owners, I didn't want to make a mistake, but on the other hand there was nothing we could point to that led to the "What's the worst that can happen?" scenario. John's off-hand remark at The Bistro, "Be brave," had nothing to do with ME, but it gave me a jolt of confidence.

"Theoretically, Sis, we probably should have, but we can't run to Doug or Steve every time we take an action. And this is a teeny-tiny step not worth accumulating billable hours with Doug's firm. Let's save their help for processing our first loans." Something else came to mind and I decided not to hold it back. "We also bring a different touch to the business," I said, "and we have to be competitive in a way that Dad was not. He didn't have to adjust to doing business online. I think we have to find our own way to approach our target market to bring in new clients and process new loans. We can't be clones of Dad—we have to create our own business style."

"So optimistic of you," Helen said. "You're assuming we'll have new businesses to work with."

"I sure am. It's either that or we let the existing contracts run their course and then we close up." Some of the loans had a few years left before they were done, but the interest on them wouldn't cover Ivy's salary for a year. "I don't know about you, but I'm not ready to give up the house. That's why I'm going to approach Janet about the part-time job. It isn't much, but it's something."

"You're right," Helen said. "If we call for advice about a friendly letter, we might as well let Steve and Doug take over ME until it dies a natural death." She sat up a little straighter and lifted her chin.

A surge of defiant energy came from my belly up to my throat. "I don't want that. From what I see, I don't think you do, either. We can do this, Sis. As you pointed out, we can make this business a part-time gig for both of us. We *can* hold on to our other dreams while we make ME ours."

My words came out not only strong, but loud. They reverberated off the walls of the office. I wished Dad could have heard them.

Helen gathered the letters to drop in the mail on her way

to lunch at the club. She'd mentioned that a new non-profit wanted her input for an upcoming event that would involve social media blasts in addition to TV and radio clips. "This could lead to a short-term consulting fee," Helen said, "but I wonder if it would take too much time away from ME."

"I'd go for it, Helen. Really. We don't know yet how much time ME is going to require," I said, "but if I can work part-time at the quilt shop, then you can work with this new non-profit."

"You're right." Helen pointed to the computer. "The loans seemed to hum along on their own, once they're negotiated and the contract is signed. Our challenge is going to be attracting new business."

"That's where you come in—and always have." Helen had been almost paralyzed with fear when we had to open the financials and assess the business. None of that fear crept in when she drafted the letter, spoke to a few clients, and came with ideas for an ME newsletter, which would focus on happenings in Briarwood. My sister was in her element.

JANET RAN HOT AND COLD WHEN I CALLED HER. COLD ON opening a conversation about the quilting class, but hot on my interest in working for her. "I'm so grateful that someone who knows about fabric and quilting wants to work here," she said eagerly.

"I'll want a little more information about the job before I agree. As you need to understand I've never worked retail before. I'll have to learn how to use the register. And—"

She cut me off with, "Easy. Money in, money out."

Knowing it wasn't going to be that simple I pushed for a face-to-face meeting until she agreed. Later that afternoon I pulled into the empty parking area at Janet's. Hmm...a bad sign for the business, but a good sign for our ability to talk freely. As much as she apparently didn't care to discuss the beginner's class on the phone, I was determined to get my thoughts about it on the table.

I pulled open the door and stepped into a silent room. A few banks of lights were on, but not the bright spotlights above the fabric area. No music filled the room, which added to the eeriness. The hair on my arms tingled. "Janet?" I called as I walked toward the office in the back of the store. "Janet?"

"Hello, I'm here." She stood in the doorway. "I was resting. I thought I would hear the buzzer on the door if someone came in." She stretched her arms above her head and did a body shimmy. "There. That's better. I'm more tired with this baby then I thought I'd be."

That was her entire explanation. She moved away from the office, and I followed her lead when she went into the main area of the shop. As if everything was dandy, she started a quick tour of the space. "I have the fabric arranged by designer or company. The trendy fabric is near the door, along with specials or seasonal bolts. Notions are..." She turned to face me when I waved my arm for her to stop.

"Slow down, Janet." I made no effort to hide my obvious annoyance. "All this can wait. The fabrics aren't my concern about accepting a job in the shop."

Janet held up her hands in surrender. "Sorry. I'm not handling this well."

"That's okay, but I can't make a decision without information. Let's start with how many hours you want me to work, and for what salary. I'm the co-owner of my father's business now, so I have to fit my job into an already rigorous schedule." I had to smile at that. Like Helen and I had a schedule. I sounded much more professional about ME than I felt.

"I get it, Tina, I really do." Janet squared her shoulders and put her game face on.

"I need to know your store policies as well," I said. "What happens if I make a mistake cutting fabric? I need to nail down those kinds of details."

She brushed the air with her hand. "You name it, you got it."

If I hadn't seen her earlier, I'd have concluded that either she wasn't knowledgeable enough to trust, or she didn't have a grasp on what was involved in hiring help. Her answers had all been made in short phrases, and I wondered if she had the energy for more than that.

Finally, Janet took a deep breath. "Here's the deal. My husband, Tom, thinks I should sell the shop, that it will be too hard to manage with the new baby. And he has a point. Carol is a great employee, but she's leaving the end of August to go back to school. And I'm..." She rubbed her baby mound. "I'm due the end of October." She sat down on a nearby chair. "That leaves Abby Higgins to mind the shop, but only part-time, during one of the busiest times of the year. Abby is an older woman who can only handle the register for a few hours before she's worn out."

Janet ran down the dilemmas and gave me more information than I needed, but it also put me on alert. If I took the job, I'd be stepping into a mess in the making. No wonder she wasn't into a postmortem on the failed class.

"So, my other choice is to close," Janet said.

Oops, that was enough to hike my alert level up into a new color box. Orange, maybe?

"Right now, given the baby coming and these staffing issues, I have to consider selling, like Tom suggests. But I have to exhaust all the possibilities before I'd take such a drastic step. Besides, this shop means the world to me. I've worked too hard to prove to myself that I could successfully run a business."

"You might close? For real?" I wanted to say she couldn't do that, but who was I to be judgmental? I'd talked about my dream of owning a shop, but I was a lot older than Janet and hadn't taken even a baby step toward doing it. I hadn't even become one of Janet's customers yet. On a nearby display, Janet had a bolt of the same fabric I'd purchased in Green Bay. A twinge of guilt trickled though me. If I'd come to her shop, I could have supported a Briarwood business and had the same fabric. "Maybe what you need is more than part-time help."

"If only the magic fairy would grant my every wish." She reached out to touch the colorful cuts of fabric in a small basket. "I need new models, a change of wall displays, and if you have money in your pocket, I could use some of that too."

I thought of ME and how a loan might ease the pressure for her, but I was thinking too far down the road. Lately it seemed I wanted to live in my future world of fulfilled hopes, and not in the sometimes-uncertain present.

"You knew eight students was a mistake, didn't you?" I pressed her for an answer.

She hung her head. "It wasn't just that I needed the registration money. I was happy for the interest from that many new customers. I'm sorry it fell on your shoulders. Heather didn't think it would be too much for you, since you've handled a whole classroom of students for a weekend."

"Not beginning students," I said, trying not to sound defensive. "Heather would have run into the same problems I did. She'd have managed it the same way I did, but that doesn't change the facts."

As I stood with Janet, listening and thinking, it didn't matter that the class was mismanaged. The possibility of having a business close in Briarwood was a bigger issue. Dad immediately came to mind. He would have reached out to help. And I was his daughter. I needed to look back into Dad's files of business profiles. Maybe he'd made notes about his process of evaluating a business to see if he could offer a loan or decline the request. Then I'd have to let Helen in on my search for a process we could use as a model.

"Let me think about your job offer, Janet. I promise I'll get back to you soon." I reached out to give her shoulder a squeeze. "Take care of yourself. You're right to make the baby your priority now."

I made my way to the front door and stopped. When I looked back Janet was still sitting in the chair, all alone in her shop. My heart saddened for her. I knew the pressure of the business and the baby must weigh heavily on her, and she had her husband to think about, too.

For other reasons, some bad memories flashed through my mind and unsettled me. But I had to let them in because they helped me understand myself. When I'd first started teaching, I'd returned home from a quilting class, waiting for Alex to ask about the students and what I'd taught them. Good or bad, I wanted to share, but he quickly turned the conversation to complain about all the losers he worked with and the stupid people that wouldn't buy the insurance he sold. I was always alone with the challenges.

When I was three blocks from home, I turned the car around and drove back to the quilt shop. An impulsive move I couldn't explain, but I was ready to tell Janet I would work full-time for her. I would also sew new models using the newest fabrics and would consult with her about updating her displays. I wanted to add that Helen would put together a new marketing strategy heavy on PR.

But the door was locked.

I slapped my hand against the glass. When I looked at the

signs on the door offering specials for the month, I noticed she hadn't removed the Help Wanted sign.

I rushed home and started flipping through the pages of Dad's ledgers hoping to find notations that would help me figure out how he decided who to help. I was sure there had been more people that needed a helping hand than he could have handled, although based on the system Helen and I had figured out, with Steve's help, much of ME was a fully automated system.

And then there was a lead. Dad's notation, "Ask Doug" had been added to a page. I knew it was Dad's because the handwriting was bold and precise handwriting. No scribbling allowed. I touched the letters and remembered the cramps in my fingers after I'd practiced writing the alphabet for hours at a time. Every time I was ready to quit, Dad would urge me to keep going. "One more time, Tina. Try to make each letter like the picture."

It made my chest tighten to remember how hard I worked to get his approval. A losing proposition as it turned out. Or at least it seemed that way from where I stood today.

When I saw movement in the flower garden closest to the house, I left the office through the French door. "Hey, are you the gardener's new hire?"

John stood up and opened his arms. I didn't hesitate to walk into the comfort of a hug. "I'm just killing a little time weeding before I leave tonight. I like connecting with my mom through these gardens." He smiled wistfully. "It always brings up a few memories."

I stiffened at the words "leave tonight." John felt that, but instead of letting me go, he held me tighter. "So soon? You haven't been home very long."

I wiggled out of his arms to look into his eyes, which often told me his true feelings. That day I didn't see any excitement.

"It can't be helped," John said, his hands lightly holding my wrists. "It surprises people to know there's such a thing as being on call with an agency, and I'm on call now."

"For what? What's the emergency?"

He grinned. "Only a major volcano eruption in Iceland. Listen to the news in the next few days because it's going to have far reaching consequences, including disruption in air travel and even tankers and freighters and summer cruise ships."

"Then how will you get there?"

"The situation is too fluid to say, but I'll find a way to hitch a ride," John said. "The wire services find ways to move people and the agency works with them to make room for me." With a quick shrug he added, "That's why I'm flying out tonight, so I can quickly get to O'Hare and catch whatever gets me close. Then I'll figure out the rest."

"Will you call?" Lately, I sounded like a desperate woman when I was near him. But then, I hadn't been near him in years.

"I promise." He leaned forward and lightly kissed me. "I'm not sorry for that, Tina." A smile crossed his face.

"Travel safe, John." I ran to the house before the tears started. John was a source of so much confusion, always had been. I went into my room to change into more comfortable clothes.

Helen's call was a welcome interruption. "Hi. Steve said he's free Sunday morning to help with Maggie's quilts. He spends Saturdays with his sister."

"John's leaving tonight," I blurted, even though the words stuck in my throat and sounded scratchy when I finally got them out.

Silence.

"Uh, I'm sorry you didn't have more time with him, Tina."

That was the best she could do, but I couldn't fault her response to my overreaction to this ordinary news. John was always leaving on a moment's notice, but I wasn't around to see it. Helen and John were like ships passing, always had been. They were cordial but not special friends like John and me.

"Are you coming home soon? We need to discuss some ME business." I impressed myself with my quick recovery and all-business tone. That was one way to get my mind off of John and to start working on what ME could do to help Janet.

"I'm pulling out of the club now. See you in a few minutes." She tagged off. Helen was a careful driver and wouldn't have considered talking or texting while navigating the busy roadway. She complained often and loudly about people who broke those rules.

Back in the office, I went through more of the bound ledgers looking for notes and clues. Mostly I was on the hunt for data about the individuals and businesses Dad declined to help. More than a list, I needed comments that explained his decisions.

I heard Helen come in the front door. "I'm in the office," I yelled.

"What are you doing? This mess looks like your sewing area." Helen tossed her purse into one of the client chairs and spun the other to face me. She flopped into the chair like she was exhausted.

"What do you know about the way Dad made his decisions?" I asked pointing to the ledgers. "What made him approve or decline a loan? Any insight about that?"

"Ha. Very funny," Helen said bitterly. "Me? You think Dad would have included me in that discussion?"

I'd struck a nerve. I understood why. Dad was so private about his dealings with other people he'd essentially built-in business-client privilege, not any different from doctor-patient and attorney-client. But more relevant to Helen's reaction, his unwillingness to explain the business, let alone prepare us to take over, hit home. "I was only hoping I could find a list or notes or something in his ledgers."

"Why? Did something happen today?"

Sitting on the floor surrounded by the early records of ME I told Helen the details of my meeting with Janet.

Shortly after I'd started, she got up and sat at the desk and pulled out a legal pad and pencil. "Slow down a minute. I need to get all these moving parts down on paper. Easier to evaluate them."

I finished by telling Helen I wanted to work full-time for Janet.

Helen tossed her pencil on the desk. "No. No. No."

"Pretty quick decision on your part, don't you think?"

"Okay, let's be honest here. Do you want to work there because you love fabric or because you have a dream of owning a quilt shop?"

"It's not a new dream." I stretched my legs out in front of me. "How did you know any of that figured into my idea about working for Janet?"

She swatted the air in front of her face. "Listen to yourself. Your words run together, your body language is all upbeat and positive when you talk about your ideas for the shop." She wiggled her fingers in the air. "You're in constant motion. But mostly I see right through you. Your eyes and your smile always tell the truth. When you're excited about something you light up like a Christmas tree."

I was turning red with the description of myself, so accurate it embarrassed me that I was that transparent. "Then why are you saying no?"

Helen bent forward and put her hands out. She touched

each finger to create a visual for her points. "One, we haven't gotten ME up and running, nor do we have a handle on our financial position. If we scrimp, can we make the money last longer from the loans already outstanding? Two, we don't know anything about Janet's financial situation other than she needed the registration money. That's pretty weak. And she didn't clarify. Three, what happens to your teaching schedule, and...and...you get the idea."

Helen swiveled the office chair to the desk and back to face me. "I can't take anymore incoming, Tina. It's too soon. And what are you? Superwoman? You can't do everything all at once even if you want to."

I closed my eyes and let her words sink in. She was right. But...now I was at a loss. I had let my mind travel into Janet's fairyland. Maybe it was to avoid the news that John was leaving, or some hidden sense of shame that the only area in which I could feel confidence rise was linked with quilting. I had a taste of understanding what I could do with that shop—with Helen's help.

Keeping my eyes forward I stacked the ledgers back onto the bookcase shelf. "When did you get so smart about evaluating a business?" I asked.

Helen scoffed. "All afternoon I've had to rein in ideas the new non-profit wanted to do to get the public's attention. Somehow, they thought everyone was willing and able to take on big projects and work for free." Helen sighed. "I had to get them to understand that this type of organization starts with a donors' seed money. They even asked about a loan from ME to get them started. I still don't know how they knew we were running the business."

"They probably read our names at the bottom of Dad's obituary," I said. "The paper did a long piece about him. What did you tell them about the loan?"

Helen picked up the pencil she's tossed and began doodling on the pad. "I dodged the question. We don't have a policy, but Dad was apparently not willing to involve ME with non-profits."

"That's true. At least not in the last several years."

"When an organization doesn't need to turn a profit," Helen said, "then the financial side is a whole different ball game. Dad was more interested in helping small business owners make a living."

The majority of loans we'd looked at were made to established retail stores and service companies, or professional practices. The rest, a smaller number, were made to families needing short-term help or longer-term loans for improving their property. Loans for new porches, new flooring, a remodeled kitchen, or an added room all fell into the category of relatively small loans.

"Under other circumstances, Janet's Quilt Shop would fit the bill, though," I pointed out.

"I suppose. But you can't work there and own the loan company." Helen frowned. "Well, at least I think that's true." Helen stepped from behind the desk and stooped to pick up the last of the ledgers I'd flipped through. "Oh, so I guess we won't be doing the quilts on Sunday. What with John not here."

I got to my feet and stretched my arms over my head. "I suppose not. I'll text him. He was killing time weeding one of the flower gardens earlier. Then he took off to get ready to take off."

"I wonder how he really feels about heading out tonight. He's been traveling for so many years. Here today, gone tomorrow." Helen picked up her purse. "I'm meeting Steve for dinner. Can you touch base with John?" She waved as she hurried out of the room.

I got up and sat in Dad's chair while I got John on the phone.

"Tina? I didn't expect to hear from you." I detected a beat of hesitancy.

"Sorry I left so abruptly," I said. "It's been a confusing day. Lots of little disappointments."

"And I added to the list by telling you I was leaving town?" John said turning it into a question, not a statement.

"No, no," I denied. "It's your job and...and..." *I want you to stay with me. I want you to be part of my life. I want you to choose me.* "I called for a reason. Steve is free Sunday morning if you want us to refold your mom's quilts. We were going to do it together, but now with your leaving..." I twirled the pencil Helen had left on the desk.

"I'd like you to wait," John said, making his feelings clear. "I want to be here when the totes are opened. They were put away a long time ago and I can't remember if I put other things in the totes along with the quilts."

"Say no more, John. Of course, we'll wait. Actually, it's not a job I wanted to do without you."

"If all goes well, I won't be gone long. I'll probably try to get to the smaller towns to see how the immediate aftermath is affecting day-to-day life there. But, at some point, I'll be done—the press corps will stay, but I'll slip out again when I can."

His brevity surprised me. When I'd happened to talk with him before he left on assignment, he usually focused on details. He'd talk about which camera and lens he'd use for monochrome panoramas versus the color of the street life he loved so much. He always mentioned why it was important to document what an event like a storm or an earthquake, and now another volcano, did to a landscape, a village or a whole country.

He minimized this trip, though. His earlier remark about wanting his mother's flower garden legacy to continue stayed with me, too. He must have seen the way Dad had continued to pay for the gardens to be maintained. That had never changed. As far as I was concerned it never would. Like Ivy's salary, the gardeners were a fixed, permanent expense of the household.

Maybe John was tiring of life on the road and wanted a career change. I had no problem wishing he'd stop traveling and stay in Briarwood. He may not love me as a life partner, but at least I knew we'd always be friends.

"Tina? Are you there?" John's voice quickened.

"Oh, sorry," I murmured. "My mind had jumped to the future of the gardens and the quilts again."

"I could use a crystal ball," he said with a short laugh.

Helen had come into the kitchen dressed in a new outfit. The sleeveless tunic top ended mid-thigh over slim slacks and dressy kitten heeled shoes. The splashes of color on the tunic and her large hoop earrings brought out Helen's bright and sassy side.

"Hold on John. Helen is on her way out to see Steve tonight, so she can let him know you want to wait to look at the quilts."

Helen nodded and spoke loud enough for John to hear. "Travel safe. Coffee is waiting when you come back." She grabbed my hand and squeezed it. "Later." And then she was gone.

"I'm going to double Helen's words. Travel safe, John, and promise you'll call when you can."

"I promise. Keep the coffeepot going." There was a beep on the line, then two. "Another call coming in. Might be flight updates. Bye."

I held the phone after disconnecting. For no reason, a

question popped into my head. Would I ever see John again? I dropped the phone on the desk and got to my feet. I crossed my arms over my chest as if protecting myself. From what? I'd never worried about something happening to John before. And why now? This trip wasn't typical. In some ways it was safer than many.

The tightness in my body built, and I recognized the signs. Nothing was going to calm me except working with fabric, so I hurried to my studio with renewed purpose. I needed new vests for teaching and perhaps to wear to work my part-time shifts at Janet's. But my enthusiasm plummeted when the reality of the huge job ahead hit. On my trip to Green Bay, I hadn't yet thought out my plan well enough to choose the fabric that matched the vision. Once again, I was searching through a stash of outdated fabric.

I turned off the lights and headed for the kitchen. I poured a glass of wine and turned on a Hallmark movie where the girl gets the guy.

Somehow, though, I was overwhelmed by the silence in the empty house. John was all but gone. Helen was out for dinner. Ivy had left for the day. Feeling sorry for myself I had the painful thought that I was so easy to leave behind.

8

For five days I couldn't stop myself from keeping my phone close by in hopes of hearing from John. Meanwhile, I sent him positive messages, not that his volcano work put him in peril, but things with John were different now. In a way, it was more like old times when we were kids clowning around and talking about anything and everything. For more than three decades, I had no definitive place on the planet to mentally put John. Now that I did, I worried about him. Silly really, since nothing had changed between us. I was in love with him, and he thought of me as his great friend. Not exactly a sister, but not his romantic partner, either. But then, there was that kiss. Light and quick, friendly more than passionate, for sure. I tried—and failed miserably—to put it out of my mind.

The online videos about the eruption in Iceland were short and gave only minimal information, mostly about the immediate day-to-day problems for the population and the economic impact. Still, I wore my diamond earrings from Dad and used them to ground me when my mind scattered.

Thankfully, during that time many of ME's clients called to

chat with us about the letter updating ME and clarifying our plans to keep the business up and running. We arranged face-to-face meetings, too, with those interested in seeing us in person and getting acquainted. Given everything else we needed to do, we limited ourselves to two meetings a day. We thought an hour or two would be more than enough time to go over the loans and see if anything else was needed. We'd use a checklist Steve helped us write.

In some cases, we arranged to drop by the business to introduce ourselves, knowing we could handle everything on the phone or through email. One way or the other, it seemed like an easy way to get a feel for the business.

We were so wrong.

True to human nature some clients wanted to rush through the checklist and be on their way. They had their businesses to run, after all. They wanted to be certain they were in good standing and that we'd consider doing business with them in the future. Others took our offering of coffee, tea, or sparkling water as an invitation to settle in and tell us their life story.

"No wonder Dad was so tired some evenings," Helen said, later one afternoon after a couple of long meetings. "He worked all day and had some evening meetings with clients, too. Fortunately, those dwindled over the years. Phone calls worked just as well, and Dad would go to their turf now and again." She grabbed the last sugar cookie on the plate and took a bite.

"I hope you made good notes for us to refer to the next time we schedule a meeting."

"Yep. Right here." She held up the legal pad she'd used to scribble notes. After attempting to take notes on a tablet, Helen realized she couldn't focus on the person when she was using a keyboard. A pen in her hand felt more natural—and friendlier. Then she'd transfer notes to the computer files after the meeting.

I didn't care what method she used as long as we had some information about each person. Over the years, Dad's record keeping, while meticulous when it came to the numbers was less so when it involved the kind of personal observations Helen and I made. We thought he was used to keeping all that information in his head, especially because he knew so many of his clients from other arenas, including the country club and the small business owners group in town.

"You have some of the same strengths as Dad," I said after one particularly successful meeting with the owner of an expanding dental practice. "You seem to enjoy meeting these people and putting them at ease. I think you can read people like Dad did. You have a real talent for it."

"Thanks." Helen smiled, but it quickly disappeared. "I think that's why Dad thought I did a good job being the PR person for ME." She snickered. "Informal PR person. I put that title on myself. I guess it made me feel like I was earning the money that showed up in my account every month. It would have been nice to have a title to acknowledge it."

"Oh, Helen," I said, trying not to show my impatience. We kept talking around the reality of Dad's strange attitude toward his daughters. "At least you were dealing with him one-on-one." My voice rose as I added, "I'm still wondering how to confront Alex, or even if I should. Doug tells me it won't make a difference in my settlement. It's not like Alex stashed away the money. I should probably forget the whole thing and move on."

Helen grimaced to acknowledge my anger. I made no secret that I was still upset about Dad and Alex and their money secrets. No resolution presented itself. I had to move on. I didn't have another choice. At least that's what I kept telling myself.

"By the way, Tina, I decided to take Steve's advice and sign up for an online accounting class from the community college. I don't have to show up and have anyone question why the co-owner of ME would be in Accounting 101. This way, I can protect my identity."

"Steve suggested it?" I asked, wondering why this was the first I heard of this. "I didn't know that."

"It came up when we were out to dinner the other night," Helen explained. "From that first meeting, he's noticed my lack of self-confidence when it comes to running ME. He thinks a formal class will give me a foundation, more or less. Then I'll gradually be more confident in evaluating the business month by month. And I can pass on what I learn to you."

"That would be great," I said, "because both of us should be able to do all the jobs." I was worried, though, because I'd decided to accept the part-time job with Janet. "I'm going to try to pick up my teaching, along with working for Janet. That's going to take time away from ME. Of course, I'll be here evenings and we can go over the totals and make decisions about new loans." It all sounded a little exhausting. "And we don't have to be in the same room to look over the financials."

"True enough," Helen said, turning her pencil end over end. "The wonders of technology." She paused, but not for long. "Are you staying busy to keep from thinking about John?"

I'd admit to no such thing. Without meeting her eye, I said, "It looks like my job at Janet's is going to eat up a lot of my time."

The call I was waiting for came at ten in the morning, just as I was about to cut fabric for a customer. But seeing the name on the screen, I excused myself and ran to the office and closed the door. "Where are you? How are you?"

He laughed. "Slow down, Tina. Catch your breath. I'm fine. Tired, but I got some pretty amazing pictures of the volcano. Ash was everywhere. It covered everything, but the daylight lasts most of a 24-hour day, so I could use all light and shadows. I've never been more grateful for the gear I have to protect the cameras."

His voice was upbeat. It was exciting to hear him happy and immersed in his work. I knew what he was feeling, because the simple act of handling fabric made the real world melt away for me.

"So, tell me what you've been doing since I left."

It never failed. His smooth voice sent a shiver through me. "I've been working at Janet's, four days a week, five-hour shifts. But she needs more help." I explained that the schedule made it impossible to make new models for the shop, so its look hadn't changed. "Oops, I just realized I was cutting fabric for a customer and ducked into the office to answer your call."

"What? That doesn't sound like you," John said. "Your boss might not want you leaving paying customers to chat with me."

"Right now, your call was more important." I heard a beep telling me our call would soon end.

"Tina, you don't know how good that makes me feel, even if I know you shouldn't have picked up. The thing is, I'm not coming home now. I'm on my way to Italy. It's a wine industry story. The grapes have been attacked by a pest and it's had everyone worried. I'll call..."

The connection ended.

When I returned to the cutting table Janet was bagging the

customer's fabric. "Sorry," I muttered. "It was an important call. I had to take it." My tone oozed defensiveness.

"You can finish up here," Janet said, not looking up. Then she turned to the customer. "I'll meet you at the register when you're ready."

For the rest of the day, I caught my mind wandering back to John's call rather than keeping my focus on fabric and customers.

When I was ready to leave for the day, I went into the office to gather my things. Janet followed me and stepped into the doorway. "I'm not happy with the way you left that customer to take a personal call this morning."

I was taken aback and stood paralyzed in place. I'd never said it was a personal call. But start to finish, I couldn't have been gone any more than three, maybe four minutes. I left the counter, true, but I hadn't gone far.

"Like I said, Janet, it was an important call." I slung my purse strap over my shoulder.

"That's all you're going to say?" Janet asked, her voice calm and quiet. "No 'I'm sorry, and it won't happen again' to reassure me?" She put her hands on the door frame essentially blocking me from leaving the tiny office.

Had I signed up to be treated like a little kid who broke a rule? Not on your life. "Look, Janet, I'm not sorry, so I'm not going to apologize. Yes, it was personal, but it was important." I was too tired to debate with her. Instead, I took a few steps toward her. "I'll be back in the morning."

Janet hesitated, but then twisted out of the way to let me pass. "No, Tina, don't come back. Your attitude is really odd. You left a customer standing at the counter. So, there's no need for you to come into work tomorrow unless you decide that in *this* shop the customers come first."

Stunned by Janet's rebuke, my face warmed as I hurried to

the front door and pushed it open. As soon as I was outside, I filled my lungs with fresh air. I already knew it would be a long night deciding if I needed to return and apologize, or perhaps quit and be done with it. I'd spend my time building ME, giving Helen the help I knew she wanted.

In my heart, I knew this was about more than feeling put upon. I hadn't worked for other people much in my life. I was reacting as if Alex had showed up to offer his criticism of me. Alex had more or less made me feel like I didn't know enough to work in the real world. That's how I felt now as I walked to the car.

On the other hand, if working in retail – or in any outside job – left no time for a short call from a special friend overseas, then I wanted no part of it. At least as a quilter and teacher, I ran my own show, set my schedule, and did things my way. As an alternative to working for Janet, I'd put the word out to the quilting community that I was available to teach classes or give lectures. I hope that teaching, along with ME, would add up to an income.

I slid into the driver's seat and laughed. I replayed my long justification and self-important diatribe and realized I had a lot of nerve judging Janet. The quilt shop belonged to her. I was the employee. She paid the bills and hired and fired—and cut the checks. But then I decided that if I owned a shop, I would give my employees some latitude.

Oh, really? My employees could pick up a call and dash away from a customer. No problem. Wow, who had lifted me up on that high horse? Why this all struck me as funny, I'll never be able to explain, but I was laughing at myself and my folly.

But now... Did I apologize and explain why the call was important, or maintain that fiction and stubbornly stick to the justification for my actions, despite leaving Janet in a difficult position with a customer?

I went from the front door straight through the house to the rocking chairs in the gardens when I got home. The more I thought about how the situation started the faster I rocked. After a few minutes of stewing, I put myself in Janet's place and understood her need to make every customer feel valued. She didn't have the luxury of a customer leaving the shop because her employee was taking a personal call. The fact that the call came from John, the most important person in my life, was beside the point.

I'd left Janet in the lurch and wasn't particularly gracious about owning it.

Janet covered my mistake, but quilters talked, and the word would quickly be passed on among them that the new employee at Janet's Quilt Shop was rude. Some would recognize my name from shows and lectures.

I didn't like facing the truth, but I cared about John even more than I wanted to admit and it was spilling over into other areas of my life. And in an unfamiliar and odd way. I'd been snippy to Janet in a manner that simply wasn't me, or at least not the person I thought myself to be.

By the time Helen joined me I was ready to call Janet and apologize.

"How's your day been?" Helen sat in the chair next to me and started rocking.

"Very bad, and very good."

"Want to elaborate?" She turned in the chair to look at me, her foot poised to push the chair into motion when needed.

"John called. That's the good part."

"Oh, really? No, can't be." Helen grinned as she kidded me about John.

I found her teasing irrationally irritating, but I knew that said more about me than about Helen. "He's done with the volcano in Iceland and is on his way to Italy."

"Ah, Italy. Sometimes I could swoon thinking about the places he goes."

A giggle escaped. "I know exactly how you feel. But I don't think this is a swoon-worthy trip. He's involved with a story about insects attacking the grape crops. For obvious reasons, the wine industry is alarmed."

"I wonder why they need a photographer," Helen said, puzzled. "The industry must have scientists documenting everything."

"I'm sure he'll explain it when he gets home." I smiled as I regained the sense of wellbeing I'd started with that morning. "Meanwhile, he sounded good. And..."

She put up her hand to stop me. "What's the bad part of the day? It can't be the wine industry's troubles that had you looking so glum when I came out here."

"John called while I was working, and I left a customer at the cutting table and took my phone into the office. I knew it would be a short call, but Janet wasn't happy. She stepped in to help the customer and then called me on what I did." I left out the part about not taking her seriously and trying to justify myself by talking about how important the call was.

"I'll bet she wasn't pleased at all. It probably threw her." Helen looked surprised as well.

"She wants an apology, and I've been debating whether I'll give her one or quit."

"Or both?" Helen said, her face a study in confusion.

I shrugged in response.

"Quitting outright is a pretty drastic move, don't you think? And just because you offer an apology that doesn't mean you can't quit. Maybe this isn't the right direction for you."

"I don't know." I hadn't thought about backing out of the job, while still maintaining a good relationship with Janet.

Helen stopped rocking. "Have you eaten, Tina?"

"Not since noon." I couldn't help but snicker. "Do you think I got cranky because I needed to eat?"

"Since you ask, I suppose that's possible," Helen said. "But I asked because I'm looking to have some fun. Ivy's gone tonight. She left chicken dinners in the fridge, but we can have those for lunch. Since John's going to Italy let's go to Maria's Table and have an Italian evening of our own."

My spirits lifted. "Hmm...with wine, preferably red."

"You know, Tina, sometimes I wonder if we drink a little too much of our favorite vino."

I swatted away her words. "Speak for yourself. It's my only vice. I prefer to think of it as a guilty pleasure." I got to my feet. "When do we leave?"

"Are you going to change?"

I looked down at my black slacks and the bright vest I wore at the quilt shop. "I hadn't thought so." I held out the lapel edges of the vest. "It has red, green, and white in it. The same color as the Italian flag. But do you think I need to change?"

"No, you look fine. I was just asking because I'm raring to go," Helen said. "I'm ravenous. After being here all day studying interest rates and analyzing Dad's profit margins, I'm ready for a relaxing dinner—warm bread, garlicky pasta."

"Well then, let's go." I'd left my handbag on the kitchen stool, so I picked it up on the way out. Helen pulled out her car keys and declared herself the designated driver. We both laughed, because all that meant was Helen limiting herself to one glass of wine so I could have two. We might joke sometimes, but both of us were moderate in most of those personal ways. Sometimes, I wondered if we'd have been better off over the long run if we'd felt young and free when we actually were young and free. Seemed we were always looking over our shoulder in fear of Dad's disapproval. Or Ivy's.

"From the day it opened, Maria's Table has been a real hotspot in town," Helen said as she pulled out of the drive and onto the street. Our house and Maggie's were at the end of the street on the edge of town, but it was a short drive to the busy center of Briarwood.

Maria's Table had taken over a one-story corner building that had seen half a dozen restaurants come and go when we were growing up. It sat empty for a few years before a couple of sisters named the Italian restaurant after their mother and transformed it into a homey but elegant place to enjoy good old fashioned Italian fare.

"I match the décor," I joked, pointing to the color scheme of the painted murals on the walls. The colors of the flag framed a flow of images of vineyards and country patios and on toward gondolas floating on canals. "These are beautiful murals," I said, wondering if John had ever been here. I didn't speculate about that out loud for fear of Helen rolling her eyes at me. It was as if I couldn't talk about much of anything without thinking of him and wondering what he'd say about the topic at hand.

Helen snickered. "So you do. You look festive." She narrowed her eyes and studied me up and down. "Now, if you had a black turtleneck, the vest would pop out and it would look stylish, in a timeless sort of way."

"Point taken," I said, following the host through the mostly filled tables to an out of the way banquette near the back. "Nice. I like being tucked away where we aren't likely to be noticed."

"Noticed by who?" Helen asked, frowning.

"Oh, throngs of your admirers," I joked. "All the people you've hit up for money over the years."

She gave me a pointed look, but it didn't last long. My sister got to work studying the menu. When the waiter came to the table for our drink order, we chose the house Chianti. Minutes later it arrived in a half-bottle size decanter with matching glasses. The waiter filled our glasses, and another brought a basket of hot crusty bread.

"We're an easy table," I said, when we ordered the lasagna dinner for two.

"They're famous for their dinner deals for two, four, or six —and beyond," Helen said. "They have smaller rooms, too, for meetings. I've been to a few."

"I've missed a lot while I was gone," I said, hearing regret in my voice.

Helen laughed, apparently thinking I was joking.

"No, no, I'm being serious. At first, decades ago now, I was excited about moving away." I took a sip of my wine and enjoyed the warm sensation in my chest when I swallowed. "That optimism didn't last long. Sometimes a fresh start doesn't necessarily mean a good start."

"But you're turning your life around now, Tina," Helen said, giving my arm an affectionate squeeze. She gestured out to the tables near us, "Look around at everyone having fun. You're entitled to some fun."

"Being out to dinner with you is fun," I said, meaning it. "We haven't spent so much time together since we were kids."

"True enough."

I didn't need to think hard to come up with my idea of fun. Anything having to do with quilting was my source of joy. Fabric, patterns, sewing, teaching. All those elements were fun. "You know, Helen, when I'm teaching, I feel like a different person in a different body. I have energy surging through me and I'm on top of the world."

"Those brain chemicals are dancing, huh?" Helen responded. "I know the feeling." She got another one of her faraway looks, as if she was thinking out every word. "I'm enjoying the work with ME, probably more than you are, but I get my highs from the charity work I do. I like writing fundraising letters and welcoming donors to events I've designed and planned."

"But what about making a living, Sis?" My tone was sharp, and I quickly took a bite of buttered bread.

"I can do both." Helen's icy tone threw me. "Can you?"

I leaned against the tufted leather back. "Yikes. I guess that was the point of taking on the job with Janet. I was trying to do both."

"I'm sorry I gave you attitude," Helen said, "but you've seemed so negative about things lately. It's like John's comings and goings affects your mood."

I started to protest but changed my mind. She was right. "John thought I was being negative with him, too. It pains me to admit that, but it's true."

"Why now? Things are finally looking up."

Helen was waiting for an answer, but I didn't have one. At least not one I cared to give.

"It seems we're at a crossroads where we both might be able to get what we want." Helen stopped long enough for a quick sip of wine. "I can visualize us sharing the job of running ME. Then I can do my work with not-for-profits, which will benefit ME, and you can pursue your quilting. We'll each work part-time."

For some reason, Helen's idea, which sounded so logical, overwhelmed me. I closed my eyes and sighed.

"What? What did I say that upset you?"

"I have trouble believing I can do my part for ME. It's so easy to look at the loan contracts and at the income and expense data. But I freeze because I can't make the leap to working with people on new loans."

"I know how you feel." Helen grinned. "Let's face it, we're impostors."

I started laughing at her remark that hit so close to home. I lightened up long enough to exclaim over the beautiful salad the waiter plunked down in front of me, soon to be followed by the lasagna with its fragrant marinara sauce.

"We can be imposters together," I finally said after mulling over the way I felt when I'd first begun teaching quilting classes. I'd had to get past the idea that I wasn't qualified enough to teach others. It was a ridiculous notion. "In this case, we fit the old expression, 'act as if'."

"Or 'fake it 'til you make it'," Helen added with a laugh. "But at least we didn't surrender and tell Doug to let the business close after the last loan is paid off."

I decided not to point out that the two of us had no other career irons in the fire that were hot enough to allow us to walk away. Sure, I could piece together a living the way I'd pieced fabric, but nothing was a sure thing.

I looked up from my plate of food and noticed Helen's troubled expression. "What is it?"

"I...I'm enjoying ME, but I wonder..." She stopped talking and waved me off. "It can wait for another time. I don't want to talk about it now. I'm enjoying myself too much."

"Okay. Whatever you say."

We finished our meal with lemon Italian ice and decaf coffee and took our time being on our way. We decided, though, that since Ivy was out with friends more often these days, we could save her some work now and again and go out for dinner together.

We were about ready to call it a night and ask for the check when two women stepped up to our table, a mother and daughter duo I speculated. The older of the two looked familiar but I couldn't put a name to the face.

"I'm sorry to interrupt your evening, but my daughter and I overheard you talking about quilting. I'm Deanna Westford." She stepped aside for the younger woman to come forward. "And with my daughter, Marci, and my two sons, I own the Log Cabin Quilt Company."

"Deanna Westford?" I repeated, but it came out as a question. I turned to Helen and said, "In the quilting world, Deanna is a celebrity."

Deanna laughed, but Marci nodded her head in agreement. Deanna introduced herself to Helen with a disclaimer about her being that famous.

"Don't be modest. You're one of the leading pattern designers and publishers in the world of quilting. I've seen your photo any number of times, but I couldn't quite place you." I turned to Helen. "And she works in her studio in the Richardson Complex right here in Briarwood. John and I walked over there from the Bistro just before he left."

"Would you like to join us for coffee?" Helen offered. She slid closer to me. "We've got plenty of room and we'll order another pot of decaf. Please. I'd like to hear more about your company."

Deanna glanced at her daughter. "Well, thank you. That's very kind of you."

I signaled the waiter to order the coffee and add it to our check. "Assuming we're not tying up a table you need tonight," I said.

"No problem. We're not busy tonight," the waiter said. "Holler if you need anything."

Two hours and another pot of coffee later, I'd learned

about the birth of The Log Cabin Quilt Company and admired the way she not only fought to make a go of it but brought her family in as well.

"When we started, we were packing orders in Mom's living room," Marci said. "We outgrew that really fast."

Finally, Deanna put out an offer I never saw coming. "Tina, I know your reputation as a teacher. I don't have time to teach classes featuring my designs anymore, or act as the company representative for Log Cabin at quilt shows. Does that sound like something that would interest you?" Deanna took a sip of coffee but kept her eyes on me over the rim of her cup.

I was too surprised to speak.

Helen nudged me under the table with her foot. "Earth to Tina? Deanna asked you a question."

I let out a short, loud laugh. "Frankly, I'm stunned. To be honest I've admired your designs, but I've never made one of your patterns, so I'd need to learn more. As you can imagine I have to be sure I'd want to teach them." That was easy to say but teaching Deanna's patterns would be a step toward rebuilding my brand as a quilting teacher.

Deanna reached into her purse and handed me a business card. "Go to the website and take a look. Leave a message in the contact box saying that you met us here and pick out a couple of designs you like. Don't forget your address. My son Nick handles shipping and he'll get the patterns out to you right away." She checked her watch. "I'll tell him he'll be hearing from you soon."

Deanna and Marci slid out of the booth. "Thanks so much for this chance to talk with you. Nothing I like better than a spontaneous meeting." Deanna had a formal tone, but she also had a warm way about her that came through when we shook hands. Marci, a sparkler herself, waved as they walked to the front of Maria's Table.

"Well, well, who's the celebrity now? She's given you one more thing to think about, hasn't she?"

My head felt heavy when doubts and possibilities mixed together. "It might be more than I can handle. My plate is already heaped with decisions to make and ME business."

"Let's go," Helen said. "You can be overwhelmed at home. I want to call Steve tonight before it gets too late. We're wrapping up plans for the benefit and I've just had another idea that will hopefully bring in more money."

"So, 'fess up. Is there more than ME and the benefit between you two?" I asked as Helen settled the bill with a debit card. "You've been brighter, happier since you met him."

"He does bring out the best in me," Helen said when we'd navigated through the tables and out the front door to the parking lot. "I don't have to worry around him when I express an opinion. He listens to me like I've seen him do with the kids at The Youth Club." She shrugged. "What can I say? We have fun together."

During the drive home I noticed the raven blue-black sky with stars filling every corner. John had talked about seeing skies full of stars all over the world. Could he be looking at them right now? I did a quick calculation of the time difference between Briarwood and Italy. It would be early morning there and John loved to get pictures of the sunrise.

Helen went to her room when we came back, but I went out to the gardens. I needed to talk to John.

9

My first attempt to connect with John failed, but the second time John sounded like he was sitting next to me in the other rocker in the garden. After wanting to hear his voice and tell him about my dilemmas and indecision, they seemed foolish and insignificant. Instead, I said hello and waited for him to fill the void.

"Hey, Tina, what's the matter?" John asked. "Something going on?"

"How did you know?" I asked, mystified, my plan to take the focus off of me thwarted.

"Hmm...let's see. First, it's been a long time since you called me. And I detected something in your voice." He paused. "So, are you going to tell me or make me ask again?"

"I will, I will," I replied, "but right now I'm in the backyard looking up at a beautiful night sky filled with an abundance of shining stars. Can you see them?"

"It's almost morning here. I'm gazing at a predawn gray sky and clouds that will soon be filled with color."

"Ah, sounds nice. I feel better just talking to you. And

speaking of color, your mother's gardens are giving us plenty of that. The blooms are beautiful right now, like the stars."

"Beautiful, like you." His voice was barely above a whisper.

"Oh, John." I took in a breath, but John didn't miss a beat. In his regular voice he asked me to tell him what happened.

I gave him a short version of how his call had put me at odds with Janet and then I moved on to Deanna Westford's offer. "So, I have decisions to make." I chuckled. "And Helen said she won't decide for me about offering an apology or walking away. Imagine that. My big sister is making me be a grownup." I paused. "It seems Helen and I are doing that for each other these days."

"Well, I hope you didn't call me looking for answers," John said, a laugh in his voice, too. "Helen is right, kiddo. You've got to call this one on your own."

"I...know," I said, deliberately sounding like a kid resigned to being grounded for a week.

John's voice was serious again when he did offer a little advice. "All I'll say is this—don't rush in with an answer. Whatever you decide may influence your future for a good long time."

I laughed and put on my pouty, childish voice when I said, "You're no help."

"Oh, yes, I am, Tina," John said. "You've got everything you need to make those personal and professional decisions for yourself."

"Easy for you to say. You found your passion before your eighteenth birthday." Without meaning to, I sounded a little resentful.

"Right. I was lucky that way. But you know in your heart what makes you happy. And whatever you decide today doesn't mean you can't change your mind along the way."

"That's true." I was calmer. I wasn't sure if that was because

John had that effect on me, or if I was finally seeing the bigger picture.

"You're not condemned to live with decisions that aren't written in stone," John said, "and most aren't, but sometimes it doesn't seem that way."

I thought about my marriage. It had felt very much permanent, etched in stone. It had taken decades to realize that I didn't have to stay. In the end, Alex made it easy for me when he walked out the door.

"So, my sage advice is to do what will make you happy," John said, his voice starting to fade a little as the connection became unstable. "You deserve a life of your making. We all do."

"You're right. I'm glad I called you. I feel better about all of it." I took a deep breath. "I don't know what I was thinking. Taking your call at the shop was my mistake."

"Whatever. It's fixable," John said. "Oops, I've got to run. It's time for me to head out."

"You're always on the run," I said. "Grass doesn't grow, and all that. Your voice is fading, anyway."

"I'm visiting not one or two, but three wineries today," John said. "There's a tight deadline on this, so I'm packing my schedule tight. That means I can get home sooner." Sounding wistful, he added. "I'm beginning to miss that small town and the people in it."

"Travel safe, John. Call when you can." I was about to say, "I love you," when I heard the disconnect. I said the words to myself instead. I rocked a little longer before going inside, but first I looked down the path at the dark shadow of a house – the Delaney house – across the yard. When John came home, I'd see lights glowing in the windows. A ripple of happiness traveled through me.

It struck me as odd that I'd spent years without regular, frequent contact with John, but now, after talking with him, I made my decision and slept better that night than over the previous few nights.

I walked into Janet's Quilt Shop the next day ready to own up to my mistake. I planned to let her know working for her was important to me, and despite the way I'd acted over my phone call, I valued her and the customers. I was taken aback by how I'd tried to defend myself and put Janet in the wrong.

Carol was at the register and immediately told me Janet wouldn't be in because she wasn't feeling well.

But now...I needed a different plan. "Did she say if she wanted anything special done today?"

"Nooo." She drew the word out probably unsure what I was asking. "I would imagine she expects us to carry on the same way we do every day." She turned when the door opened, and the buzzer rang. She went to greet the customers, which left me to manage on my own.

I hadn't been given the okay to reorganize the fabric that I thought should be changed at the end of the month. But I did make sure the bolts that had been used yesterday were restocked in their rightful place. I didn't get the job finished before the shop filled with a carload of women out for a day of shopping and lunch. "More shopping than food," one said with a laugh.

John would have described the women as having high spirits. In a way they reminded me of Helen. She had a certain joie de vivre—an expression John used to describe people he'd observe while on assignment. It came back to the colorful street life that made so many societies tick.

Meanwhile, this high-spirited group of shoppers turned

out to be a very enthusiastic bunch. I tried to focus on cutting fabrics they chose while also answering their questions. Carol dealt with specific requests and handled the register and packing their shopping bags. When they left Carol and I did a high five and rested our backs against the counter and took deep breaths.

"Best day in a long time. Janet will be happily surprised. I'll call her right now." Carol grabbed her phone and made the call.

I wanted to eavesdrop but forced myself to walk toward the cutting table and at least pretend I wasn't invested in being part of the successful morning of sales.

Later, Carol came to find me straightening the baby fabrics. "Janet doesn't think she'll be coming in tomorrow and wanted to know if you'd be willing to work an extra day. She knows you're not scheduled but hopes you can help out. Can you?"

Janet couldn't be too upset with me, but maybe she was desperate. I told Carol I'd check my schedule. Helen and I agreed we wouldn't talk publicly or casually about ME, so I wasn't sure how much Janet and Carol understood what I meant by commitments. I barely did.

More quilters came in the afternoon, but busy as we were, I really wanted to help Janet out. I couldn't think of anything specific for ME on the calendar. I told Carol she could reassure Janet that I could work the extra day. Near closing, Carol and I worked furiously to right the shop for the next day. If I was working, I wanted everything in its rightful place, to save me organization time.

I was ready to cut a few pieces of fabric to begin making new vests, but after agreeing to work the next day I decided the old ones would work for as long as needed.

Carol stepped up next to me as we cleared the cutting

table and arranged the bolts of fabric. "I like that combination you chose," pointing to the stack of bolts I had picked out for my new vests. "By the way, Janet knows I have an appointment in the morning and can't get here until noon, so she said to give you the keys. We'll lock up together tonight, but you can open in the morning."

"Are you taking the cash with you?" The shop did very few cash transactions, but even so, I was a part-time employee. Janet had already questioned my loyalty, so I thought it best for Carol to be accountable.

"You'll need it when you open," Carol said. "We'll take the cash and the checks and credit card receipts out of the register and lock them in the office like we always do."

I didn't like the arrangement, but I agreed. I followed Carol out to the parking lot, and she turned one way and I turned another. I had a buoyant feeling, so different from the mild dread I'd had coming in. I almost laughed out loud. This had been a really good day.

I was still feeling good when I opened the front door and Helen called my name from the kitchen. "There's a package from Deanna Westford on the table by the door."

I brought it with me when I went to see Helen. "That was a quick turnaround, wasn't it?"

"A guy – I think his name was Nick – said Deanna wanted you to have this right away so he brought it over instead of mailing it."

I opened the package and laid the patterns on the kitchen island. Each one was eye catching. The pictures on the pattern packaging showed interesting designs and vibrant colors, like a show of autumn leaves at their height. The note included was short and to the point: Give me a call when you decide – Deanna.

"Which of these do you like, Helen?"

Helen turned from warming a coffee in the microwave. "Wow. All the patterns are beautiful. Look at the table runners, too. Everything is so elegant. But that's not surprising. Deanna has a certain kind of elegance about her, doesn't she?" Helen folded her arms and studied the patters. "So, which one will you go with?"

"I'm not sure I can…I may not be up—"

"Listen here, sister." She put her cup down and grabbed my shoulders. "You are good enough to do any of these patterns—or anything else you really want to do."

I moved out of her grasp. "Whoa, you sound like John. And Steve's thinking has rubbed off on you, too."

"Maybe it has, and what of it?" A new defiance brought life to Helen's voice. This wasn't a familiar Helen.

To avoid making a quick, possibly wrong, decision I gathered the patterns and put them back in the package. "Janet isn't feeling good, so I agreed to open the shop tomorrow."

Helen's eyes opened in alarm. "Oops. Did you forget Melvin Tully is coming in the afternoon to review his contract with us? Steve calls Mel a money maker for ME. I looked back through his file and every time he satisfies one loan, he asks for a new one—it's how he stays stocked and orders in bulk. I stopped by his gift shop the other day. Lots of items are either locally made or from the region. We need him, and Melvin needs us."

"Well, will you listen to you? My big sister is becoming quite the businesswoman."

Helen blushed at my compliment. I hoped that diverted her attention to the fact that I'd double booked myself. "I have to give Steve some credit," Helen said, smiling like she always did when his name came up. "He's a great coach and is patient with my long lists of questions."

"Are we paying him for all that information?"

Helen looked out the window. "Not so far, or not directly. This is part of the work for the firm, and Doug will charge ME for some of the services. I think he enjoys our times together, so it doesn't seem like work for him."

Then, as if she remembered, Helen threw her hands up in the air. "Hey, what's with this making commitments to Janet without checking the ME schedule first?"

"I know, I know. I'll see to it that this doesn't happen again." On the other hand, if I brought in a salary, I could contribute to the household account. To be determined. "But you don't have to sell Tully on the business. He knows how we operate. We can keep the same terms, can't we?"

"That's true, Tina. So, it's okay this time. I've shopped at his store from time to time and he had a long history with Dad. I can handle him alone." Helen said, sounding reasonable. "But we need new people for first-time clients and that means you need to be here, too."

I was aware of all that, but I wasn't sure how it was going to work out to match Helen's vision. On the other hand, I had a feeling Helen had bumped into her calling without knowing it. "I get it, but for now, send me a text when the meeting is over, and I'll call you when I get a break. I'm interested in what Mel Tully wants."

"The lending account at the bank is growing because we haven't made new loans," Helen said, "so it's probably time for us to reinvest some of our profit. This may be our first contract, and we have a model for it."

I caught some of Helen's excitement. Signing our first contract was a milestone. I touched my earrings. I hoped Dad would be proud of us.

I RELOCKED THE DOOR OF THE QUILT SHOP AFTER ENTERING. I'D chosen one of Deanna's patterns and was hunting for the right fabrics. I promised myself I'd be patient and follow her directions rather than impulsively jump ahead and do it my way. Instead, it would be like teaching a class, only I'd be the student. I browsed the bolts of fabric, going from solids to patterns and from winter and holiday themes to nursery style patterns. I lost track of the time because I jolted to attention when someone pounded on the door. I ran to unlock it. "I'm so sorry. I don't usually open the shop, so I lost track of time."

"No worries," the woman said with a laugh. "I get lost in fabric too."

"Are you from around here?" I asked, noticing a difference in her accent.

"No, I'm visiting my husband's family and needed a break." She gave me a knowing look, as if certain I'd understand. "I can only take hovering relatives for so long, and then I have to escape."

I didn't want to get into chummy talk about a family I knew nothing about, so I quickly asked if she was looking something special.

"Oh, I suppose I'd like to gather Christmas ideas." She scooted over to the row of bolts of fabric all of which were seasonal designs. "You have different fabrics than I see at the shops at home." She moved away quickly when a bolt caught her eye on a nearby spinner.

"Browse all you like. Call if you need help. I'm Tina." I went back to the stack of fabrics I'd picked out earlier for one of Deanna's patterns. One of the fabrics made the others appear dull. I kept adding and subtracting bolts trying to get the best combination.

"I'd try a rust or a brown in place of the yellow," the shopper offered.

I stood back and considered both rust and brown. "Both are worth a try. I'm making a wall hanging from the Log Cabin Quilt Company. It's my first time using one of their designs."

"Wow, those are excellent patterns. I've made a few myself. The owner came to our quilt show a couple of years ago," the shopper said. "I understand Deanna, that's her name, is way too busy now with the company to do a lot of traveling anymore. But she used to fill a room when she gave one of her presentations."

I wanted to probe and learn a little more about Deanna, but the buzzer rang, and customers filed in. Between handling the cutting table and the register I didn't have much time to chat with the women. Carol arrived at noon, which gave me a break, but we had our hands full when a line formed at the cutting table.

It was over an hour later before we had time to say hello. Carol was holding the bolts of fabric I'd chosen for Deanna's pattern. "Someone must have forgotten their pattern. I don't know why Janet doesn't carry Log Cabin designs. Deanna Westford is from Briarwood, after all. It's too bad, because I do like her designs."

"No, no one forgot. That's my next project. I came in early to get the fabric, but customers kept arriving and I never got back to cut it."

"I'll do it for you," Carol said, reaching for a rotary cutter. "How much?"

"Half a yard of each."

The buzzer rang again. Janet walked in looking pale and tired. She grabbed the first chair and sat. No hello, no how's it going. She dropped her news without easing into it. "I'm on bedrest until the baby is born. Doctor's orders, and she wasn't subtle about this." She sighed and blurted, "I'm closing the shop—I don't see any other choice."

That was drastic. Janet's eyes filled with tears. It did occur to me, though, that the old saying, "When one door closes, another opens," came to mind. Janet might close the shop, but Deanna offered me a marketing position. Doors were closing and opening, but what did that mean in the long run? All this was circling in my head as I said, "I'm so sorry, Janet. I know this is a difficult decision for you."

She offered a wan smile.

"I suppose I could work more hours while you can't, but there have to be other employees to help." I turned to Carol, "You?"

Carol shook her head. "As much as I love working here, I love teaching more and I'm registered for school."

Carol and I stood next to Janet, each at a loss for a solution to Janet's predicament. After Janet said she wanted to stay in the shop a little while longer, Carol and I sensed she wanted to be alone and we left together.

"I wonder how long the shop will be open," Carol said. "I need to work to get money for school. I hope this job lasts a little longer. I enjoy it so much." She hurried to her car and drove away.

I sat in my car looking at the shop—one woman's dream. Did it have to come to an end? What would it really take to keep Janet's Quilt Shop a viable business in Briarwood? A text from Helen made me laugh – Not talking to Tully alone again!

Oh, dear. That exclamation point convinced me she was serious. I called her to ask about supper.

"Meet Steve and me at the club. I want you both to hear about my day." She stopped a second. "Over wine."

I laughed. "I thought that was my vice. See you at the club."

As I drove to the country club I thought about the woman from the beginner's class, who I'd run into at the club. I'd never called her back. I wonder if she expected the call, or had she figured out she'd made her feelings known. Surprisingly, too, neither Janet nor Heather ever mentioned the second class, or if it was even held. I never asked about it, either, and I'd had many chances to. Maybe it was a topic better put to rest.

When I left my car in the club's parking lot and headed for the door, a blast of frigid air circled me and made me shiver. I hurried back to my car to get a summer sweater. I met Steve going inside on my return trip. He offered a friendly greeting, typical of his pleasant demeanor. "Helen said you were joining us. I'm glad to see you again."

"Glad to see you. A lot has happened these past weeks."

He looked up at the sky. "All this change makes life exciting, huh? I think Helen is finding new purpose with ME."

"Hmm…let's wait to see what she has to say about her meeting today." I didn't know if Helen was going to conclude this business was right up her alley or decide to pack it in.

Helen was already at the table with a glass wine for herself and one for Steven and me already on the table. As soon as we sat, she held up her glass as a greeting. "If you don't want wine, Steve, no problem. Tina or I will drink it."

Steve returned her salute, but then he scanned the room. "I was thinking on the way over that if we're going to talk about ME tonight, we should get to-go dinners and head back to your place. We can't risk being overheard talking about clients in public, and the dining room is crowded tonight. Some of these folks are clients."

"Agreed." I lowered my voice and said, "I have news that's not public yet—it's not a done deal, either, but it could have implications for us."

"At least we don't live far from here." Helen handed a

menu to Steve and me. "I'm having the special, whatever it is. I'm not fussy tonight."

Our order was handled quickly, and we caravanned back to the house. I rummaged in the fridge and saw that Ivy had left a green salad for us. I put it and Ivy's homemade dressings on the dining room table where we could spread out. We didn't use it often, mostly just on holidays for the last several years, but it was a pleasant room with a large table and comfortable chairs.

Helen barely waited to unload the containers of chicken dinners before she immediately started in about Mel Tully. "Like I told you, I'm never meeting him alone again." she said shaking her head and passing around the containers.

"It was all stupid flirting and patronizing. Mel all but told me not to worry my pretty little head over his loan." Helen imitated his patronizing tone. "Dad always renewed it, so our little meeting wasn't even necessary. Ha! We'll see about that."

I groaned, but Helen wasn't done. It turned out Mel Tully wanted to adjourn the meeting and head to the Bistro for a drink—or two. "And he wanted to know what I did for fun, and if I was free this Saturday night." Helen snorted. "I made it clear my calendar was chockfull. Then he wanted to know if liked to dance." Helen curled her lip in disgust. "Ugh."

"How did you handle it?" I asked. "I mean, how did you finally get him out of here?"

"I stood and grabbed my purse and told him I was headed to another meeting." Helen laughed. "I shouted into the kitchen to tell Ivy I was leaving and wasn't sure when I'd be back."

"So, he had no choice but to leave," Steve said, thoughtfully, "and he knew you weren't alone here."

"Actually, I was. Ivy was at the Farmer's Market at the Richardson Complex."

"Did Melvin make any moves on you—physically, I mean?" I asked.

"No, but he would have if I hadn't made up an excuse to leave." Helen's disgusted expression still hadn't left her face.

"You shouldn't have to leave your own office just to make a jerk like Mel get out of your face," Steve said, his face reddening.

"I know, I know. But Tina and I knew going in we'd have to put up with some of this," Helen insisted, "especially from a few of the older men who haven't grown up yet."

"I don't think either of you should meet clients or discuss contracts alone for a while, at least until you get to know the clients better," Steve said. "Let's call it propriety, a bench word now. We have no way of knowing which clients are capable of crossing these lines."

"You're right, Steve." Helen said before turning to me. "We need to team up on these face-to-face meetings. I don't want to deal with that kind of harassment."

"Then we'll need to coordinate our schedules," I added, worried but trying not to show it. As much as I knew Steve was right, I wondered how all the pieces of our days would fit together. Fortunately, we didn't have many face-to-face meetings with existing clients anymore. Melvin Tully was an exception, because he was such an important client. We couldn't afford to lose him, either.

"By the way, what happened with the loan?" Steve asked.

"He wants the same arrangement," Helen said. "He's already getting good interest rates from us. He still has another sixteen months on a smaller personal loan. The twelve-month business loan rolls over soon. He'll sign the contracts, and we'll deposit the money in his account. It's automated, fortunately, so we may never need to see him in person again."

I sighed in relief. "I'm glad it worked out."

Ready to pivot the conversation, Steve asked me, "Have you talked to John lately? I'm anxious to see his Iceland photographs."

"You're two countries behind," I teased. "I talked to him when he was off to the wineries, but he soon texted to say he was done there and on his way to India."

"Man, all those frequent flyer miles," Steve said, his tone envious. "It would be a lot of fun to take off someplace exotic. Well, exotic to me, anyway. It's obviously not exotic to the people who live there."

"Just give me a warm beach in January," Helen said, taking a final bite of chicken before putting her fork on her empty plate. Then she frowned. "Wait...didn't you have some secret news, Tina?"

"Secret, yes, and in its own way as dreary as your meeting with Mel," I said. "But strangely, it could be part of the puzzle we're putting together."

I explained what Janet had said about closing the shop, which would have an impact on the community. "Quilters come from all over to get their supplies at Janet's shop, and she has a good mail order business she runs online. So that means we'd lose the quilters who tend to come in groups and plan around seasons and holidays. The ripple effect would hurt Briarwood, because these shoppers stay around to visit other shops and have lunch at one of our eateries."

"That's not good news, Tina." Helen's sympathetic tone showed she was puzzled, too. "But are you saying this is more than a financial issue?"

"Absolutely. Quilting is a specific type of sewing. The women who quilt look to shop owners for information based on experience. The staff needs to be familiar with the language and some of the techniques."

"Who do you know that could help out?" Steve asked.

"Being newly back in Briarwood myself, no one comes to mind except Heather. I don't know that many women in the craft community. But for sure, Janet's shop is too large for one person to handle. I worked by myself this morning until noon and there was a line of customers wanting fabric cut when Carol arrived. I was at the register working as fast as I could."

"Do you think Deanna might know someone?" Helen told Steve about our chance meeting with the owner of The Log Cabin Quilt Company and her daughter.

"She might, but I need to get an okay from Janet before I start talking to other people about her plan to close the shop."

"Is it too late to call Janet now?" Helen seemed driven to help.

"I don't think so. I'll be back in a few minutes." I went into the office and made the first call. Janet said she was posting a sign on the door the next day about closing at the end of the week. That was only three days away, not much time to reverse her decision if she could.

When I called Deanna, she was surprised about Janet's situation, but asked if she could call me back in a few minutes. "I need to talk to a couple of people about this."

Helen and Steve had taken their glasses of wine and moved to the living room while I was on the phone. They sat next to each other, a cozy scene. I had a feeling Steve was a keeper and I also suspected Helen knew as much. The way Steve looked at Helen was certainly a strong clue. I sat in the chair across from them.

"Steve's agreed to sit in our meetings with a couple of the clients that hold large loans from ME," Helen said. "He thinks we might not have quite enough experience to counter their requests."

"Why do I feel like I'm Little Red Riding Hood about to meet the Big Bad Wolf?"

Steve laughed. "It's only a handful of clients. And you don't need to meet them regularly. Just the one time to introduce yourselves. You don't want them looking around for other sources of financing."

"Why would they do that?" I asked.

"They might not realize you two are steeping yourselves in the business and intend to keep it going," Steve said.

"It makes sense, Tina. It's even more important we send out regular newsletters and have some other PR things in the works." Helen nodded in agreement. "We need to make sure ME stays prominent in their minds."

"I'm sure your dad had his own way of handling them," Steve added, "but it wouldn't be unusual for clients to be both fearful of change and curious. Some might decide to look elsewhere rather than renegotiate their contracts with you."

I was grateful for Steve's offer. "I still feel unsure about these meetings," I said. "Your presence will help. I'm glad we don't have to do this all at once." I was still unsettled about Janet and the shop and what might happen if Deanna wanted to take over.

"So, include me in your plans," Steve said. "And Helen and I can make a list of the businesses with bigger loans. We can start there—preferably evening meetings, or late afternoon, or before eight a.m. We'll figure out a way to add this work to the arrangement you have with Doug."

"Sounds like a good plan," Helen said.

Steve stood and held out his hand. Helen took it and in one quick motion he pulled her off the couch. "Time for me to leave."

My phone buzzed so I waved and headed to the office to

take Deanna's call. We dispensed with pleasantries in a matter of seconds.

"I know this is an unusual request," Deanna said, "but can you meet me at my studio in the Richardson Complex before you're due at the shop tomorrow? Say around eight?"

I was surprised, but I saw no reason to say no. I got directions from her and that was that.

I had to laugh—and so did Deanna—when we simultaneously said, "Looking forward to meeting with you."

10

DEANNA MET ME AT THE DOOR WITH A MUG OF COFFEE AND A smile. I heard other voices coming from the living area. "Come in and meet my grown kids." I guessed her tall, lanky sons, Jared and Nick, to be in their late twenties or early thirties. They were in the chairs opposite the couch, and Marci, mid-twenties tops, waved from her place on the floor.

I thanked Nick for delivering the patterns. "I wish I'd been home when you came by."

"You're welcome. I'm doing my part to keep Log Cabin alive." He had an open friendly smile and aimed it my way, as he tossed a pen in the air and caught it. Nick was definitely a people person.

Deanna offered me a seat next to her on the couch and turned the floor over to Jared, the IT brains of the company. According to Deanna he also managed the long-range plans for the company.

I sat back and listened to Jared's tale of the rapid growth of the family business. "We've grown quickly in the unique niche of quilting. But we have to branch out to grow for the long haul," Jared said in an all-business tone. He then tossed out all kinds of ideas like having Deanna develop a fabric line and explained why they rejected that idea. For one thing, that would dominate Deanna's time.

"The other idea we've tossed around is a retail store," Jared said, still serious. "Mom hadn't wanted to go into competition with Janet, but things have changed, so we might have found a resolution that's good for Janet and for us."

I sat there wondering what any of this had to do with me, but I didn't interrupt Jared's presentation. He was succinct with the Log Cabin plans. His mom nodded in approval.

"So, bottom line, Mom already offered you the Log Cabin's marketing position," Jared said, "but now if we acquire the quilt shop, we'd like to make you the manager—if that interests you."

I sensed big changes were on the way, and my heartbeat picked up speed in recognition of that. I acknowledged the offer. "As I see it, the real problem still exists regardless of who owns the shop," I said. "Right now, it's seriously understaffed."

"You're right," Jared said. "What we don't know is how Janet finds her help, and if she's advertised. Now that's a moot point."

"I'm not in a position to ask her," I said. "I've worked for her a handful of days, and I don't want to leave an impression that I'm criticizing her in what is a real crisis in her life. With the complications in her pregnancy, she needs support not faultfinding. Unfortunately, Carol can't increase her hours. I already asked."

We talked more about the details of ownership, the hidden responsibilities that were part of dealing with the public. I pulled my vest closer to my body, knowing what I was about to say would add other complications. "It's only my opinion, of course, but the quilt shop needs a major overhaul." A little voice taunted me, you should talk? Yeah, yeah, it was true, my quilting business needed an overhaul, but we weren't talking about me. This was about the shop.

"After working there, I can describe the outdated models, and wall displays that have hung for a long time without any rotation or change. For lack of a better word, it needs energy, lots of energy. The old fabric needs to be weeded out and sold at seriously slashed prices. That will make room to feature the latest fabrics and patterns." I sighed. "Janet has what it takes—look what she's done with a shop in a small market and an online store. But right now, she's torn between wanting to keep the shop and being pulled toward selling it."

"Babies have a way of taking over," Deanna said, playfully gesturing to her kids.

"The question is do we have the time and energy to do all of that now?" Marci asked, looking up at her mom.

Jared closed his tablet. "All we're doing is speculating. If I'm going to evaluate the long-term value of owning a shop, I need to see it as it is now." Jared turned to me. "Are you working this morning?"

"I am." I glanced at the clock on Deanna's wall. "I have to leave to get the store opened up and ready to go. But you can follow, and I'll be happy to show you around and you'll see what I mean."

"Let's go." Deanna stood and grabbed her shoulder bag—a briefcase really. A woman on the move. And one who meant business.

JARED FOLLOWED ME AROUND THE SHOP, ASKING ONE QUESTION after another, almost before I had finished with my answer. I second-guessed my decision to invite Deanna and her family to peruse the shop. Since Janet hadn't finalized a decision to sell, I worried that I'd seriously over-stepped. On the other hand, it was possible Janet had a willing buyer if she wanted one. Jared carried his tablet and took copious notes. He reminded me of a doctor charting on a screen, almost as if he had a checklist of his own. Maybe he did. Deanna and Marci quietly wandered the shop checking fabrics and notions.

Nick was at the pattern spinner and remarked that Janet didn't stock Log Cabin patterns. "We could announce that addition as a way to introduce the shop and link it to Mom."

Since Deanna had built a sterling reputation as a designer and teacher, a link to the shop could only be a benefit. I'd wondered why Janet hadn't thought to feature Log Cabin designs in the first place. A person with a national reputation was down the street, so to speak.

"Let's slow it down, Nick," Deanna said. "We need to talk to Janet before we make any decisions. She might have come up with a different plan for herself and the shop. This shop may be outdated now, but she built it from scratch, more or less, so she's probably not easily defeated."

I didn't doubt Janet's backbone, but I sensed her health issues and fears for her baby had made the shop far less important to her, at least temporarily. But that was for Janet and Deanna to discuss, so I kept my observations to myself.

"If Janet is interested, Jared and Marci will put together an offer proposal," Deanna said, speaking directly to me.

I heard knocking on the door. "Oops, I need to unlock. We're officially open." I hurried to the door and opened it for a man holding rolls of paper.

"I don't believe we've met," he said, surprised.

"I'm Tina Montgomery. I work for Janet and I'm just opening the shop for the day."

The man's face relaxed a bit. "Good to know. I'm Tom

Spier, Janet's husband. We've hit another bump in the road with the baby."

"Oh, no," I said. "I hope it's not serious. Janet mentioned the bed rest issue."

Fatigue rolled off his shoulders. "No, no, it's another complication. They may have to take the baby before the due date." He looked at Deanna and her family approaching.

I introduced everyone and explained who Deanna was and why she and her crew were in the shop. "Janet told me she might be forced to close the shop and I'm trying to see if there's an alternative. Deanna wanted to learn more about the shop. These people may be interested..."

"It's yours." Tom raised his arms and waved the rolls of paper. "These are For Sale signs for the door. Unfortunately, there's simply no way Janet can come back."

I thought about Janet building a business from her passion for quilting. "Janet's decision?" I asked.

He glared at me, but only for a second. "Of course. We've been talking about this for many weeks now, and this new reality made the decision for us." Tom handed the signs to Nick who in turn passed them to me. "It's heartbreaking, too, especially for Janet. But I have faith in her. She'll get back into the quilting business one way or another. She likes to quilt and teach. The shop didn't give her much chance to do either."

The room was totally silent while he spoke. The space seemed to grow smaller. My heart went out to Janet, but I had a feeling she was making the right choice over the long run.

"How wonderful to have a new baby," Marci said, breaking the silence.

"Yes," Tom said, his face lighting up. "We're hoping all goes well from here." He pulled business cards from the pocket of his sport coat and handed them to Deanna before turning away from the counter. "Let's talk. I have an attorney who can handle the paperwork. I have to get to my job."

Deanna and Tom exchanged a few words about timing and contracts. Finally, Tom turned to me and thanked me for smoothing the way to solve the quilt shop problem without a lot of drama.

He took in a breath and left without looking back into the shop.

"Wow," Jared said, "what a lot of mixed emotions, huh?"

"I'll say," Marci said, looking around. "We've got a lot to do, but she sure left us a good foundation to build on."

"I'll get started on some contract terms," Jared said.

"All of us have things to do today." Deanna shook my hand. "We'll go over the numbers before I make a final decision, so give us three days. Then we'll know for sure what we intend to do. Thanks for being so forthright about the shop."

My phone buzzed. It was Janet. I waved as the Westford family left and then filled Janet in on Tom's visit and the Deanna's plan to buy. "It's not final yet, of course. But the lawyers will be talking soon."

"Okay." Janet's voice sounded like a whimper. I knew she was fighting back tears.

"I'm sorry you had to make this difficult decision." What else could I say? "Why don't I give you a call later? I'll tell you about my day here. Oh, one more thing. Can I move the fabric around?"

"Sure—you do what you think the shop needs." Janet's voice was stronger now.

I wondered what it took to pull up that strength, especially after such a defeat. I decided to wait to move the bolts of fabric that had been by the front door for weeks. Carol often did that kind of organizational work.

The first customer started a very busy day, filled with

special order pickups and packing some orders for the delivery company to pick up. When I had a free minute, I started to hang the For Sale sign on the door, since the sale wasn't final yet. Carol arrived when I changed my mind and decided to wait.

"Are you alone here again?" Carol asked. "Janet told me Abby Higgins would be here this morning."

"I've never met Abby, but Janet mentioned her weeks ago," I said. "She hasn't worked when I've been here."

"I think she's Janet's neighbor or something, but it doesn't matter now. I think she only worked when she wanted to," Carol said, frowning. "She had a regular schedule."

"Maybe that explains it." I unrolled one of the signs. "Just in case you were wondering. It's official." I decided against telling Carol a deal was in the works. It wasn't my place to do that.

Carol held the corners while I taped the sign to the door. At the end of the day, I'd fine out from Janet if Deanna or Jared had been in touch.

"Three more days and we're done." Carol shook her head and grimaced. "Sure could have used the money for school."

"You don't know what's going to happen. Who knows? Maybe the new owner will want you to stay onboard." I really wanted to tell her about the potential deal, but I couldn't.

Meanwhile, my mind raced, overrun with confusing thoughts made me jittery. I even entertained the notion that I should be the one to buy the shop. Was this my dream slipping through my fingers? Was this really my dream at this point in my life?

"I guess there's no reason to rearrange the fabrics and models today?" I said. "Could be wasted effort. Let's hope for lots of shoppers to clear some stock."

I had an idea about moving fabric and texted Janet. When

she texted back, I asked Carol to make some signs indicating that until the door was locked for good everything in the shop would be sold at 20% off.

But now... I needed to make sure Deanna knew how small the window of opportunity was. Three days. I went into the office and closed the door and got Deanna on the phone. I told her the For Sale signs were up and reminded her about the closing date. I also mentioned the sale we'd initiated.

"We both grasp how hard it will be to get customers back if they come and find a locked door," I said. "I'm not presuming to know what you should do, but after all these years in the small quilting world, I do know an opportunity like this doesn't come along every day."

"Thanks for giving me your take on this. We're debating the pros and cons now, as a matter of fact." Deanna laughed. "Family business, family decision."

I ended the call when a knock on the door interrupted my conversation, and I opened the door.

John stood there with his arms open wide. I walked into them as if that was our typical way of saying hello. In the background I heard "Go, girl" from one of the customers, which sent a few titters through the shop. I buried my face in his chest. I wasn't the kind of woman to put on displays with a man. Especially one I insisted was only a friend. But I couldn't deny my face was hot and beet red. I pulled him into the office.

"Hey," he said, "What's to be shy about? I'm a life-long friend that's been overseas for a while. Maybe they're jealous of you." His voice rumbled in his chest. I held him tighter from a minute longer then stepped away. "Why didn't you call?"

"And interrupt you again in the middle of all this?" He waved through the open door into the shop. A couple of women were actually watching us. What was this? High school?

"Oops, I have to get out there. I need to help the customers. Will I see you tonight?"

"Dinner? The four of us? I've got news. Bye." He sauntered out of the shop as if moving through a crowd of fans.

Oh, brother. I wasn't used to so much going on all at once. I took a sip of cold coffee from my cup on the desk. Then I closed the door behind me and became a sales associate/fabric cutter again. A few women were chatting about the shop closing, and a couple offered me teasing remarks about my handsome guy. My protests about him being my good lifelong friend fell on deaf ears. I guess it's true, everybody loves a romance. Real or imagined, in my case. But just the sight of him put a smile on my face the rest of the day.

I was glad the day passed quickly, and it seemed like a déjà vu moment when I walked into the club and saw John, Steve and Helen at the same table we had before. Once again, John stood and held out his arms for me to walk into. It made me laugh. "We can't keep doing this in public. You should have heard the women after you left the shop."

"I don't see why not. It's a free country," John quipped. "Sit down. The waitress is bringing champagne."

"Really? What are we celebrating?" I looked across the table to Helen, but she shook her head. Steve pointed with his chin to John.

"I've told Steve and Helen already, now I'm telling you." He took ahold of my hand. "I'm retiring and returning to Briarwood for good."

Where were my words when I needed them? All I could focus on was the warmth of John's hand holding mine.

"When? And why?" I was about to question the use of the term "retiring." John? At what, age 52?

"Oh, not retiring as in heading to the desert to play golf or to the Florida Keys to fish." He flapped that idea away. "No, I have lots of ideas. I'm going to figure out a new direction and that means talking to other people about how to implement them."

Steve poured the champagne and raised his glass for a toast. "Welcome home, John."

We clinked our glasses in the center, like the four of us making a pact. Who knew, maybe we were, like John and I had done when we first met as kids.

Regardless the three-word toast made my heart sing.

"Home. That's a pretty nice sounding word." John said and we all touched glasses again.

The evening passed quickly. We ordered the pasta dinners and mostly talked about the work Steve and Helen were doing for the upcoming benefit for The Youth Club. "We'll have lot of auction pieces and raffles and donation drawings to keep the evening buzzing. The community is so generous for this event." Helen glanced at John. "Would you like to add one of your photos to the auction? It's not too late. I have an inside line with one of the members of the auction committee." She smiled slyly at Steve.

Steve picked up on the idea. "That would be terrific, John. Local resident, national – oops, international photographer – supporting the youth of his community."

"I'd like that." John sat a little straighter in his chair. "Good. I'll pick out three or four and you can decide which one you want."

"How about you, Tina? You have those cool patterns from Deanna? Could you get one finished before the benefit? We could promote Deanna's design, Janet's fabrics, and you as the quilter. Three more locals to showcase."

I mentally threw negative vibes Helen's way. As if I didn't

have enough on my plate. And I'd have to add being present for the ME client meetings, too. "C'mon, Helen. You know what my days have been like. I don't know if I could get it finished anywhere close to on time."

"But it's for the kids." Helen used her most persuasive voice.

"Why don't I just throw in some money, instead, if it's 'for the kids' as you say?" Even John looked a little taken aback by my tone. Did Helen really think quilters could just throw together pieces in a rush? "These things take time, Helen, that's all I'm saying." I could feel the angry tension building in my body. I didn't want to be shamed into pleasing Helen for no good reason.

Three pairs of eyes bored into me. Okay, I'd do it, but I intended to be clear about how disrespectful of my time—and talent—Helen was being. I'd deal with her alone and tell John about it later. I wasn't letting this drop. "Okay, you trapped me. You have me backed into a corner." I tried to smile and keep my voice light. The only thing keeping my temper in check was the desire to do a Deanna Westford design. "I'll need time to sew so I'll have less time for ME until I finish." And less time for John, if he wanted to spend more time with me.

Helen didn't like my tone. "I'm doing most of ME right now, anyway, and you don't know what's going to happen with the shop. Besides, you won't be sewing twenty-four hours a day." She glanced at Steve. "I'm scheduling evening meetings so Steve can join us. I don't want another episode like the one with Mel."

"Mel?" John asked. "Who's Mel?"

"I'll tell you later," I said. "Let's not get sidetracked, Helen. You win. I'll do the wall hanging." I softened my voice when I said, "You know I appreciate how organized you are. And when is the benefit again? With everything else I've been doing I seem to have forgotten."

"Nice try, Tina." Helen gave me a teasing smile. "It's next Saturday." She leaned across the table and patted my hand. "And don't claim you aren't good enough to get it done. I know you are."

Suddenly, the day overwhelmed me, and I pushed my chair back and got to my feet. "Whew, if I'm going to be burning the midnight oil, I better get home and get some sleep."

"You two stay," John said to Helen and Steve. "I'll walk Tina to her car and go on home myself. I'm seriously jetlagged." John tucked my elbow in his palm and kept it there until we reached my car. "I'll be in the gardens early in the morning if you want to join me for coffee."

"I'd like that," I said. "And make it early. I have to be in the shop tomorrow. I so want to hear more about your retirement."

"Still in the planning stages." He wrapped his arms around me. "I don't think I'll ever get tired of holding you." But he did the opposite when he stepped back and closed the car door.

I went right to my bedroom when I got home, first to check voice mail messages, then to wind down. I was a little embarrassed by how I handled Helen's request, but I felt justified in being annoyed with her. I resolved to talk to her about it the next day. Right. When I had five minutes.

Janet and Deanna both wanted me to give them a return call. Janet had called first, so I returned her call first. She was upset, not at me necessarily, but at circumstances. "I'm rethinking selling the shop," Janet said. "Will you take the sign down?

"Of course, but are you sure?"

"Deanna Westford called me, and the reality hit. If I sell, so much of me goes with it." Anger and tears filled her words.

"I thought that because of the baby... I mean, Tom was worried about you and told us you wouldn't be coming back. I was just trying to help ease a path out for you that would benefit everyone."

A little calmer now, Janet said, "I'm thinking that when the baby comes, I can bring her to the shop while I'm working. Other women do that."

I wasn't touching that with the proverbial ten-foot pole. "Look, all of this is up to you. I'm here to help—we had a busy, productive day with lots of sales. Tomorrow, with the discount going is likely to be the same."

Silence. I was about to say more when I realized the call had been dropped. I'd try again later.

Deanna was more confused than angry when she picked up my call. "We decided to make an offer and I called to ask if I could drop it off at her house. Janet said the shop isn't for sale."

"I just talked to her. She's having second thoughts. I don't know what to tell you."

"This is business, Tina." Deanna's tone didn't sound so much cold as overly businesslike. "There are a lot of moving parts to this offer, and we don't want the shop to be closed more than a day or two. September starts the holiday buying for quilters." She sighed, and her voice softened when she said, "But you know that."

So, I found myself in the middle of the two parties wanting ownership of the quilt shop. Being in the middle was not a comfy spot.

But now...How did I remove myself without either of them having hard feelings toward me? I was working for Janet and

Deanna had offered me a position in the shop if Log Cabin owned it.

"Look Deanna, the best I can do for everyone is try to keep the shop in good shape while all this shakes out between you." I gathered my thoughts and finally spilled then. "If you want my opinion, and maybe you do, maybe you don't, I think she's reluctant to give up her dream. An actual offer threw her for a loop. Suddenly, it was a wrenching decision again." I assured Deanna that I'd touch base with Janet after opening the shop in the morning.

I sat on the edge of my bed wondering how such a wonderful day could also be such a tough one. I couldn't think about ME or a wall hanging for an auction. My mind was searching for a solution to a problem that wasn't even mine. I slipped out of my room and went to rock in the gardens and look at the stars. I was hoping John would come by, maybe to do a little rocking and thinking. But I was alone.

When I turned to go inside, the lights were on in Helen's room. I wanted to ask for help finding a solution, but this was my problem, one I'd had a hand in making because I didn't want a business in Briarwood to close. Still, I couldn't sleep. I pulled out the Log Cabin pattern I'd chosen from the package of samples and read the directions. I had a week. Not much time to make this kind of quilt project even if I worked on it every day. I resented Helen all over again for asking me to do this, especially because her obvious lack of quilting knowledge was showing.

An uncomfortable feeling washed over me. I was ascribing the indifference Alex showed for my work to Helen. No wonder I lashed out. Even worse, her reminder that I was good enough brought Dad's lack of confidence to the surface. She hadn't meant that to hurt, but it did. It cut deeply into me. All I could do was talk to Helen about the buttons she pushed. And push them she had, and hard.

I opened the bag with the fabrics I'd chosen. Running my hand across them calmed me, but in a heightened way. The fabrics excited me. The design was a posy of flowers wrapped with a colorful ribbon. I had chosen two light reds and mauve for the flowers and five greens for the stems and leaves. But I was missing two critical pieces, the fabric for the ribbon and the border fabric. I gathered the fabrics to take to the quilt shop with me that next day.

I had seven days to figure it out.

11

"Got a broken clock?" Carol greeted me when I arrived at the quilt shop an hour earlier than my scheduled start time.

"I need fabric." I pulled the Log Cabin pattern from my tote. "Ribbon, border, and backing. I'm making the piece for the auction at the benefit for the Youth Club."

Carol's eyes widened. "Are you crazy? It'll take more than a week to do the hand sewing and the quilting."

I swatted that thought hanging in the air. "No, no, no. I can't think that way. My sister is counting on me. I can't let her down. She's handling our family business while I work here, so I owe her." I guessed that was accurate enough. My mood had quieted down a little. I didn't like the pressure, but maybe it was practice for whatever I intended to do with my quilting and with ME.

Overnight, I'd decided I needed to learn to handle pressure that came from a source that had to do with me and my life. Pressures from Alex had never been that way. Everything was about Alex alone. I spent years cooped up in our apartment thinking about what I could do to please him. No more.

Carol left me when the buzzer announced a customer.

That freed me to find the fabric that would draw the design together. I was deep in thought when I looked up and Marci Westford approached. I nodded when she put her finger to her lips in a "don't let on that you know me" sign.

I looked both ways to find Carol. She was with the customer on the opposite side of the shop. "What are you doing here?"

"Reconnaissance. Nick would say I'm snooping," Marci said. "I've been wondering if I could manage the shop since we started talking about acquiring it. Because of my mom, I know a little about quilting and fabric. I've done a lot of quilting on the long-arm machine, but I've never made a quilt from the beginning."

"Your mom can show you."

With a shake of her head, she said, "She's way too busy designing patterns. She doesn't teach anymore."

"Then take a class." No sooner than the words were out of my mouth when I regretted saying them. Not only was I being short with Marci, I thought about the less than stellar beginner's class in the small classroom in the back corner of the shop. Thoughts of Heather quickly followed. I hadn't heard from her since I taught the class what seemed like months ago. I pushed those thoughts away and focused on Marci. "Sorry for the way that popped out. I realize you must be very busy with the company."

"We all are, but Log Cabin needs one of us in this shop if we acquire it. I'm the one, the only one."

Was Deanna so sure I was going to turn down her offer to be the assistant manager? So much was up in the air at the moment.

"Tina, can you help me here?" Yikes, there was a line at the cutting table and one forming at the register. Carol looked a little frantic.

"I have to run." I turned away, but rotated back to say, "It would be fun working with you."

At the register one woman told me she bought more fabric than she'd planned. When I asked why, she said the For Sale sign threw her and she wanted the shop to stay in Briarwood. The extra fabric was her way of showing support for a store she considered her hometown source of supplies. As the customers came and went, I heard the same sentiment over and over. At some point, we were so busy that Marci must have slipped away.

I hadn't called Janet yet, but shortly after lunch there was a lull, so I went into the office to make the call. But Janet's name appeared on my screen almost immediately after I closed the door. "I was just going to call you," I said.

"I didn't want to keep you hanging and wondering what I was going to do." Janet's tone was quiet, calmer than I'd heard before. "Tom and I came to a decision, and I just called Deanna and accepted her offer. I get it now. I can't enjoy the baby and do the shop justice. It's not a regular job. It's more like a calling that I'll need to put on hold. I'll stay involved in quilting another way."

Her decision didn't surprise me, but her sensible attitude did. She'd been so torn and emotional about letting go of this business she'd built. "Well, you know the expression, 'When one door closes, another opens'."

"You're right. Tom and I are blessed to have a baby coming and if I need to stay in bed, well, so be it."

"I'm sure there will be lots of communication during the transition. I can tell you the customers are very sorry to see you go, but they'll be relieved when they learn the shop isn't going away." I repeated the comments, but my phone buzzed for another call, so I begged off to take the call from Helen.

"We have an emergency at ME," she blurted. "Correction,

we don't have the problem, Mary Forrester from Cones 'N Scoops called. Her ice cream freezer quit, and she needs another one immediately to stay open. She was Dad's client a couple of years ago. Her loan was paid in full and on time. Plus, she has good credit."

"And?" I asked, knowing Carol was alone on the floor.

"I want to help her, Tina."

"Wow. Go for it. This is a great opportunity for us. This will be our first fresh contract—not like Melvin, where it was essentially repeating the same loan year after year."

"Good. I thought you'd agree," Helen said, slightly breathless. "I've got the model contract and will enter the figures now that I have your okay. You and Steve can both review it tonight, and she can electronically sign it. We can do the fund transfer in the morning."

"Can't ask for any faster service than that," I said. "This is very good news. It's not the biggest loan in the world, but it's a good start. Really, two good starts this week."

"We won't take long. All you'll have to do is look it over. I'm aware you have the quilting hanging over your head...ha! Pardon the pun." Helen paused. "Just think, Tina. Our first start-to-finish contract. I guess Dad would be shocked, huh?"

I touched my diamond earrings. "And when he got over the shock of his daughters pulling this off, I hope he'd be proud."

"Yeah, I hope so, too." Helen snickered. "Interesting. It doesn't matter what Dad would think. *I'm* proud of us."

We ended our call, and I rang Deanna, hoping to talk with her, but it went to voice mail. Darn.

The rest of the day flew by. I wasn't free to think about anything but the customers in front of me. We barely had a lull. Back home after closing, I wasted no time changing into a blouse and comfy shorts. Ivy handed me a glass of iced tea and got our dinners on the table in short order.

Ivy smiled as she sat at the table. "I'm told you're sewing a special piece, so no drawn-out dinner talk. And I want to see it when you are done."

"And no interruptions," Helen added with a grin, "not even John."

But now...with John arriving home late yesterday, I wanted to spend more time with him before he took off again. I kept that thought to myself. "He's probably still sleeping off his jet lag," I said. After the long day, I wanted to sleep myself, but first the contract, and then the sewing. I was halfway through dinner, when Deanna returned my call. The sale of the quilt shop was in the hands of the lawyers. She hoped I would continue working there and help Marci with the transition. Then she asked if I wanted the assistant manager's position with a salary of more money than I'd ever earned in my life. I said yes.

Helen and I poured ourselves mugs of coffee and went over the contract with a fine-tooth comb. We saw no problem, so we sent it to Steve, who replied in a matter of minutes. The deal was completed with the electronic signatures, and I was free to sew for whatever time there was left.

I'd probably been working on my setup for about an hour, when I went upstairs to get more coffee. I knew I had barely half an hour of energy left in me. But when I got to the kitchen, I saw John come through the gardens with a bottle of wine in his hand.

I went out to greet him and made a quick decision to put sewing aside for the evening and unwind with a glass of chilled white wine. "Helen's not going to be happy with us meeting like this."

"Uh, oh, I'm scared," John said. "Can't you tell?" He waited by patio door while I carried out two glasses and we settled in the rockers. "I wouldn't worry about Helen. She's probably on the phone with Steve."

"Could be," I agreed. "We actually have something to celebrate. A big, huge something. We wrote, or I should say Helen wrote our first contract today. It's a local business and it had to be done fast."

"Did you get background on the client?"

That was his first thought? I stared at him, furious with the question. "Of course. Helen did the work. It's a former client with a good record. She had an expansion loan with ME four years ago and never made so much as a late payment." I shook my head. "Sorry I sound annoyed, but that doubt in your voice is exactly what I'd have expected from Dad."

"Sorry. I mean it, Tina." A puzzled expression settled on his face. "Why would you say that about your dad?"

He sounded contrite, so I cut him a break. "It's okay. But you *know* Helen and I have been so shaky about the business because Dad didn't think we were capable of running it. That's why he never talked to us about it. Apparently, he had no faith that we'd understand it." Suddenly, I was filled with pride for my sister. "Helen has put in a lot of time to be ready for this moment. And you should see her PR plan. It's subtle, but she builds on ME's prominence in Briarwood. Being well known in town herself, she's ceding no ground to the idea that ME is a lesser business because Dad is gone." When I finally stopped talking, I exhaled. "Okay, I'm done with my speech now."

"I get what you're saying, Tina, I do." John stared into the gardens. "I'm glad you and Helen have gained some confidence but give me a chance to catch up with all this. I've been gone, remember?"

I wasn't used to exchanging sharp words with John. "It's just that there's so much history here. And it's not all pretty and it doesn't reflect well on Dad. For that matter, it doesn't put Helen and me in the best light, either."

John shifted the pattern of his rocking to sync with me. "Let's see if I can get us back on the same page," he said, smiling. "Helen was serious about making sure you have time to sew, wasn't she? Should you be sewing now?"

I flipped my hand in the air. "Yeah, yeah. I'll work on it tomorrow." I didn't say it out loud, but that night was for rocking in the gardens with John.

BEFORE I LEFT FOR THE QUILT SHOP, HELEN SAT ME DOWN AT the computer to sign the contract for Mary's loan. I could feel her excitement in the air mixing with my own.

"You'll need to sign hard copies, too, but that can wait. For now, the electronic signature is good enough to get the money transferred."

"What will Mary do until the freezer is installed?"

"She has two smaller ones, so she'll shrink her menu for a few days. Insurance will cover the product losses," Helen explained. "She's going to call when it's installed. I told her I'd stop in for some ice cream when she's at full capacity again."

"Good idea. A little personal touch. I like it." I got a kick out of Helen. She was good at this. "I'm glad we're able to help her. She'll help us spread the word about ME."

"You and I need to spend some time looking over the accounts again." She held up her hand before I could speak. "But not until the benefit is over. How's it coming?"

I hedged with a shoulder shrug. "Okay. I'm underway." It wasn't a lie exactly. I had all the fabric, and I knew the stems and leaves would be the most time-consuming section. I promised myself I'd start sewing as soon as I got home from work.

I entered the shop to find Deanna, Marci, and Carol stand around the cutting table, talking over each other, smiling, laughing. They looked so relaxed and easy with each other. I wondered if my more reserved personality would be a fit. I could talk quilting all day long, but I'd never been good with social banter. Deanna, as professional as she was, had a buoyancy about her. And Marci, my new boss, had energy to spare.

"Tina, come quick," Marci said. "We're sharing ideas for changes we can probably make in the evenings so we can stay open for customers during the day."

Yikes! Evenings? When would I sew?

But now...I didn't have time for regrets. I joined the women. "Tell me your ideas."

Deanna studied her list and then ran down a few ideas for rearranging the shop and prominently featuring her Log Cabin designs with its own spinner. That made perfect sense, of course. This shop was more or less a division of her company. "We'll need models using the fabric in the shop and the new bolts that will arrive soon."

"Um...Deanna? About the evenings."

"Jared and Nick will help us. The whole revamp should take two, maybe three evenings." She touched the bolts of fabric as she moved between the displays.

I saw the handwriting on the wall. Deanna was making short work of turning Janet's Quilt Shop into the Log Cabin Quilt Shop. It was a matter of days. I'd be the assistant manager, working for The Log Cabin Company. I had to drill that into my head.

At the sound of the door opening Deanna said she'd take care of the customer. I followed behind her to see how she conveyed the change of ownership to the customers. With that customer, and a few more that came in over the next couple of hours, she struck up a friendly back-and-forth as she asked them for suggestions. “We want the shop to remain your go-to place for quilting fabric and supplies.”

I worked between the cutting table and the register. Marci shadowed me and with her experience with fabric she was soon able to cut fabric for customers. Carol and I took turns at the register, and without needing to rush to keep up with the line I had time to chat with the quilters about their projects.

After Deanna and Marci left, Carol and I handled the traffic and finished the day by moving Halloween and school themed fabric to the display closest to the door. All in all, a high-five day. When we locked the door Carol confided that Deanna had asked her to work until she left for school. “She even wants me here when I’m home on semester breaks. Can’t ask for more than that.”

“I’m glad for you,” I said, “and for me. With you here, I can adjust my schedule so I’m not here every day.”

On the drive home, I mentally began sewing the wall hanging. Helen and Ivy were gone so I headed to my quilting studio, to begin working. I started with the stems. Feeling energized I cut out the leaves. Because leaves aren’t perfect in nature, I sewed uneven edges and tipped a few ends of the pointed leaves.

I lost track of time and got one flower done. My eyes were tired, but I kept at it, knowing that if I put in a few more hours, I’d be finished sewing the design.

Sometime later, I startled awake. My hand was poised to take a stitch, but the tip of the needle had poked my skin to awaken me. I went into a near panic when a small blemish of blood appeared on the fabric.

Was I a good enough quilter to cover my mistake? If I twisted one of the flower petals to cover the error maybe no one would know the difference. Who was I kidding? Deanna Westford would know, and others, if we displayed the pattern next to the wall hanging like Helen wanted.

"Tina? Are you downstairs? The lights are on." Helen called from the top of the stairs. Her footsteps echoed in the stairwell as she came down the steps. "Tina?"

"I must have fallen asleep. I was working on the wall hanging and lost track of time." Helen stepped closer to look at my progress. I quickly put my hand over the blood spot. I didn't want her to know that I had made a beginning quilter's mistake. And in my sleep, no less.

"This is beautiful. Maybe I'll have to bid on it at the benefit. We should have more of your work in the house."

I was speechless. "If you want the hanging, give some money to the Youth Club. The pressure will be off, and I can get some sleep."

"I was only saying..."

"I know, I know, but you know how I feel. I'm glad you want my work in the house, but we've got loads of time ahead for that." I'd put in a long day that morphed into a long night.

"You're being a little touchy about this," Helen said defensively. "I'm obviously not going to bid on your hanging. I'm sure it will fetch a bigger price than I can pay."

"I know. I'm sorry. I fell asleep in the middle of working on this." I folded the wall hanging and started to clean up the mess I'd made. "I won't be home for dinner tomorrow night. Deanna is having her sons come in to help move the heavy displays. I have to be there."

"There's coffee ready upstairs," Helen said turning to leave. "And Mary's freezer is arriving today. She's really happy with us."

"If she feels good, I feel good. So far, we renewed Tully's loan and negotiated a brand new one." I smiled. "Let's go for ice cream soon. Soon, defined as after the benefit." I followed her up the stairs. "I bet this is how Dad felt early on when he realized he was able to help someone."

"Now I wish I'd forced the issue with Dad," Helen said. "I folded so easily when he avoided my questions. If I had it to do over, I'd have taken a whole different path to get him to either explain the business or admit he didn't trust me with it."

Helen's voice was calm and low, so I couldn't decide if she was angry or wistful.

I crossed the room and wrapped my arms around her. "None of that matters. Just like the money Dad gave Alex. It's done with. I'll never know the real reason he acted behind my back."

I followed Helen upstairs and poured a cup of coffee, but I didn't bother sitting at the table. I didn't have that much time.

"Are you really that accepting?" Helen asked. "These last days you've never mentioned Alex and Dad's money. I haven't wanted to bring it up, but since you did..." She shrugged and looked expectantly at me.

"Well, all I can say is that there's nothing I can do to change the situation, and I don't want to contact Alex, even to rage at him over it." I'd been too busy and stressed to think about it. Excited, too, because I'd landed a job that suited me, maybe not forever, but for now.

"And didn't Doug say it was a done deal, anyway?"

"Exactly. But still, I had fantasies of telling him off." I took a gulp of coffee and enjoyed the sensation of the hot liquid warming my chest. "I'd really like to dump years of resentment on him, but I won't do that. He doesn't care what I think and it's not good for me to keep going over my failure to protect myself from his shenanigans."

Helen nodded. "You're taking the same road with Dad. I

keep feeling like he did us wrong, but I have to take responsibility for not pushing him."

"That's the key, isn't it?" I asked. "I've never felt like I was calling the shots in my life." I hooted. "But now I do, and I'm responsible for my choices. Accepting this new job was good. I can make a contribution into the household account."

Helen shook her head. "Let's hold off on big changes in ME. We have time to figure out the finances in the next couple of months. I'll keep learning the business and courting some new clients."

If that's the way she wanted it, I was good with it. I took my coffee and headed to my room to get ready for the day. It barely felt like yesterday ended. When I touched the prick spot from the needle, I thought maybe it was a sign that I needed to find a way to slow down. Maybe I'd start by not saying yes to every request.

The day passed in a blur with customers buying yards and yards of fabric. After we closed, Deanna began the transition to the new Log Cabin Quilt Shop. As I watched Deanna direct her sons and Marci—and me—I could see how precisely she'd planned the makeover. She'd put a great deal of thought into the new design for the shop. I better understood Marci's admiration of her mother. We tried to do an inventory of the fabric bolts as we moved them, but that stopped Nick and Jared from moving the displays.

"This isn't getting the job done, Mom. Leave it for later." Jared stood with his hands on his hips.

I saw that big job in my future, maybe even the next night.

Deanna agreed and quickly revamped her plan. It took only a few hours to give the shop a fresh, new look and atmosphere. Even the locks would be changed by the end of the following day.

I was tired, physically tired, that is, but mentally energized.

I could have taken on the world at that moment. But, by the time I reached the house fatigue caught up with me and my energy had evaporated. All I really wanted was a long night's sleep. I recognized Steve's car in the driveway and soft music greeted me when I went inside. Not wanting to interrupt, I peeked into the living room, immediately surprised to see them slow dancing.

"Practicing for the benefit?" I smiled and waved. "Maybe the committee should add a dance contest."

Helen stepped back but didn't break the dance hold. "Hey, Tina, we didn't think you'd be so late. You missed dinner."

"Is something wrong? I had my phone."

"No, no," Helen said. "I was worried because you didn't get much sleep last night."

"I intend to make up for it tonight." I turned to leave.

"I showed Steve the wall hanging," Helen called out."

"And the mistake?" That jumped out of my mouth. My fatigue talking. They didn't know about the tiny blood stain.

"All we saw was a beautiful piece of handwork." Steve continued to hold Helen's hand as if ready to restart their slow steps around the room.

"Mistakes? You don't make mistakes," Helen said in a teasing tone as she put her hand on Steve's shoulder, "and if should such a travesty occur, you're good enough to hide it."

If she only knew. I blinked away the tears. Maybe Helen believed I was good enough, but I wasn't so sure. I was too tired to argue or debate my self-concept. I left them to their dancing and hurried to my room.

12

For three days, Carol and I worked with Marci during the day, but we were able to finish the makeover in the next two evenings. Deanna was satisfied that we didn't need another session. Only the displays on the four walls remained untouched, and they wouldn't stay the same for too much longer. When Jared and Nick carried out the portable wall that formed the classroom, I had a twinge of sadness. My thoughts of teaching for Deanna went out the door with the wall.

I had mixed feelings about all that had transpired, even the role I played with my new job. Teaching quilting techniques had been a lifeline for me when I was married to Alex and so desperately in need of a purpose, something that I was passionate about. Now I thought of Heather and the botched class I'd taught as a substitute. Then there was the woman I never called back. Steve hadn't mentioned his sister after his first request for me to show her some basic techniques.

That evening after leaving the shop I put all thoughts aside to finish the last flower and the bow on the wall hanging. I'd admitted the mistake and replaced that piece and had worked deep into the night after coming back from the revamping work at the shop. Now, I had one more late night of work and it would be ready for the benefit. Then, I could sleep.

I'd never been more grateful for Helen's wardrobe than I was the night of the benefit. I mentioned wearing a black skirt and one of my dressier vests, but Helen had different ideas and wasn't shy about her opinion—outdated was her favorite word, at least when it came to most everything I owned. "At least you have a great job now," she said, more than once, "and you can buy yourself some new clothes." When I protested that I liked my look, she pointed out that I could update my closet but still keep the same style.

While we weren't exactly the same size, I remembered her having a glittery dark blue tunic top that would fit me and she had a dressy black flared skirt that looked fine with my one and only pair of heels. I rummaged through her closet until I found both pieces. And it only took three passes to finally get my hands on them. I wore the diamond earrings from Dad and a gold bracelet.

John and Steve had cooked up their own plan for the evening. They arrived at the house within minutes of each other. Steve was barely dry from his shower, with droplets of water scattered in his hair. Both men carried white boxes.

Through the clear plastic cover, I saw a white orchid. A memory of John's senior prom flashed through my mind. John had gotten me a white orchid that night. I saw the smile on his face and returned one of my own. "I remember, John."

Helen joined us in the entryway and put her arm around Steve's waist as they watched John slip the corsage onto my wrist. "Well, John Delaney, aren't you the man of the evening," she said.

Steve quietly handed Helen the box he was carrying. "For you," he said softly.

Both hands went to her face.

"Guess I'm a man of the evening, too." Steve laughed.

She bent forward and kissed his cheek before opening the box. "You didn't have to, but I do love flowers." She gave the miniature bouquet of tea roses to Steve along with the pin to secure it the wide strap of her silky dress.

"Not me. I'll stick you for sure." He immediately wanted to pass the flowers and pin to me. "You work with pins every day. I'm sure you won't have any difficulty."

I laughed and went ahead and did as he asked. When I'd accomplished the mission, I moved closer to John. "So, we're off to the prom, huh?"

"Next year we'll call it the Youth Club Prom and Auction," Helen said. "Why not?" She gestured to us in our dressy clothes and now our flowers. "Look at us. All we need are some flouncy organza and some music from the eighties."

"Maybe a disco ball, huh?" Steve joked.

"I hope not," John said with a groan.

We drove in separate cars, which gave me time to both remember and forget those dances John and I used to go to. I still had two years of high school to endure after he left, which started three decades of a friendship consisting of phone calls with long months in between. He went his way while I tried to make a go of life with Alex. So far, the night was almost a duplicate of an earlier time.

"I'm glad we're alone," John said, giving me a quick glance before returning his attention to the road. "I have a feeling that Helen and Steve will be busy tonight greeting the guests and playing their part as leaders and organizers of this shindig. They look like guests at the party, but don't let their fancy clothes fool you. This is all about coaxing donations from attendees."

"And how would you know that?"

"Steve told me he's worked really hard to get auction items people will want to bid on, and he's had to lean on people to keep upping the bids to make this kind of gala worth the effort," John said. "Apparently, the people of Briarwood are getting tired of being asked to give to this or that charity—it's true, it never ends."

"But isn't this different? It's for local kids. I find it hard to believe people here in town would withhold support for children's programs." Would I bid with abandonment? I hadn't thought of bidding at all. Helen and I agreed to a lump sum and ME would be listed as a corporate donor. Maybe I had been outspoken before I knew all the details. "One the other hand, as much as I believe in this program, I wouldn't know about being inundated with requests for money. Dad took care of that, and Helen wants us to develop a clear policy about giving our support to various charities in town."

"I think my mom handled a lot of the outreach work for your dad, a little the way Helen does," John said. "Seriously, it was probably part of her job description as his assistant."

"Funny you should mention that. I have some memories of Maggie, all dressed up and ready to go out for the evening," I said. "I always thought she was so beautiful. Do you think she enjoyed events like this?"

John laughed. "Truthfully, my mom was okay with working for your dad, but other than her family, she had two great loves, flowers and quilting. I have a feeling she considered these PR type of events as one more duty of her day job."

"I don't think that's true for Helen. She's a natural and so easily stepped into that role for Dad," I said. "Lucky us, she's good at it."

"She might feel inadequate when it comes to the nitty-gritty of the business, but not with the community side." John finished his sentence as he pulled into the country club drive, one of many cars. "Wow. Look at the number of people here already." John made a circle through the rows of cars before finding a spot near the outer edge of the parking lot.

I had brought a black woven shawl, another find in Helen's closet, and I pulled it tight around me to keep me warm in the crisp, fall air. I inhaled the scent of logs burning in the country club stone fireplace in the lobby. When we went inside, we saw that the fireplace had already attracted a crowd.

Inside, Steve and Helen stood side-by-side in a receiving line with the other members of the organizing committee. They pretended they didn't know us until John spoiled the ruse when he gave Helen a huge hug and she let out a burst of laughter.

"Well, that's a joke on us." She gave John a friendly tap on the shoulder. The guests behind us laughed and smiled.

The country club ballroom had been loosely divided into three areas: the auction platform where the items were displayed for viewing, round tables for dinner, and a wooden floor for dancing. Spotlights focused on the auction items formed a brighter zone than the more subtle lighting for dining. The glow from the centerpiece candles added points of light on the linen tablecloths.

John and I registered for the auction and were given a brochure and paddle. The brochure listed the pieces donated for auction. I was impressed by the quality of the local items, like a vase of cut flowers each month for a year from Briarwood Florists. "Look John, coupons for free ice cream, two cones a month. Now that's a valuable gift."

"And here's your wall hanging," he said, grinning. "You have a real eye for color, Tina. It's gorgeous.

"And your framed photos."

He'd put together a grouping of four photos of street life, a vegetable market in Bagdad, a pickup basketball game in Prague, girls playing soccer in a refugee camp in Jordan, and a woman in Lima with dozens of flowers stuck in the brim of her hat selling bouquets from her cart. I took in a breath imagining John capturing these scenes, these faces. He'd seen it all, yet he was giving it up. But I guess if he wanted to see markets and kids making their own fun, he could see that on the streets and parks of Briarwood. Different children, same exuberance.

Another of John's photos appeared by itself, poster size. It showed the rocking chairs in the gardens with a white porcelain teapot on a table next to the chairs. The garden was in full summer bloom so the reds and purples, along with orange and gold, dominated the scene John captured.

Deanna's Log Cabin Pattern Company was represented with a fabulous quilt done in one of her signature designs and the brilliant colors. There were gift certificates from an auto shop and one of the small food markets. The same cleaning company that had worked for us for decades auctioned a package of its services. The country club was auctioning passes, and Daisy, a local jewelry artist, offered stunning silver earrings and a sliver and obsidian necklace. Another fiber artist donated a package of her one-of-a-kind needlepoint designs she sold printed on the backing with the supplies needed to make it.

"We should bid on gift certificates from Maria's Table and the Bistro," John said, pointing to the cluster of gift certificates from local restaurants and two bakeries.

"I know, family favorites, huh? I think Steve and Helen have met for lunch and dinner at both places." Since I'd been away from the house so much, I didn't know exactly where

Steve and Helen went, but I knew they saw a lot of each other. I pointed to another cluster of certificates. "I think every salon in Briarwood donated a gift certificate. It reminds me I need a haircut."

"I think it's beautiful the way it is," John said.

Before I had a chance to respond, he was singing the praises of an enormous wine and cheese basket compliments of a local winery and a specialty food shop.

"There's some of everything here, even Molly's in-house daycare services."

Within minutes Steve was at the podium announcing that dinner was being served so we should find an empty place at one of the tables. The auction area emptied fast.

John grabbed my hand and bee-lined to a table near the back of the room. He leaned over to whisper when I tried to pull him in a different direction. "This is a better spot to see whose bidding." He wiggled his eyebrows. Now we were co-conspirators in something. I wasn't sure what.

We stood behind the two chairs John had chosen and watched others move past us. Helen and others from the committee were seated at the head table at the front of the room. When the room settled down Steve continued. "Welcome, welcome. I'm announcing a slight change of plans. Because our community has been so generous, we have more auction pieces than we anticipated. So, we're going to start the auction when the servers bring the dessert carts around. We want to make sure everyone has a chance to enjoy the band and dancing later."

John and I chatted with our tablemates while we ate exceptional tenderloin tips served over noodles, curried chicken, and side dishes of autumn vegetables. Molly, who'd offered two weeks of free infant-care, was seated at our table, and filled our glasses with the bottle of red wine already opened and on the table on a tray with glasses. Chelsea, the needlepoint designer, did the honors for those who preferred the white wine.

I was secretly thrilled to meet Chelsea, a presence at every fair. Her work was sold in gift shops all over the region. I was so happy to meet her because I'd admired her for a couple of years. Still in her twenties she'd carved out her own niche and was featured in several craft magazines. She handed me a brochure, and I saw that she'd gone international. Her designs were getting reviews from Ireland and Australia, and two from Germany. And she lived nearby on a small orchard outside of Briarwood.

"I think we can come up with some ideas for cross promotion," I said, when we'd finished the main course.

"I'd like that. Or at least we could share a tent, perhaps with other fiber artists at nearby festivals," Chelsea said, eyeing the dessert cart. "Are you going to bid on anything in particular?"

"Oh, perhaps one of the gift certificates for a salon or a restaurant," I said, keeping quiet about bidding on one of John's photos. "How about you?"

"I know the jewelry artist, so I might start with her." Chelsea sparkled as she spoke and lit up over the iced poppy seed cupcake she picked from the cart the server brought our way.

"Pumpkin pie for me," I said, moving aside to have one plate whisked away to make room for the pie. "And black coffee."

I had taken my first bite of pie when Steve tapped the microphone. "Doug Baker has volunteered to be our auctioneer, and he's starting in five minutes. Please have your bidding paddle in hand and open your wallets. This evening is all about the youth of Briarwood."

"He wasn't kidding about starting, was he? I'm barely going to get to finish this cupcake." John leaned across me to confer with Chelsea about their superior dessert choice. "Maybe we should bid on the leftover cupcakes—if there are any. I warn you, though, I've got deep pockets."

Chelsea laughed, finding John especially amusing. She kept looking back and forth between John and me. I expected she thought we were one of the old married couples filling the room. In fact, I made a note that when it came to age, Molly and Chelsea were a minority. A few younger people were clustered around, but not enough to keep an event like this going year after year. I'd mention that to Steve and Helen to consider when they planned next year's events.

I opened my booklet to the listing. I wanted to follow along with the bidding until John's picture was offered. Then I would bid for a chance to have an original John Delaney photograph for myself.

John bent over to look at the notes I was making while the bidding progressed. He pointed to the listing of his picture where he saw I'd circled it. "You don't have to bid. I'll give you one."

I whispered, "It's the only item I want, and I can't not bid. What would Helen and Steve think?"

"Bid on something and then after paying for it give it back to be re-auctioned."

"That's rude. What would the donor think?"

John and I sat back while the bidding wars went on for the smaller items and it didn't take long for the wine and cheese basket to be off the list, and the ice cream and flowers and gift certificates. Most all the donors were present, and Doug had everyone stand and be recognized.

Lots of paddles shot up when the necklace Chelsea wanted was up for a bid, but she finally had to shake her head.

She lost out to a very high bid. “I guess I’ll have to buy one similar to it, but at least I won’t have to pay six times more,” she whispered to me.

The needlepoint designs brought in many times their retail value, which brought her spirits back up. Molly’s services were snapped up, too.

“What a table,” John said.

In the background I heard Steve call John’s number. “I’m holding two offerings from Briarwood’s renowned photographer John Delaney. He’s been documenting events all over the world for many years. We’ll start with the single photos of the gardens at the Montgomery house, originally planted by John’s mother, Maggie Delaney. The rocking chairs were her idea, too.”

The bidding was fast and furious for John’s first work. Three others bid before I got my paddle in the air. The game was on. I raised the bid over the others and Doug egged the others to outdo me and join in the fun. When the man at the next table doubled the already high bid the rest of us conceded.

I squeezed John’s arm. “Darn. I was looking forward to hanging the picture in my studio.”

“I’ll give you as many pictures as you want.” He reached to take my hand. “I’m going to surprise you with a special one soon.”

“Don’t be such a tease,” I said, responding to the twinkle in his gray-blue eyes.

When John’s next work came up, Steve started the bid so high, only a few raised him. But it was clear, Steve wanted John’s street life scenes and he came back and finally prevailed.

As it happened, the final item was my wall hanging. Doug described it—and me—with his typical flourish. He also explained that Janet had sold the shop to Deanna and described them both as winners, Janet and her baby, and Deanna and her expansion.

Deanna raised Doug's first bid, and then the owner of one of the bakeries went higher. A woman at the next table then bested that bid, but the bakery owner won out.

I was feeling a little heady from the bidding war and was lost in thought when John touched my arm. "Tina? Are you okay?"

I laid my hand over his. "I'm fine."

I didn't offer more explanation. Then I overheard the bidder at the next table tell her companion that she'd like to learn more about quilting after seeing the wall hanging. I was ready to turn and begin a conversation when the other people at our table stood up. Mary Louise, who owned the high-end bakery on Briarwood's main drag, sought me out, and had four other women follow her.

"Rumor has it you're quite a quilting teacher," Mary Louise said. "I love the hanging. I can't wait to get it home. I know exactly where I'm putting it. I have a collection of fiber art at the top of my stairs to the second floor. And now I'm adding yours."

"Thanks so much," I said, recognizing her now that she introduced herself. "We're bakery regulars—my sister thinks your blueberry muffins are the best in the world, bar none." Mary Louise had a friendship vibe about her. I had a feeling she'd be a fun lunch or coffee partner, and the quilt shop and the bakery weren't so far apart to make it difficult to get together. I told her I'd drop by and she took off, but a couple of women lingered.

"My husband and I just moved to Briarwood and I'm so excited to see you again," one of the women said. "I went to one of your lectures when I was visiting my sister in Michigan.

I was still working then and didn't have time to start a new hobby. Are you still teaching?"

I didn't like my answer, but it was the only one I had. "Not right now. I'm managing The Log Cabin Quilt Shop for the new owner, Deanna Westford. Do stop in soon. You might enjoy looking around. And there are teachers around. I know a couple who offer classes."

As I heard myself talking about other people's teaching, I was hit with the truth. It came to me like a river of water rushing in to nourish a parched and barren land. I wanted to teach quilting. I enjoyed it. I was good at it. I wanted my own teaching studio. I reeled a little from the power behind my realization, but I didn't think anyone would notice what was going on.

The women drifted away when the band started with a slow, easy song to encourage the reluctant dancers to the floor. I looked over at John, suddenly aware he'd been waiting for me to end my conversation with the women. He gave his head a nod toward the band. I seemed to float over to him and take his outstretched hand. We moved onto the dance floor, and even after all our years apart we moved as if we'd danced together for years.

"Want to tell me what's going on in that head of yours?" John held me tighter and spoke into my ear." You are about to burst."

"I've found my future. I want to teach quilting again. I want to give lectures and...and..." I squeezed John's shoulder. "The ideas are running through my head so fast I can't remember them all."

"What about working at the quilt shop?" He drew his head back and looked into my eyes. "You can't quit after agreeing to take on a major position in the shop."

"Not exactly the reaction I hoped for." I was determined

not to let anything deflate my excitement, so I kept going. "My idea is too new for me to burn any bridges. But, when the time is right, the quilt shop is the perfect place to advertise my classes." I could see quilters picking up my business cards and calling to schedule a class. "I can see my business card in my mind's eye."

We had danced to the edge of the wooden floor. He laughed when he bumped into Helen and Steve chatting with the guests as they were filing out. "Well, benefit organizers, how do you think the evening went?"

"Nothing official yet, but I think the coffers are filling up and we'll have plenty of money to support the programs for the coming year." Steve didn't let go of Helen's hand when she turned away to say goodnight to more guests on their way out.

"That's great news," John said. "All your time and effort was worthwhile then. Glad to have been a part of it." John rubbed his thumb over the back of my hand.

Helen turned back to us. I had to put my thoughts of teaching aside and focus on Helen and the evening she was part of making such a huge success. "You did such a great job, Helen. As for me, I was sorry my bid didn't win John's picture, but he said another one is in the works and it's just for me."

Helen gave me a private smile. "Okay, everyone. One more dance and the evening's a wrap. Are you leaving or staying 'til the end?"

I started to say we were leaving, but John had other ideas. "Staying."

He twirled me under his arm, so we headed back to the dance floor. Steven and Helen joined us. The band played a bluesy rendition of "Moon River." It should have been romantic and fun. Instead, it made me think of John going off to see the world. Without me.

On the ride home I surprised myself when I blurted, "Are

you really staying in Briarwood and changing careers? Or are you leaving town again?"

"What are you really asking, Tina?"

"I'm not asking anything of you, John, but you should know you send me mixed messages all the time." I hesitated, but finally added, "You always have."

"What are you really saying, Tina?"

"I don't want things to get awkward between us. I'd do anything not to lose your friendship. I think you know that, but it's hard when I don't really know where I stand."

My heart had never thumped along this fast or hard. "I want to teach quilting again. I know that. But I also want to know about us. If there's any chance our friendship changes and we become more to each other, I'd need to know you'll be supportive of my passion, even if was demanding and took me out of town."

"Why are you asking me this?" John said. "I don't understand."

If he didn't understand it was because he really gave little thought to what my previous life had been. This wasn't going the way I expected. "From things I've told you, you're aware that I had no encouragement from Alex. He ridiculed and derided every dream I ever had. So, I want to be sure that if you and I have a future, it would be different."

"That's quite a mouthful." He turned the signal lights on to enter the driveway to the house. He put the car in park but didn't turn off the ignition. I guessed he wasn't coming into star gaze in the garden. "So according to you, the agreement goes something like this: 'This is my plan, and we can be together, however you define that, if I'm willing to compromise'."

Whoa, when he played that back to me, it was clear he saw

my plan as ridged, uncompromising, and one-sided. His tone had been uncharacteristically cold.

"I didn't mean..." What was a better way to say what I actually did mean? I was at a loss for words to get him to understand that my words had condensed a lifetime of dreams and hurts and failed expectations, which had become a cocoon that protected me.

At the same time, a sense of calm I hadn't felt in months washed over me in those few minutes when my bond with John was hanging in the balance. I was confident that I was good enough to be a good teacher. Whether John was part of my life going forward was the big unknown, but I wasn't going to let that stop me as I had let Alex do.

John stopped the car and kept his distance as he saw me to the front door. "Goodnight, Tina." He rushed back to his car and left me standing in the moonlight.

13

THE NEXT THREE DAYS I WAS LIKE A SLEEPWALKER. EARLY IN THE morning I poured my coffee into an insulated cup and slipped into a warm jacket before heading to the rockers. October mornings had a tendency to be cool before the sun rose above the treetops. For some reason, I assumed that John would join me, that we'd clear up whatever happened between us. But I was wrong. Eventually, I had to go inside and get ready for my day ahead. But even before the landscapers arrived do their final garden cleanup, I noticed some of the spaces were cleared of spent flowers. Someone, John, I was sure, had mulched a couple of beds so the perennials were protected from the harsh Wisconsin winter on its way. He was caring for his mother's legacy.

By the fourth day, I chose a trip to my studio over the rockers. Their presence only brought me down and I had to adjust to a different life. Whatever I thought might be developing between us was not to be. I didn't understand John's mixed messages, at least that's what I persisted in labeling them. Somehow, my new job and the prospect of teaching were going to pull me out of my malaise.

Those mornings in my studio were set aside to begin creating my new teaching wardrobe, my updated new signature look. At the quilt shop when Marci asked about the fabrics I was buying I was quick to shift the conversation toward holiday gifts. I didn't want Marci to think I was planning my escape when I'd barely begun, because I was doing no such thing. I needed the quilt shop as it needed me. It was helping me discover the kinds of classes that quilters wanted so I'd be prepared when the time came to strike out on my own. That wouldn't be for quite a long time.

I figured that my reputation – past and future – hinged on my commitments now. I'd promised to help manage The Log Cabin Quilt Shop and so I would, no timetable attached. Once Marci became comfortable with fabric lines, though, and with ordering stock and supplies, along with addressing shoppers' questions I'd focus on teaching. As a goal for myself and not shared with anyone else, I set aside one full year in the shop to get Marci ready to run the shop without me acting as tutor. She could also improve her quilting skills in that time. A year would take her through a complete cycle of quilt shows, designer traveling shows to display, and showcasing Deanna's new patterns.

After a long day of cutting fabric with pumpkins and ghosts and helping a customer alter a costume for her daughter with a broken leg, Marci asked me to stay after closing. We pulled chairs to the cutting table where she had laid out patterns and papers. She didn't waste any time getting to the point of our meeting. Of course, she and Deanna had seen the wall hanging I'd made for the auction. They'd also heard me recognize Deanna's designs. She arched her arm over the cutting table. "So, as you can see, the shop is in dire need of models. We have all these new fabrics coming in, but all the models are yesterday's news."

That was certainly true. She'd get no argument from me. I figured she either wanted me to make some models or teach her how. Or maybe both.

"So, Carol's going to be on a school break for almost a month," Marci said. "She wants to work in the shop during that time, so I'll get the benefit of watching her way of working with the customers here."

"Where would you like me to fit in? We're in our busiest days now, and as we get closer to the holiday, we'll likely move more gift certificates than fabric. You know the cycles." I saw the three of us stumbling over each other on a slow day.

"And that's more or less what we're counting on. We'd like you to make these models using the new fabrics," Marci said. "You pick the fabrics you like."

So far, so good. "I'd need to work at home, since there's no place to sew here."

"Exactly." Marci quickly added that my salary would stay the same. "Work is work. It doesn't matter where it's done."

I stood up to more closely look at the patterns, surprised that not all of them were Deanna's designs.

"Mom wants models for all levels of quilters – beginners to advanced." Marci let out a quick laugh. "Of course, she wants them yesterday, but if you can have them ready by the beginning of the New Year, that would be great. We're planning a "New Owner" celebration." She finger quoted the words. "I'd be really grateful for the update. Meanwhile, you and Carol can keep coaching me on the ways of a quilt shop."

"There's a lot to learn, but you're doing fine so far."

"I wish my stodgy older brothers could hear you," Marci said, pursing her lips in disgust. "They're not ragging on me much right now, but that's because Mom has told them to back off and give me time to learn all the moving parts."

I couldn't imagine what the brothers had to complain

about. But maybe there was a lingering older brother-little sister dynamic they hadn't outgrown. Whatever it was, it had nothing to do with me. Facts were facts, and Marci and the shop were doing very well.

"I'll make the models for you while Carol is here. I have to look at the pieces more carefully to assess the time, but I can do the work. And between the three of us, we'll get the shop to be...well, everything you want it to be."

I thought of our age difference and how I wished I'd had a mentor when I was her age. How different my life would have been. I pressed the pause button on my thoughts. Was that true? I couldn't say. I'd been so brokenhearted over John leaving Briarwood and, as I saw it, rejecting me, I'm not sure I would have recognized a mentor if one had fallen into my lap. Instead, I fell under the spell of Alex's charm and expected him to give me a life.

But now...as I gathered up the patterns and the notes Marci had made for each one, I thought of the freedom I'd have making the models. I became energized when I realized I'd be working with the newest fabrics on my own time schedule in my own studio.

Marci and I left the shop at the same time. I took a few minutes to check messages and listened to Ivy say, "I'll be gone tonight. Supper in fridge. Package from John on front door table." My hands began to shake—for no good reason other than it was from John. And there was no phone message from him. Disappointment snaked through me. Ridiculous. I'd had a good day, even a great day that was all about my career and my future, and something that involved John set me back. That had to change. I had a life of my own that was more important than a relationship with John. Couldn't I have both? From the moment I'd stepped into his open arms in the gardens, I assumed we'd been building toward something even deeper than our long friendship.

I hurried home and sat in the chair next to the table still wearing my coat, tote bag and purse at my feet. I took a deep breath and opened the large brown envelope. It was filled with a packet of photographs. I quickly pulled them out and flipped through them. They were shots of Maggie's quilts. John had hand-written the final page.

Dearest Tina,

I've thought a lot about our last awkward "conversation." So this is what I have to say: I've lived on my own, alone, but I thought that was necessary for my profession. I was wrong.

Solitude wasn't required, and now I realize I made many mistakes and I can't undo them. Now I find I want to try to get back what I lost. And the world has moved on without me. You made it clear you have your own work and commitments.

I'm willing to learn how to adjust to another person's life and dreams, but I need your help. I also have some lingering questions that, at least for me, are blocking my way forward with you. Are you willing to hear them?

I accepted an assignment and I'll be away for a while. As always, I can't pinpoint when I'll be back. I'll call you soon.

I've loved you for as long as I can remember.

John

I reread his note, with a heart filled with the joy of his words, but painful regret and hurt competing for attention. Oh, what my life could have been if he'd told me of his love years ago. I wondered what mistakes he was talking about and what questions he wanted to ask. I was an open book, or thought I was. That part of his note was as surprising as all the rest of it.

I moved into the living room and looked at the photo of each quilt Maggie had made. They were colorful and bright, like her flower gardens. One was dark and sorrowful. I guessed it had been made the year Susan, Maggie's daughter and John's sister, died from leukemia.

The longer I looked at the photos the more I wondered when John would have taken the pictures. Months had passed since we'd talked about opening the totes and refolding the quilts. I was interrupted by a text from Helen. She wouldn't be home for dinner.

Good. What a relief I'd be by myself that evening. I could bask in my joy of John wanting to be with me. Now, as an adult woman, not as a young teen with stars in her eyes. Whatever questions John had for me, I'd answer. I had nothing to hide. If John still wanted to accept assignments that took him away sometimes, I'd adjust. More than anything I wanted us to share our dreams for the years to come, but first I was sure John wanted to deal with the sadness of what kept us apart. It's as if I needed to mourn the mistakes I made and the years we missed being together.

My thoughts swirled and took me on a rollercoaster ride. I went to the kitchen and warmed the chicken rice soup Ivy had left for me. I rummaged around in the cupboard for crackers and helped myself to the cheese cubes she always had ready. I poured a glass of white wine and danced myself around the island waiting for the microwave to beep.

When I finished the last of the soup I cleaned up after myself and grabbed a couple of Ivy's sugar cookies and headed to the studio. As happy as I was, I didn't want to waste any time before sorting through the patterns for the quilt shop models. Forcing myself to focus, I soon saw that Marci was right about the patterns. They ran the gamut from beginner level to challenging. Best of all, they'd be fun to do. While John was away, I'd have my own dream to work on.

But now...With no new spring fabric available in my supplies, I couldn't start. I turned off the lights and went upstairs and decided to idle the evening away with some surfing and streaming. Helen was always mentioning a good series she'd watched. I settled on a game show that held my interest until I knew more answers than the contestants. Then I found a movie that looked promising, at least until shoot-outs and car chases took over the storyline. My mind kept jumping to John. Where was he? How long would he be gone? Then I jumped to the past and wasted time dreaming about a life of adventure and traveling around the world with him. Is that what our marriage would have been like? Or would we have held each other back? The same questions became an endless loop in my mind.

Just like I was no longer a teenager mooning over a boy, I was no longer that unsure woman who left her miserable marriage. I had a plan, and I was making it happen. Well, sort of. I wasn't teaching again, not yet, but my drive to work with anyone who wanted to learn quilting was strong. Young or old, it didn't matter.

I still hadn't worked out some details. Like where I would teach. The quilt shop no longer had a classroom. My studio was a possibility, but of limited size and accessibility, it had limited value. Helen used the office almost every day, but it offered some expandable space, room for tables. Helen would have a vote.

It had been a long time since we'd worked together on the accounts, but Helen didn't seem to mind. At least she hadn't mentioned it. In fact, she was thriving. I believe she'd found her niche. Still, working at home for a month or so would give me a chance to help with the ME business. I'd had a ready excuse when Helen was counting on me to produce the wall hanging. That excuse was over, though.

I walked over to the French doors that opened to the flower gardens and the area in the far corner of the property. For years we had played there, building forts and castles, having picnics, and in the summer, camping out and watching the stars on warm nights. Now that area seemed lonely, wasted.

On the opposite corner of the property John's house was a shadow in the darkness. Soon he would be home, he'd said so in his letter, and lights would glow in the windows.

The longer I stood staring into the gardens, the more a fuzzy image became clearer, and my ideal teaching studio emerged. One built with a large classroom for students to move about, where the latest notions and gadgets would be available for the students to use, and cubbyholes for their supplies. I thought of Maggie's quilts and in my mind's eye I could see them displayed in a gallery type of room, maybe with couches in the center. And we'd build a kitchenette. Some of my classes were day-long and we needed breaks.

I wanted to share my idea with John, but I didn't know where he was. Did it matter? By now he'd know that I saw the pictures and his note. I sat at the desk and punched in the sequence of numbers for his satellite phone at the bottom of his letter.

After a few beeps I heard his groggy, "Hello."

I chuckled in spite of myself. "Oh, John, I didn't think you would be asleep."

"It's okay, Tina. I hoped you'd call."

"We have so much to talk about," I said eagerly. "Of course, whatever you want to ask me, I'll answer. I've got nothing to hide."

The words came out faint, but clear enough for me to hear his response. "That's good, but we can't reach an understanding over satellite phone."

I was disappointed in his matter-of-fact tone. I wanted a little romance, no matter how far away we were.

"Time enough, Tina, to hash all this through when I get back."

I bit my tongue. Hash out? What was he talking about? "Well, okay, but I just had a vision while I was looking at the vacant corner of land behind the house. The field where we played as kids."

"What about the corner? I couldn't quite hear you." His words were muffled through a yawn.

"I want to build a learning center where I can teach quilting."

"You're going to put up a building?" John's voice was still faint. Sometimes he sounded as if he were sitting next to me, but not this time. He really was thousands of miles away.

"Not by myself. I'm a little rusty in the hammer and nails department," I joked. "I'm going to start making plans to add a building. Let's put it that way."

"Got it. I have to go soon. I'm in Hungary. More winery business. But we can talk about the building—and us—when I get back. Love..." Static masked his voice. The call disconnected. I thought about redialing, but John said he had to leave. We didn't seem to be on the same page, anyway.

I went back to the window and peered into the darkness.

In my mind's eye the building was there, sturdy and strong, and I saw myself teaching in the classroom. I don't know how long I stood there before Helen interrupted my thinking.

"Hey, Tina, why are you standing in the dark?"

"Teaching," was my quick response. "Over there." I pointed into the darkness.

"Do you feel okay?" Helen stepped next to me and touched my arm. "You've been extra quiet since the benefit."

"I'm fine. Things are happening," I mused. "Fast, but maybe not fast enough. You know how it is when you're trying to figure out how you want to live for the rest of your life."

"What? Aren't you happy here? In Briarwood? In our house?" There was genuine surprise in the questions blurted staccato style. The woman was demanding answers.

"I don't want to live anywhere else." I turned and looked directly at her. "Especially with John changing his life so he can be around more." I smiled. "He dropped off a packet of pictures of Maggie's quilts. In a roundabout way in a note he wrote with the photos, we've at least *started* to finish a conversation we had the night of the benefit. I love him, he loves me. We're going to be true partners now. Like life partners—for real."

Helen hooted and raised her hands over her head. "Well, it's about time. Steve and I have an ongoing conversation about when you two will see what we see when you're together."

I shook my head. "That's too complicated." I cradled my head in my hand. "I called John to tell him my decision about building a teaching studio. He sounded like he was sleeping. He's doing more work about the wine industry, this time in Hungary. I wanted to tell him I finally have a plan for my future."

"Does it include John and the building you mentioned?"

"It does." I frowned. "John says he has questions he needs to ask. It sounds like they're important to him, but I don't know what they could be. But I can't think about them now. I've got this new project for Deanna to plan for—starting tomorrow."

I pulled Helen to the desk and in a stick drawing with lots of commentary I told her about the teaching studio and the gallery for Maggie's quilts. "Remember Dad asked us to show off Maggie's quilts and make sure the community knew what a treasure we had in our town."

Helen waited for me to wind down before asking, "How are you going to pay for the building?"

"I haven't thought that far ahead." A yawn escaped. It had been a long, emotional day and I was sure the upcoming days would be busy at the quilt shop. A fabric shipment was scheduled for delivery and that meant Marci would have a chance to learn how to handle major shipments, while I would help the customers. I couldn't wait. While I worked, I'd think about the design for the learning center. And about John and his lingering questions.

14

I SPENT THE NEXT WEEK DIVIDING MY TIME BETWEEN THE QUILT shop and my quilting studio. The spring fabrics that arrived gave Marci and me enough variety that I could begin to sew the models for the grand opening. Marci came up with a few patterns for Christmas that she wanted done first, and I didn't care which models I worked on. I put in long hours because I didn't want to feel guilty when I took time away from my studio to be with John when he was finally home.

Mostly, I carried a smile with me wherever I went. After months of turmoil and indecision I had a new path of my own choosing to follow. Why wouldn't I be filled with hope and contentment? The ugliness of my past and the emotional drama with Alex seemed like a lifetime ago.

On a rare evening at home Helen came downstairs to join me in the studio and chat while I worked. As she brought me up to date with the accounts she was managing for ME, I was impressed by her confidence. She was so sure of her decisions and when she explained her reasoning behind each one, I agreed. She'd attracted two new clients for medium term, business expansion loans.

"When people want to expand their space or the product lines or services, it's a good omen for the future," Helen said. "Steve wonders if Briarwood isn't at the beginning of a renaissance. The Richardson Complex triggered a quick boost in local business, but now tourism is up and that increases demand all around."

"I hope he's right," I said, thinking that with the quilt shop, plus the number of other fiber artists in town, we might become a craft hub. "It could be perfect timing for a quilting school and gallery."

"Pretty exciting, huh?" Helen said, beaming.

"We should make you CEO and President of ME. I could be your backup—and co-signer. I think being the sister duo is good for the company's image."

She slapped her hands together. "Oh, no, we own this company together, we make major decisions together, and if we make a mistake, we do that together, too."

"Yes, ma'am," I gave her a mock salute. "But you deserve compensation at least equivalent to what was automatically deposited in your account." I frowned. "Why can't we convert money in that account back to the business, and you can be paid a real salary?"

"Steve said we should ride the old way a little longer. We can reconfigure the accounts for next year. Not very far away. But we should take all this into consideration." She grinned. "I do know for sure that Ivy isn't ready to retire, but she would welcome some reduced hours, and we can adjust her salary to fit what she wants."

I'd wondered about Ivy, the woman who essentially raised us. I was glad Helen had been thinking about her, too. Then I decided to change the direction of our conversation. "What have you and Steve been up to?"

"He roped me into organizing a Halloween party at the youth club," she said with a wide smile.

"Roped you, huh? Probably the easiest thing he ever did." I couldn't help but tease her. "So, I assume you'll wear a costume."

Helen sighed. "I haven't had a minute to give that any thought, but I suppose I should. I've been busy with the plans. Some of the kids are helping and I'm finding it hard to say no to their ideas. They want to put on a skit for their parents."

I sat back in my chair to look at her. "You enjoy working with the kids. I can tell."

"I am. More than I ever thought I would. And I'm comfortable around Steve, too, even when he's working and serious."

"No kidding. You two looked easy in each other's company from the day we met him here in the office," I said.

"Funny thing, I don't miss the country club," Helen said. "I'm just as happy doing my part at the club itself, not just raising money for it." Helen described doing some informal tutoring with a young girl who was having some trouble with her reading homework. "You should have seen her smile when she read a whole paragraph without my help."

The smile that crossed Helen's face was a gift in itself. Being with Steve had led her to a new direction and purpose. "And how is it between you and Steve?"

"I hope..." She flipped her hand in the air and mumbled something about returning a phone call and took off up the stairs.

"I know all about hope, Sis," I called out. If she heard me, she didn't respond.

A few days later I was busy putting more bolts of Christmas fabric near the front of the shop when the door chime rang. Then I jumped when I felt a tap on my shoulder. "Hey, Tina."

I knew the voice and turned to see John. I took the couple of steps into his open arms. "Why didn't you call to let me know you were on your way home?"

"More fun this way, but I can't stay. I've a couple of appointments this afternoon."

"With who?" I clapped my hand over my mouth. "Sorry. None of my business."

"That's not it. I don't want to bother you when you're working. I'll come by the house this evening. We'll build a fire and talk."

"And you'll finally ask those questions you've been hinting at all this time?"

"Yes." His voice was firm, but he was smiling and the twinkle in his eyes – oh, those gray-blues – told me I was headed into a danger zone. I'd waited years to be there.

At closing time, Marci suggested we stay to chat and decide the best role for Carol to play in the shop, beyond the normal business of selling fabric and supplies. "She'll be here for Thanksgiving weekend, always busy no matter what. Her winter break will soon follow."

I forced myself not to agree to stay late, which had always been my fallback position before. Instead, I said, "Can we schedule for another time—tomorrow or the next day? I have plans this evening, and they aren't easily changed." I liked the sound of the new me. All I could think about was crackling wood and dancing flames and a cozy room. Intimate came to mind.

"With the man we've been seeing you with?"

"Yes, he's a...friend from high school," I replied before I

thought about what I really wanted to say.

"Well, for a guy who's just a friend, he sure knows how to slow dance." She waved her hand in front of her face as if cooling her skin.

I felt heat rise up my neck. Busted. "I'll let you know. I can't promise you'll be the first to know if things change, but one of the first." I grinned, feeling foolish for no reason. I didn't give her a chance to change her mind and hurried out of the store.

I changed into comfy clothes and started a fire minutes before John arrived. He carried a bouquet of flowers in one hand and a take-out bag from the new Thai restaurant in the other. He held a bottle of wine in the crook of one arm.

I laughed when he shoved the flowers at me to catch the wine that was slipping downward. "Come in. Let me help you." I reached for the food bag. I breathed in the strong scent of ginger. "One of my favorite smells."

"Nothing like the real thing," John said.

"The Briarwood version must seem like a poor substitute after you've tasted the original."

"Then let me taste an original." He put the wine on the table by the door and pulled me into a toe-curling kiss.

I leaned into him and rested my head against his chest. I wanted to stay there forever. When we broke apart my tongue slipped across my lips. He had left behind the taste of peppermint. "I'm sure glad you're back." I touched my diamond earrings to settle the emotions about to surface.

"Are you hungry?" he asked.

I gave him a smile.

"For food, I mean," John said, with a laugh in his voice. "We'll save the other for later."

"Let's catch up first," I said. "I'll put the food in the fridge, and you can pour the wine." In the kitchen I grabbed a vase for the flowers and John took out wine glasses. He knew this kitchen about as well as the one in his own house.

John added a couple of logs to the dwindling fire before sitting next to me on the couch. There was an awkward silence until John held up his glass. "To us, Tina. We'll figure out what's best for us."

"After the night of the benefit I didn't think you'd want to see me again," I said. "I was so confused."

He scooted back to create distance between us. "Look, Tina. Hearing you talk about me going away and now wondering what my intention is toward you is getting old."

"Wow, tell me how you really feel," I said, smarting from the remark.

"I will. Give me a minute." John gulped back a mouthful of wine. "There seems to be a myth that I abandoned you and went off for my big life."

"Myth? That's what happened." Now I was getting agitated. "You left Briarwood after you graduated from high school. You didn't tell me you were leaving."

"You were sixteen, Tina, and hadn't set your own course. I was only eighteen myself."

"So? Lots of teenagers fall in love..." I trailed off, wandering into dangerous territory. I had a feeling what was coming next.

"I wasn't in love with you. I'd known you forever. I didn't know what I felt for you was love." He groaned and threw his head back.

"Well, I knew what I felt." The crackling of the fire drew my attention. The sound reverberated in my ears. This wasn't what I'd expected to happen.

"Maybe so, Tina, but I had to leave and let you grow up. I became immersed in my work. I had to fight for every assignment." His face became animated with the memories. "I was little more than an apprentice for years."

"What does this have to do with anything? So, okay, I loved you, but you didn't love me back. I accepted it and moved on." Moved on in the worst possible way.

"And this gets us to the part where I was missing you so much. I'd come home a few times and I kept waiting for you to go away to college and set a direction," John said, putting his glass on the coffee table and letting his hands do part of the talking.

I was embarrassed thinking of my aimlessness, not making a plan, or maybe waiting for Dad to ask me to help him with the business. And then Alex...

"I wanted to come back long enough to find out what you wanted," John said, his voice hoarse and earnest. "*I* had visions of us getting married and living in a studio apartment somewhere near an airport where I could fly in and out."

"What? You never once hinted at that," I gasped. "Why didn't you let *me* in on that vision?"

"First, because we were still so young. But I wondered what you'd do while I was gone." He let out a low guttural sound, a mix anger and frustration. "Stupid me, I thought it would be unfair to drag you into a life of wandering around, lots of uncertainty. I never knew where my next assignment was coming from."

"I would have gone anywhere with you." My chest ached as I almost spit out the words. "I'd have found something to do. I might have done work of my own, quilting and maybe writing about quilting all over the world." Wow, talk about a smashed dream. Not that I'd given much thought to quilting at the time. But I would have come to that.

"The silence was my big mistake." John shook his head. "By the time I realized what I'd done it was too late."

It would never have been too late. "What do you mean, *too late*?"

His features were almost distorted in disbelief, as if I'd said something ridiculous. "*You* married Alex. Remember? You were so happy, at least that's what you told me."

"I lied. I married him, yes," I said, my voice rising. "A huge blunder, the biggest mistake of my life. The only reason I did it was because *you* made it clear you didn't want me."

"That's not true, Tina, I backed off because you told me you were madly in love with him. Alex this, and Alex that," John said, flicking his hand this way and that.

"I was never in love with him the way I've always loved you." I buried my face in my hands. "And I stayed almost thirty years trying to make the miserable marriage work."

I got up off the couch and kept my hands busy poking at the logs and stirring the embers. "So, the question is, why did I marry him?"

"And why did you stay? All of it kept us apart."

"I didn't know that," I nearly screamed. It was a good thing we were alone in the house. "Why did you need to tell me this?"

"So you finally get it, Tina. I had more in mind for my life than simply traveling the world. You were always on my mind." John ran his hand over his hair "No, not when I was eighteen, but later. And I waited too long to let you in on my fantasies."

"So that's the myth, huh?"

"Right, Tina. And we can't go forward now without it on the table. I didn't say anything because I thought you were committed to making a life with Alex." He scoffed. "At least until you came back to Briarwood and got such a quick divorce. I'm sure you knew the truth about Alex many years ago but didn't make a move to get out of the situation." His voice lowered when he added, "By that time, I had all the work I could handle, and you were settled on the other side of the state, still trying to make it work with him."

"My foolish pride kept me there," I said bitterly. "But what changed for you?

"What do you think? You finally *divorced* Alex. That meant it was time for me to come home. In all these years, I've never found anyone else I wanted to share my life with, Tina." He gave me a look that told me I should have known all this. "And with this kind of life, I've had all kinds of opportunities. It's never been the fault of the women I've been involved with. I wasn't being fair to them. I finally had to face the fact that it's always been you."

I sighed and wiped away tears. "Like you've been for me, even though we had a three-decade detour." I spoke with regret rising and filling every cell in my body. I started to apologize, but then I realized we were way beyond that.

John let out a cynical laugh. "Most people think being away on these assignments is so glamorous. Trust me, it isn't. I've been alone so much, even if I'm part of a crew or locals are working with me." He mocked a puffed-out chest. "And I'm good at it. I've hung on to more than one crag in a mountain to get a picture no one else had the nerve to shoot. But..."

I rolled my hand toward him. "But what? Finish the thought, John."

"It's not only that I'm beyond the age of being hungry for those challenges. I want to stay home and be with you." He stood and moved toward the fireplace to stand with me. He gave my hand a squeeze. "When you mentioned your teaching and some travel, it dawned on me that it isn't either-or. I don't have to give it all up. I can slow down the travel and pick and choose my assignments. I can say no to a series on wineries, but yes, to an assignment where I can get back to Lima or Manila or Miami and document street life."

"I'm jumping ahead, but what will you do when you're home? And where do you want to live? Here in Briarwood?" With each question my voice rose higher. A log in the fire settled and sent sparks up the chimney.

"Slow down. Don't panic." He put his hands on my shoulders. "After losing each other for so many years, are you really concerned about how we'll handle a tiny little issue like where we'll live? You own half a house, and I own all of one. I think we can figure that out."

I had to laugh. "That's really funny. I guess I'm still reeling at the idea that all this time we've felt the same way about each other," I said. "And I blew it. I saw everything in black and white. I got married, so I had to make it work. Like now, you travel or you don't travel, as if there's no in between. I've been gradually reawakening since I've been home. I faced the truth about Dad and his lack of confidence in Helen and me."

"I know it was tough to find out he'd been funneling money to Alex," John said, his eyes filled with empathy.

I nodded. "That was even worse than knowing he didn't think Helen and I could run ME. But that money is gone now. For good. But in a way, knowing the truth helped me embrace the idea of having dreams. It no longer matters what Dad would think, or that Alex would mock me."

"That's big, Tina. A huge step."

"And now, a life you and I can plan together? I'll take it!"

John laughed. "Let me tell you about my afternoon."

As it turned out, John had talked to the head of the art department at the university, and she would be thrilled to have a guest lecturer on the caliber of John. He was known everywhere. "Turns out, they want to have graduate seminars, and open it to people who have studied photography at the university, or other places, too. They think they could attract people from out of town."

"Adding to the arts and crafts reputation of the region," I interjected.

"She couldn't offer a faculty position, but I'd have turned it down. I'm not interested in that. I don't want to commit to any university's schedule." John smiled slyly. "I want to use the reputation I've earned to teach the whole package, including the business side and how to manage a life like this. Things have changed in thirty years." John closed his eyes and took a deep breath. "But I know I want to teach. Like you, I have that drive now. There's something I want to show you."

Holding my hand, we went back to the couch and sat close together. He reached into his shirt pocket and took out a folded piece of paper. "I've given some thought to this situation, but I want your opinion before I go any further." John passed the paper to me.

I drew in a breath. His drawing was a smaller version of the stick drawing I'd done for Helen.

"What's the matter, Tina?"

"Your drawing is almost the same as mine." I got up to get paper and a pen and quickly drew a basic diagram of the teaching building I designed in my head. I added a few lines that created a mirror image of the sewing rooms. "We only need to add a darkroom and another classroom."

I turned the paper so John could see the whole drawing. "Just think, we'd be independent teachers with our own building." I pointed to the backyard. "We can rent the space to other craft teachers and have a full house every week. We have the land beyond the gardens. The property actually goes back pretty far. We'd need to extend the driveway and perhaps landscape to separate the house from the building. But the biggest challenge is finding the funding to build it."

John frowned. “The other night you mentioned a building. I hadn’t realized you’d thought this far out.”

I laughed. “You were asleep when I called.”

“What did you expect?” he kidded. “I was on the other side of the world.”

“And how was I to know where you were?” I pulled my hand from his. “Will that change? I mean, when you take assignments will I know where you’re going?” I didn’t like my needy tone. I shook my head. “Oops, sorry. I always feel a little at a loss when you’re gone.”

“You’ll know as much as I know, and sometimes, the client isn’t sure where we’ll be, or where they’ll send me alone without a crew,” John explained. “But I’ll be in Briarwood most of the time, spending my days with you. And when I’m not, we’ll work out communication.”

I curled my legs under me and turned to face him. “Let’s get back to the building. I don’t know the first thing about construction.”

“I’ve taken pictures of thousands of buildings,” John said, “but the fort we made as kids was my only attempt with lumber and nails.”

Finally, we set the table in the kitchen and kept talking about our joint venture over steaming Thai food and our coffee and sugar cookies. When it finally came time for John to leave, we stood at the door wrapped in each other’s arms. After a final kiss, John broke into a jog and headed for his house.

15

Over the next week, John consulted commercial builders during the day and narrowed the list by eliminating the bigger firms that did large complexes or multi-floor commercial buildings only. Showing his frustration John mimicked one of the architects when he adjusted his pants and pretended to have suspenders, "Won't happen. Can't put a building like that in a residential area."

I laughed at his antics, but John was serious when he put a two-month deadline to get our ducks in a row, so we could be ready to apply for permits, hire an architect, and design the building inside and out. With any luck, John could start teaching by summer.

I still had commitments to Deanna, so I couldn't be so precise. As it turned out, we also had slightly different visions. But John came around to my idea of a retreat center that offered some housing for weekend seminars and longer events. But as much as we wanted to think that big, money held us back. We finally decided that would be our expansion plan. "Imagine, an expansion plan already," I said, as excited by the idea as I'd been from the start.

When we told Helen more about our plans over coffee one evening, she pointed out that we'd be bringing business to the B&Bs in town and to the larger hotels on the highway coming into Briarwood. "The Briarwood business association will love this."

"What should we name our building?" I asked, looking first at John and then at Helen. She was good at that sort of brainstorming.

"Got any ideas in that head of yours?" John asked.

"Yup. Right before he died, Dad asked Helen and me to find a way to showcase Maggie's quilts. He didn't want them stored somewhere that would keep them hidden from view."

"But he was so ill I didn't want to tell him we didn't have the quilts with us, but you had them at your house." Helen added.

John frowned. "I really have kept them packed away. Mom would want them displayed."

"Perfect. We'll need something on the walls of the gallery when we open. We've agreed on having gallery space as part of the design," I said. "It would be a strange school if we didn't display photograph and quilts—and other fiber art."

"Quilts and gardens..." John mused.

"Your mom gave you your first camera and she taught me how to quilt," I said, "so she's the force behind all this, anyway."

John smiled. "Then we should name it, the Maggie Delaney Learning Center."

I leaned over and gave John the kind of kiss that would seal any legal document. Helen quietly slipped out of the room

---

THE WEEKS PASSED AND THANKSGIVING WAS A FEW DAYS AWAY. John left town for a short assignment in Florida but promised to be home for the holiday. I focused on models for the shop, starting with seasonal pillows and table runners, and three teaser models made from the spring fabrics. Pleased with my production and the quality of my work, Marci had tote bags ready with more patterns and fabric for me to sew. She wanted many models to display after the holidays.

Helen and I were working hard in the same house, only crossing paths at meals. She was in charge of ME, and doing a great job, with Steve providing help when needed. I showed up to okay a few new contracts, and to proof the first-ever ME newsletter, Helen's baby. John and I had talked with Steve about our building project, which we'd dive into in earnest when the holidays were behind us.

Thanksgiving arrived with a dusting of snow and a cold wind. Steve was serving dinner at the local homeless shelter. Little did we know he was a master arm twister and enlisted Helen, John, and me to help. I was impressed by the way Steve combined his professional life with his community work. We were only a small part of a team he had assembled.

After we'd served a long line of men, women and children, we fixed our plates. As the four of us gathered at one end of a long table, Steve insisted that Helen take the seat sat next to him. Then halfway through our meal Steve's napkin fell to the floor. When Steve bent over to retrieve it John grabbed my hand under the table. Steve was on his knee next to Helen's chair, and she turned toward him with a puzzled expression.

Steve spoke quickly. "I love you, Helen. Will you marry me?"

She dropped her silverware on the plate producing a loud clatter, but she used her free hands to cradle his cheeks. "I... I..." She looked at me across the table, a smile filling her face.

"I told you he was easy to look at when he came to the house the first time."

Steve wiggled on the floor and slid back onto his chair. "Maybe I..."

Before he finished Helen moved to sit on his lap and put her arms around his neck. When she kissed him, John and I got to our feet and started clapping, immediately drawing attention to the pair. Applause and whistles followed.

Helen raised her arms in the air. "Yes! Of course, I'll marry you."

I squeezed John's hand and blinked to keep the happy tears for my sister from falling. "I'm so happy for them," I whispered in his ear.

A few days later Helen called me into her room. I found her packing suitcases. "Steve and I are leaving early tomorrow for a short vacation. He won't tell me where we're going so I don't know what clothes to pack."

I pushed aside a pile of folded clothes and sat on the edge of the bed. "Hey, Sis, you're a rising star in the business life of Briarwood. Why don't you take some basics and buy some new things when you get there?"

She beamed at me. "Yeah, I could do that. This year is shaping up to be a much better year than I ever imagined."

I gave her an "I'm so excited for you." look. "First you're making ME work and learning so much along the way. Now you have Steve. Wouldn't Dad be happy?"

Helen frowned. "Well, I assume so. It's hard to know what he'd think."

"Let's assume Dad would have eventually changed if we'd pushed him." I said, hoping she'd agree. "I don't want to spend the rest of my life resenting him."

She nodded. "Like you, I'm trying to make up for all the years I've wasted. I love running ME and seeing the way I can make a living, while also being useful in Briarwood. Steve gets credit for encouraging me when I felt like an impostor."

I knew exactly what she was saying. "You've done a great job being the face of ME, and you were here when Dad needed help."

Helen dismissed all my words with a fast flick of her hand. "That's the past now. I've got my eye on the future. I'm actually going out of town. Do you know how seldom I've gone away? I used to envy Ivy her cruises."

We were interrupted by a call coming in from John. "Have they left yet?"

I stepped out of the room before Helen heard his voice.

"Nope. But can you tell me where they're going?"

"You can't tell her. Promise?" John lowered his voice even more. "I mean it."

"Okay, okay, I promise."

"They're flying to Vegas to be married—if Steve can convince her."

"What?" I was stunned. "Without me...us. And without all their friends?"

John hesitated. "The idea is they'll have a big bash at the country club when they get back. I wasn't supposed to tell you any of this, but we're supposed to help organize the party." John cleared his throat. "I mean, if Helen agrees. Steve's supposed to let me know."

I knew my sister. "She'll say yes because she's crazy about him—she floats around the house now. As for Steve, he's brilliant. She'd spend months organizing a real wedding. And this will make a fun, romantic story Helen can tell. I don't blame Steve for wanting to move this marriage along."

"How long do you want to wait before your wedding, Tina?"

My heart picked up speed. "Shush. You'll have to do better

than to trick me into an answer. And not now. This is Helen and Steve's time."

"Oh, okay," John said, pretending to be disappointed, "but I still love you."

"Every time you say that I want to hear it again." I laughed. "Good thing I love you back."

Not long after we ended the call, I waved goodbye to Helen and Steve. Then Carol called to tell me about a mini-party planned at the quilt shop the following day. Janet was bringing baby Drew for a visit. They were serving punch and cupcakes and Marci was going to post a video of customers enjoying the new mom and baby.

I didn't like interrupting my work on the samples, but this was about Janet. "I'll be there. Janet gave me a job when I came back to Briarwood...well, you know the story."

The day flew by. My focus on my work only wavered when Helen came to mind. Sure enough, around dinner time, my phone buzzed and Helen's name appeared. "Mrs. Helen Montgomery Anderson wants to talk to her sister."

I enjoyed a good belly laugh. "So, he talked you into it. And?"

"It's been great fun. More fun than I've ever had in my life." Helen had more news. They'd live in Steve's condo for now and maybe buy a house later. "I'm a little nervous about packing up my things. It'll be strange at first. I've never lived anywhere but in our house."

"I'll miss having you here." I heard the wistfulness in my voice. We hadn't seen each other much lately, but I always felt comforted when I heard the front door close, or I'd hear her stirring in her room in the morning.

"I'll miss you, too."

When we finished our conversation I sent a text to John, who texted back that he'd already heard from Steve. A few minutes later John called. "Any other news from the newlyweds?"

"Helen's excited about seeing one of those famous Las Vegas shows, a country-western star. Her name escapes me at the moment," I said. "I suppose that's what Las Vegas newlyweds do."

"Wouldn't know. But I don't have time to think about it right now. I'm on my way to visit an old school friend of ours, Matt Kramer. He and his wife, Jane Kettering, run a home construction business here in town."

"I know who you're talking about." They were nearly finished repaying a loan, but that was confidential. "Are they expanding beyond houses now?"

"Maybe. Our building isn't all that different from a house. Easier to build, actually. I thought I –we – might get a few ideas from him."

"Good. Stop by on your way home, so you can tell me all about it."

I was in my studio when I heard pellets of ice hit the window and mentally told John to be safe on the road. A few hours later I was lost in my sewing when the front doorbell chimed. I rushed up the stairs to answer it and found John huddled in his jacket under the porch light. He'd turned the collar up to keep the ice from going down his neck.

"Hurry in. You're about to become an icicle." I pulled on his arm to get him inside.

John's smile radiated through the cold as we made a fire. "I wish you'd been with me tonight. I didn't remember much about either Matt or Jane, but they laughed about their names being so close they sat next to each other all through school. Even their parents thought it was funny they ended up getting married."

I already knew Matt's dad had built homes and Matt took

over when his dad fell on a job and couldn't work anymore. But I feigned ignorance and listened as John repeated back what Matt said.

By now we had a fire going and John was rubbing his palms together and rotating his body to get warm.

"In a nutshell he agreed with the other builders who claim we won't be able to get a permit to build the type of structure we've planned."

I was heartbroken. All our dreams and plans were in that drawing and now we had to start over. My face must have shown by disappointment.

"Hey, wait a minute. Hear me out." John sat down next to me. He took my hand and lifted my chin with his finger. He reached into his shirt pocket to withdraw folded pieces of paper. "Jane used a program to create diagrams from ideas people feed her—obviously their clients." He handed me the papers. "It's amazing."

At first, I was confused. There were two buildings connected with a covered walkway. "This isn't..."

John held up his hand again to stop me until he could finish. "Matt said if we built the center to resemble a house it wouldn't look out of place in the neighborhood."

I pointed to the diagram. "But..."

"I even mentioned the possibility we'd want to add a B&B style residence for students, which is when he suggested connecting my house to the learning center."

As it turned out, it wouldn't take much to convert the rooms and we could eliminate – or downsize – the kitchen in the center.

My mind jumped ahead again. "Can he build it for us? On our timeline?"

John nodded. "Jane says she can get the permits for us."

I grabbed his face. "I love you, John Delaney."

"I don't know a better way to say it, so how about this? I love you, too, Tina Montgomery. And I want to spend the rest of our lives together in your house." He shrugged. "Seems I'm losing mine."

That gave me a little painful stab in my chest. I could imagine John must have mixed feelings. I told him about Helen and Steve's plan.

"But before we deal with all those practical arrangements, what do you think about Matt and Jane's ideas?" John looked at me through eager eyes.

"I love them!" I thought I'd made that clear. This was everything we wanted and more. We'd even gotten more gallery space in this new design.

When it came time to leave, John went outside to start his car only to find it encased in ice. He came back in for a warmup, and another kiss, before deciding to walk home. After another kiss or two, he left through the French doors in the office and quickly disappeared into the darkness. The only light came from his flashlight beam.

He'd left the drawings of the learning center so I could study the diagrams Jane had made. The longer I stared at them the more excited I got.

It was strange not to wait for Helen to come home. I hoped one day soon, I wouldn't watch John go off to his own house. When would John finally make it official? I was still waiting for the proposal.

16

Time moved quickly through December. Although she could do most of ME's work at her new home, Helen still came to the house frequently to work in the office. We had meetings with a couple of new clients and the office in our house still had an official look. But it was clear that in running ME Helen had found her niche. That development, along with being in love made Helen glow. No other word did her justice.

"I didn't know I could be so happy," Helen said one morning when we'd finished up the work we needed to do together and shared a pot of coffee in the office. "Every day is a new adventure with Steve." She sat back in the chair with a happy sigh. "Tell me what going on with you?"

"Same as before," I said. "I'm sewing and quilting for the shop and working there about half the time. John and I are having great time planning our learning center."

"Have you found financing for the center?"

"We won't put a lot of energy into that until after the holidays."

"Have you considered ME?" Helen offered. "Steve cautioned that it would be a little tricky to be the lender and recipient, but John could be the sole borrower. On the other hand, looking at a loan that size, are you and John certain you'll be able to teach enough to cover the expenses?"

"No, not yet. And it's going to be more than a teaching site. We'll have a gallery, too. And it's going to be great space to rent out to others, at least in the early days." I paused to gather my thoughts. "In the bigger picture, I don't want the kind of stress of an arrangement like that would put on the two of us. You and I still haven't configured our permanent arrangement with ME, with you in charge and taking a salary, which would be a larger share of the profits."

"We don't talk about this often, but we still have Dad's life insurance waiting to be used for a good cause." Helen fiddled with a pen.

"Half is yours. Maybe you and Steve will want to use it to build a house—or something."

"Actually, I think investing in my sister is a sure bet. Steve wants to analyze the numbers, do the feasibility study, as ME does with any loan. But for the most part he'd on board. And it won't be an ME loan. It would be between us."

My cells buzzed with excitement because it would be a perfect solution. "I'll talk to John tonight while we're out for dinner and Christmas shopping."

Helen's phone rang so I left the office and headed to my studio. Marci had handed me yet another tote filled with new projects she wanted available by January.

All morning, the aroma of Ivy's vegetable soup had traveled through the house, and I joined her for lunch in the kitchen. We ate lunch together more often now that I was buried deep in my studio at least half the week.

Halfway through lunch, Ivy said, "You seem extra happy lately, Tina. Is it because John's been home more?"

I wasn't able to hide my moods and feelings from Ivy so I told her about the learning center and went to the studio to pull out a sketch to show her. She put her spoon down and studied the diagram. "Well, well, isn't this something. I like this idea."

I pointed out the gallery where Maggie's quilts would hang, then moved onto the mirror image rooms for photography and quilting. The breezeway joined the building to John's house. "We could glass that in or make it into extra gallery space, but for now we'll keep it basic. At some point, we'll offer B&B type of housing for overnight students." I grinned. "We're repurposing John's house."

Ivy rested her elbow on the table and put her chin in her palm. She looked so focused I wondered what she was thinking about with such intensity. Finally, she spoke. "I want to be part of this new venture. With your dad gone and Helen married, there's not much for me to do around here. I need a purpose to keep me going."

I listened to her, really listened, when she told me about saving her money all these years. She'd lived in the house with us and other than her vacations with friends, she spent little. Now she needed a new direction. Investing in teaching was like investing in the future. "I'm proud of you, Tina. You're adding something special to Briarwood, just like Deanna did with her quilt company and now she's keeping Janet's place alive."

I saw the excitement in her face. "Do you know that way back in the beginning John suggested that you could run the B&B part of this venture? We didn't know we'd use John's house."

"Sound like it's right up my alley," Ivy said.

I told her that we were still in a planning stage, so she couldn't say a word to anyone about the idea.

She rubbed her palms together. "Ooh, secrets. I love them."

Later, when I was done for the day and waiting for John, I found Ivy in the living room surrounded by boxes of Christmas decorations. "Here you are. An artist at work." Ivy had made all the holidays special for Helen and me when we were little kids, but Christmas was her favorite.

"This year will be fun because of Helen and Steve, and you and John. Change is in the air. Your dad would have enjoyed seeing his girls happy."

I touched my diamond earrings. Yes, despite everything, Dad wanted us to enjoy life. He had, even after losing our mother.

Ivy had a glass evergreen tree in her hand and keeping with a Montgomery holiday tradition she placed it on the fireplace mantle. "You have a wonderful evening. Tell John about my offer. It's time I did more than dust and cook."

"The B&B will mean a lot of dusting. Maybe not much cooking, though," I joked.

"But I would be part of that Band B. Think of it, Tilly Iverson, part owner of a Briarwood business."

I smiled at the reference to Tilly. When she came to work for Dad and take care of Helen and me, she hadn't wanted us to call her by her first name, but somehow, turning Iverson into Ivy suited her. Helen and I would forget it wasn't her actual first name.

But now...How would I tell her if John had changed his mind and refused her offer? I tried not to let any hint of doubt show when I said goodbye to her as John pulled into the driveway

I decided to wait to talk to John until after we were done shopping and had stopped for dinner. He was on a mission when we entered the mall. He knew what he wanted to buy for the people on his list, many of whom were part of the team he worked with at the agency who got him the majority of his assignments. He had colleagues he often worked with in the field he wanted to acknowledge. "I hope some of these folks will visit us one day," he said as he dramatically scratched a name off his list.

"What a production," I teased. "I don't remember you ever fussing so much about gifts."

"We were kids. I had other stuff to fuss over." The slight wrinkle that appeared on John's forehead stayed put. His body was in front of me, but his mind had drifted away."

"What's going on?" I asked. "You've gone far, far away."

John shook his head. "Oh, it's nothing. I'm about done. Let's get a quick dinner at the food court."

Half the shoppers in the mall must have had the same idea because the food court was crowded and without an empty table in sight. We picked up takeout tacos and rice and beans and headed to my house. Ivy welcomed us in the kitchen with cups of hot cider. She winked at me before hurrying out of the room.

"Ivy could have joined us," John said as he took containers out of the shopping bag. "There's more food than we can eat."

"That's a conversation we can have later." I pinched my thumb and forefinger together and drew them across my lips.

"Later tonight or later, like in a month from now?"

"Tonight, if you must know. So, tell me about your meeting."

John unwrapped an overstuffed taco shell. "I met with Doug."

That made sense, but I wondered why he hadn't told me.

"I assume we'll use him for the legal work for the center," John explained, "but I wanted his opinion about using mom's life insurance money to partially finance the center."

"Funny, Helen and I had the same conversation," I said.

As we compared notes, we were on the same page, more or less, but John intended to use the accrued interest, which Doug thought was a great use of his mother's gift to him. He was the sole owner of those funds, though, unlike me.

"I'm with Doug on that kind of issue," I said. "Helen suggested we have ME back us, but I said no, and I don't want to use all the life insurance money, either. Besides, if ME fails, or our idea sinks, we'll need money."

"ME is fine, and the center won't fail, honey." John tapped his fingertips on the table for emphasis. "We're strong and good enough to overcome all the obstacles. We already have."

I drained the last of the cider from the cup. "I have news you'll like to hear." I rolled up the wrapper from the taco and let it drop on my plate. "Ivy wants to be one of our investors and work in the B&B when it's occupied."

John chuckled. "My idea, remember? I'm such a genius. Tell me more."

I did and in great detail. Ivy had been part of John's life, too, especially with his mom working for Dad. "But, with Ivy wanting to invest, I realized this project is getting far too big for us to handle without advisors. We should meet with Steve and let him help us."

"And Doug wants a share of the pie too. We could have a meeting of potential investors already."

"Doug? Why would he be interested in our center?"

John's expression turned thoughtful. "He said something about a promise to your dad, but he didn't elaborate."

"Doug knew how Max felt about Briarwood. He'd spent his whole life here and had a silent role in making so much happen." I smiled at John. "I think it means that Doug believes this is good for the town."

I suggested we have a preliminary meeting with everyone

involved so far. "This is moving quickly, and it's too important to put off until after the holidays."

John agreed and we came up with a date to meet at my house. I texted Helen, Steve, and Ivy, and John took care of Doug. The six of us agreed to meet the next evening, Doug's only available time for several days. It was one of my in-shop days, so I knew it would be hectic and I'd have no time for sewing.

But now...I was one step closer to my dream.

WE SAT AT THE TABLE IN THE OFFICE, WITH HELEN TAKING notes on her laptop. We asked Doug to walk us through the agenda, which included reviewing the drawings Matt and Jane had already done. We agreed to interview architects the builders suggested to get scaled drawings and perhaps a rendering that would give us a whole picture. John had taken pictures of the land and its proximity to the gardens. It was easy to picture the building nestled past the gardens and connected to John's house.

When it came to financing, Ivy gave us a figure of what she'd be willing to invest—and she anticipated Doug and Steve's questions. "No, it's not all the money I have. I knew you're going ask that. You don't want me risking everything, and I certainly won't."

Doug rolled his pen between his fingers. "Got it, Ivy. We'll work out the percentages of investment later, but you'll have an owner's share."

Doug looked over at John. "And you? Are you okay with what we discussed yesterday?"

"I am." John explained that our center was a good use of the profit from his mother's insurance money. If we need it, I'll use some of the principal, too," John said, looking at me. "But I've left this money alone for all these years. I finally have something that means enough to me to use all of it if necessary."

I felt a thrilling shiver run through me. I knew for sure that John's dream and my dream were compatible and that he'd go to any length to make our shared dream happen.

When he gave Doug the number he would invest from the profit to date. I suppressed a gasp. I sensed others around the table were surprised, too.

"I had no need to touch the insurance money," John explained, no doubt sensing our surprise at how much money he could throw into the pot. "I never spend money on anything other than top-of-the-line cameras and good boots and jackets."

Helen spoke up and added our dad's money as our contribution. Steve agreed that was a great idea and then he added in his own investment. He wanted a piece of the center, too.

"I don't think there's any better way to continue Dad's legacy than to move forward with ME and to make the best use of the house and gardens," Helen said. "Tina agrees."

Doug sat forward and told us about an investment he and Max had made in a venture in Briarwood. They'd both made a huge profit, and Doug had salted his away, the same way John had done with Maggie's life insurance. "So, we made the money investing in Briarwood, so I might as well invest it in the town again. So, count me in on the center—it's going to be great for the town. And a fun project for us."

The room became eerily quiet. I looked from Helen to Doug to John, and I grabbed a tissue from the box on the sideboard and passed it to Ivy. This was a game-changer for her, too.

"I think we have enough money to start building. We can always go to the bank in the future, if needed." Steve said.

Ivy left the room and came back with a bottle of champagne and glasses. "I've watched all kinds of wonderful things happen in this office, and tonight I'm part of one. Let's have a toast." With a towel wrapped around the neck of the bottle, Ivy expertly popped the cork and Steve held up the glasses for her to fill.

"Your words are our toast, Ivy," Helen said. "It's a wonderful new beginning for all of us."

BEFORE WE ALL KNEW IT, CHRISTMAS WAS REALLY UPON US. As she always did, Ivy had a tree delivered and Helen and I helped her load it with ornaments. This year Ivy added a sprig of mistletoe by the front door. I laughed the first time I saw it.

On Christmas Eve, Helen and Steve came early, weighed down by loads of presents they put under the tree. "I haven't seen that many gifts since we were little kids," Helen said. "Don't you remember, Tina? We counted our packages to see if we had the same number. Drove Dad crazy."

Steve grinned. "That's why all the kids at The Youth Club get one gift apiece at their party."

"I wanted to give them more, but Steve reminded me we supply other things at other times, like all the sports equipment," Helen said.

Ivy had left earlier to spend the holiday with friends, but she'd set out bowls of snacks on the coffee table with a note saying there were trays of cheese and cold shrimp in the fridge.

"So, let's get this party started." John picked up a gift and read the tag. "To Steve, From Tina." He grabbed another one.

"To Steve, From Helen." He passed three more to Steve. "What is this? Didn't Santa know I was in Briarwood this year?"

"Move over, John." Helen kneeled down and made four piles of gifts. "She patted a box at the top of one pile. "There, John, all these are for you."

John laughed—and blushed.

"I think we all feel like kids tonight," I said, putting my hand over my heart. "So much has happened. So many really wonderful things. It's holiday magic for real."

Steve and Helen reached for each other's hands. "You got that right, Tina," Steve said. But he wasn't looking into my eyes. The tender moment between Helen and Steve made me yearn for such a moment. Somehow, John and I still had to push aside all the distractions and allow ourselves to focus only on each other.

By the time we finished opening boxes filled with scarves and sweaters and tore the covering off carefully wrapped books, the room was filled with paper and bows in every color. I started to fill a trash bag with the debris, but John snagged my hand and tugged on it until I was in his lap.

"I've got one more gift for you, Tina." There was a small box in his hand. "We decided to name the building The Maggie Delaney Retreat and Learning Center and since you're an owner and soon to be teaching there, I thought it was time for you to add the Delaney name to yours." He opened the lid to show me a simple diamond ring between a double wedding band. "Will you marry me, Tina? Finally? At long last?"

Helen gasped, but Steve shushed her.

"It's okay. Make noise. Shout and cheer," I said, laughing. After all the years of loving John, here I was with my arms around his neck and whispering yes into his neck.

"Could you say that louder, please? I want to have

witnesses that you really said the word." John caressed my face as he spoke.

I closed my eyes and let this moment soak in. I didn't want to become overwhelmed and miss any of what I was feeling.

"Why are you waiting, Tina?" Helen was frustrated and didn't hide it. "Tell him..."

"Helen, let her answer." Steve's calm nature was serving him well.

"Tina?"

I looked into those gray-blue eyes that curled my toes and made my knees weak. "Yes, John, I will marry you."

EPILOGUE

I HELD THE INVITATION TO THE GRAND OPENING OF THE MAGGIE Delaney Retreat and Learning Center. The event we'd been waiting for was happening in a few hours.

John was off on a rare assignment. It was supposed to be for a few days, but it had stretched into over a week already. I'd tried to stay positive when I dialed his satellite phone day after day trying to reach him. I'd even called the satellite phone company to see if there had been a technical problem with his phone. They'd returned my call after finding no internal errors, but they, too, hadn't been able to connect with him.

Fatigue washed over me. I hadn't slept for days, nor eaten much. I managed to work on some quilting projects, but everything else had been put aside. All I could think about was that John was in trouble and couldn't come back to me. It was irrational, but I was incapable of shaking that thought.

I twisted my wedding rings as I remembered the warm early spring day that John and I were married in the gardens. The tulips and daffodils tipped down in the light breeze on that sunny day. Helen and Steve were our witnesses while

Doug performed the simple ceremony. Now, hoping to calm my fears I touched my diamond earrings from Dad.

I was staring into the gardens when Ivy touched my arm. "It's time for us to go." She'd been looking forward to this event as much as everyone else—she'd been with us through each step of the planning and construction.

Helen and Steve joined Ivy and me and stepped into the gardens on this golden autumn day with a sky as blue as I'd ever seen it. It had rained around dawn and the scent of damp earth lingered in the air as we started down the path to the building. Late season flowers swayed in the light wind that ushered out the rain.

Doug met us partway down the path. I could tell from the way he looked at Ivy he was hoping she'd have news. I dabbed the tissue on the corners of my eyes. "We have to do this, Doug. We can't keep all these people waiting any longer."

Doug took my arm, but after a few steps I heard the French door open.

"Hey, wait for me," John called, managing a smile. One arm was in a sling and his face and neck were covered with bruises.

I ran to him, and he embraced me with his free arm. "You know those mountainsides I've bragged about? Well, I got my shot, but then I fell off. I watched my phone tumble down into a ravine so far below I could barely see it."

John told us how he was eventually found two days later. It had taken almost a day to get him medical help. "All I thought about was surviving and coming back to you." He struggled to breathe and talk at the same time. "I wouldn't let them call you, Tina, knowing you'd come to be with me."

I put my arm through his. "Lean on me, John. It's time to honor Maggie and Max by launching our baby. Then I'll take you home and you can rest."

We let the others walk ahead of us and I hung on to John's arm and steadied him as we walked the path to the center. Our grand opening had drawn almost a hundred guests, among them Janet and Tom, Deanna and her kids, Carol, and many faces I recognized as Ivy's friends.

"We'll be walking this path from the house to the center a lot in next few years, won't we, John?"

"Absolutely." He leaned in to plant a quick kiss on my lips before we reached the front of the Maggie Delaney Retreat and Learning Center. "And now this is our moment to share."

I smiled up at John and then Doug began to tell the story of how we came to gather on this fine September day.

Thank you for reading *The Quilt Garden.*
If you enjoyed this book, please tell a friend or leave a review online to help other readers discover my books.
Thank you!

ABOUT THE AUTHOR

In a world abundant with books, Gini Athey always finds herself reading three or four at the same time. While she reads across genres, her favorite books involve families with all their challenges and rewards. She writes the same kind of stories she likes to read.

Gini and her husband are avid world travelers and enjoy summers at their camp in Canada. They live in a rural area west of Green Bay.

Gini Athey is the author of the Wolf Creek Square series. For more information, visit her website at www.giniathey.com.

Made in the USA
Monee, IL
17 February 2023